MW01481929

THE
GLASS
LAKE

THE GLASS LAKE

SUSAN JANE WRIGHT

ROAN IMPRINT

Copyright © 2022 Susan Jane Wright

All rights reserved. No part of this book may be reproduced in any form by any electronic or mechanical means, including information storage and retreival systems, without permission in writing from the publisher, except by reviewers, who may quote brief passages in a review

ISBN 978-1-998782-01-7 (Paperback Edition)
ISBN 978-1-998782-02-4 (eBook Edition)

Characters and events in this book are fictitious. Any similarity to real persons, living or dead, is coincidental and not intended by the author.

Editing by Pip Wallace
Front cover image by Dominik Dombrowski
Front cover design by JCVArtStudio

Published by Roan Imprint
1500 14 St SW Suite 119
Calgary, AB T3C 1C9
Canada

Visit www.SusanJaneWright.ca

To Tivola
All the best
Susan

For Roy, Kelly, and Eden
As Always

The Day It Happened

November 12, 9:42 A.M.

CHAPTER 1

The ice was clear and smooth like a sheet of glass. Kirsten Gula hesitated, tapping the heel of her hiking boot on the glassy surface, once, twice, before gingerly stepping forward. Would it really support their weight, or shatter, dumping them into the freezing water below? Tyler and Jack did not share her concern. The twins shot out from behind her, their skates carving filigree patterns as their shadows rippled over the brown rocks below.

"Mommy," Amy watched her brothers glide farther and farther away, "why did the lake turn to glass?" She huffed, trying to squeeze her foot into her skate, her face was tipped down into her scarf muffling her words.

Kirsten took Amy's skate, opened it wide, pulling out the tongue, and slipped it over her daughter's thick woolly socks. "Ooh, that's getting a little snug. You're growing up, young lady." She scowled at Amy with a pretend frown.

"I'm a big girl now," Amy said, tugging at a mitten that was sliding off her small hand.

"Yes you are, four is getting right up there, you'll be an old lady soon." Kirsten tweaked the little girl's nose and they both giggled.

"How does that feel?" Her mother adjusted the other skate and sat back on her heels. Amy nodded, her eyes following the twins who were shouting and crashing into each other on the middle of the lake.

"What turned the lake into glass?"

Kirsten smiled. Amy wouldn't stop asking the question until she got an answer. Her little girl was tenacious and not easily distracted. A thoughtful child who moved through life at a slower pace than her ten-year-old brothers, two mini tornadoes.

"What turned the lake into glass?" Kirsten repeated Amy's question. She was an engineer, not a meteorologist, and struggled to find the right words to explain congelation ice to a four-year-old. "Well, when it gets cold, the top of the lake turns to ice and sometimes when conditions are just right, magic happens and the top of the lake freezes perfectly clear, like glass."

"Instead of snow white?"

"That's right."

"Was everything just right last night? For magic ice?"

"Oh, I think everything has been just right for quite a few nights now." Kirsten's neighbour, an avid cross-country skier, called last night to tell her about the phenomenon. 'Kirsten,' he said, 'you've got to get the kids out there right away, before the city folks show up and wreck it.' So this morning just before the soft pink sunrise Kirsten woke the kids early, stuffed them with toast and honey and bundled them into the SUV for the quick drive down snowy backroads to the lake.

Kevin would have loved this. He'd been the cool dad who dreamed up brilliant family adventures; she was the boring mom who dragged them to their dental appointments and reported back from parent-teacher meetings. She'd become even more rigid after Kevin had died. But four years was a long time. She'd fallen to bits at the time but was better now. She owed it to the children to bring a glimmer of joy back into their lives. So this morning they were skipping school to go skating on the magic lake. Kirsten stood up, arched her back, then hoisted Amy up onto her feet. The little girl wobbled out onto the ice, a small red puffball in a white plastic helmet, and immediately dropped to her hands and knees.

"Mommy. I see fish."

Kirsten raised her eyebrows. *Fish?* She hadn't given much thought to how fish survive the harsh Canadian winters, which seemed to be longer and nastier with each passing year, but if Amy said she spotted fish they'd be down there, dozing among the smooth round rocks in the lakebed.

"Amy, whatever you do, don't lick the ice," Kirsten said as she pulled off her boots and wedged her feet into a pair of beat-up figure skates. She'd found them in the garage behind some unpacked moving boxes. The white leather was creased and smudged with dust. She hadn't worn them in years but when she stepped out on to the ice and pushed off, it all came back. Just like riding a bicycle, she thought as she sailed effortlessly over to Amy. She lifted the child back on her feet and tightened the strap of her helmet more snugly under her round chin. "We can't have you cracking your head on the ice now, can we?"

"No," Amy said firmly. "No more goose eggs."

"Stay close to shore, sweetie, so you can rest on the snowbank if you get tired." Amy nodded, grey eyes serious.

An angry yell shattered the still morning air. Kirsten snapped to attention. The boys were rolling around on the ice, arms and legs thrashing, as they fought over a hockey puck. She pushed off, the swish of her blades propelling her smoothly across the frozen lake.

"Tyler, Jack, stop it! Someone's going to lose an eye."

She was almost upon them when she heard it. An explosion. Loud, a sonic boom that shook the birds out of the trees. Then came the tremor and the ice shuddered beneath her feet. Her eyes darted to the orange and white markers at the edge of the lake, then to Amy who was still on her knees, piling snow in tiny mounds on the ice, then back to the boys who were frozen in mid tussle.

The ice vibrated again. A silent thud under her feet.

Fear shot through her, hot like molten metal. She swooped down on the boys. Black hair flying, eyes wild as a Valkyrie, she yanked Jack off Tyler, hauling them both to their feet and pivoting toward the shore. "Go," she screamed, "get off the ice, go!" and shoved them ahead of her.

Tyler lost his balance and stumbled; his skate clashed with Jack's blade. Jack skidded sideways, Kirsten caught his jacket, tugging him upright.

"Mom!" Jack yelled. "What the hell?"

Her heart was pounding. "Amy!" she screamed. "Get off the ice. Into the snowbank. Now!"

Amy looked up, eyes round with confusion, then set her lips in a tight line of determination. She pushed her hood back, planted her mittens on the ice and started crawling to the shore.

Kirsten flew up behind her, the boys flailing and scuttling beside her. She flung them like rag dolls into the snow and scooped up her daughter, trying to shield Amy with her body.

Then it happened.

Nine Months Earlier

January

CHAPTER 2

I'm not a reckless driver, quite the opposite in fact, but here I was roaring down Elbow Drive well above the speed limit with the river flashing by the windows and the radio cranked up high. I couldn't wait to tell them.

My law firm was on the cusp of going global—in the reputational sense. What delicious payback! Five years ago, after a horrific experience at one of the biggest firms in the city, I'd left 'big law' to set up the city's first green energy law firm. I convinced Keith Lawson, a top-notch regulatory law partner, Madeline, paralegal extraordinaire, and Bridget, the finest administrative assistant I'd ever had, to come with me. A year later AJ Braxton, known as Alexander James to no one but his mom, joined us as an associate. We'd built a solid reputation in the province as a boutique firm. And soon our name would be known around the world.

The Mini skidded to a stop on the hardpacked snow in the parking lot. It was January, four more months of winter before the gentle breath of spring. The crows and magpies squawked overhead as I crunched down the narrow strip of paving between the parking lot and the office building and flung open the front door.

"Good Lord, Evie!" Bridget shot to her feet. "That's

quite an entrance." She waved a hand in the direction of the parking lot.

"Gather everyone in the conference room," I said. "I have an announcement!"

By the time I'd tossed my coat onto my desk they were assembled in the sunlit conference room facing the river. Keith was perched on the edge of the conference table, his arms crossed and a knowing smile on his face. AJ was seated, one arm slung over the back of a chair. Madeline was beside him, a leather-bound notepad resting in her lap, and Bridget, her eyes wide with excitement, paced in front of the windows.

"We got the Phoenix file!" I'd intended to build up to it slowly, tease them a little, but they knew I'd been meeting with the company and I couldn't contain myself.

Everyone leapt to their feet, filling the room with cheers and applause. The Phoenix file was a green energy lawyer's dream. Phoenix, a large intercontinental pipeline company, was modernizing twenty-six compressor stations on its pipeline that stretched from western Canada and all the way down into the American Midwest. It had selected Vesper, a small Italian company, as its supplier because—and this was the magic part—the Vesper compressors were unlike anything on the market; they would transform Phoenix into the world's first net-zero pipeline company. Every big law firm in the city wanted the file and Michelle Yu, Phoenix's Chief Legal Officer, had awarded it to Lawson Valentine, to me.

"That's fantastic!" Keith grabbed my shoulders awkwardly, in a combination hug and handshake. "Congratulations!"

"This is a credit to all of us, Keith." It was true that I had a personal relationship with Michelle Yu, I'd spent a

two-month practicum in Phoenix's in-house law department when I was in third year. She'd become a mentor and
a close friend. And a major client, after we set up Lawson
Valentine, sending us work that was too specialized for
her lawyers to handle.

We'd submitted a bid for the Phoenix file and were
over the moon when Michelle invited me, the lead lawyer, to meet with Alistair Bannerman, Phoenix's CEO.
Hiring outside counsel was Michelle's purview but this
was a landmark transaction—small dollar value relatively
speaking but of global significance to Phoenix's reputation—so it wasn't surprising that the CEO wanted to
weigh in on what he called 'the talent.' One last hurdle
and the file was ours.

The meeting lasted all of ten minutes. Bannerman's
assistant, a woman with piercing blue eyes and short white
hair, ushered Michelle and me into Bannerman's office.
We sat in the visitors' chairs waiting for him to arrive. The
muffled sound of running water. The door to the executive
bathroom, a small room behind a rosewood wall, clicked
open. A thin middle-aged man in a smartly tailored suit
rounded the corner. Michelle and I stood, he nodded and
I waited for Michelle to introduce me to her boss.

"So you're the lawyer who's going to help us make
history." Alastair Bannerman shook my hand. He had a
high shiny forehead and glittering brown eyes. He looked
amused.

"That's certainly the objective." I smiled.

He chuckled, said a few words about the importance of
the Vesper compressor project to the company, "and to the
climate of course," then pronounced he was glad to have
me on board. Michelle's face relaxed in a broad smile as
we strolled back to her office.

"That's it then," she said. "You've got the file." I was so excited I gave her a big hug, right there in the executive lobby.

Madeline interrupted as I relayed the story. "What's Bannerman like?" She arched a brow. "He's an eligible bachelor, you know. A very wealthy, eligible bachelor." If anyone would know Bannerman's net worth it would be Madeline, a single woman in her mid forties, who, as far as I can tell, was highly sought after by every eligible bachelor in town.

"It was hard to tell," I said. "We only talked for a few minutes."

Bridget asked about the executive bathroom, these quirky privileges of rank fascinate her. Before we went down that rabbit hole, Keith interrupted.

"How are the in-house guys taking it?" he asked.

"You mean Dave?"

"Who's Dave?" AJ sat forward in his chair, a puzzled expression on his face.

"Dave Bryson is Michelle's second in command," I explained. Dave and I had history but I didn't want to go into it right then. "She didn't say much other than that Dave worked on the file initially, but she preferred to send it outside. Hey, it's her call. That's why they pay her the big bucks; Michelle's one of the top five executives at Phoenix, dealing with the bruised egos of her subordinates comes with the territory."

AJ scratched his head. "True, but this is a landmark file, that's got to hurt."

"Not my problem." I was practically vibrating, I couldn't help myself. "We got the file!"

Another round of cheers and applause, then Bridget

asked if she needed to make any travel arrangements. "I assume you and Ray will be flitting off to Rome, right?"

"Not yet," I said. Ray Cook, Phoenix's Chief Operations Officer, was still finalizing some technical specifications with Vesper's CEO. Ray would bring me in to draft the contracts after they'd been settled.

*   *   *   *

That was in February. Nine months later Amy saw a dragon in the lake. And two months after that, I discovered who put it there.

CHAPTER 3

Raymond Cook is always late. I've worked with him on various projects in the past and not once has he made it to a meeting on time. If he were a mid-level manager, I could nudge him with pointed comments about the meter running whether he shows up or not, but he's a high-ranking executive, he'd show up when he was good and ready. As my sister Louisa says, sometimes you've got to go with the flow. I was in Rome, standing in the entrance to the breakfast room at the Hotel Monte Cenci, my usual table overlooking the boxwood terrace was free; I would go with the flow.

The tiny garden provided a soft green buffer between this venerable Roman hotel and the terracotta building next door. The breakfast room windows were slightly open and the delicate scent of Madonna lilies graced the air. I set my laptop on the linen tablecloth and stood in the middle of the room, surveying the buffet table. Every morning I promised myself I'd try something new—the hotel offered everything from muesli to fish—but again I returned to my table with my usual: crusty rolls, soft cheese, and pineapple. Why tamper with perfection.

Isabella was waiting for me when I sat down. She shook her head, tut-tutting. She's in charge of the breakfast room and took me under her wing when I arrived.

"You eat like a little bird," she said, setting my cappuccino down on the white tablecloth. "This is not breakfast. Have some apple cake. The Torta della Nonna is nice, cake with cream and nuts." I managed to negotiate her down to a small cup of yogurt and she darted over to the buffet table to scoop it up before I changed my mind. She returned with two yogurt cups and an apple tart and waited with her arms crossed while I peeled off the first tinfoil lid. "A busy day today?" she asked.

"Yes, a busy day. We're meeting with Signore Clemente today."

"Not Signore Calisto?"

I tried not to choke on my coffee. Had Isabella overheard me grumbling to Ray about the odious Signore Piero Calisto? He was Faro Clemente's partner, an older man, soon to retire and clinging to his law practice and the prestige it conferred with the stubborn tenacity of a limpet. On my first day here, before Ray arrived, Calisto professed to be shocked that a big company like Phoenix would entrust such an important file to a 'little nothing girl' like me.

I'd pulled myself up to my full five-five-or-so height, pushed a lock of hair behind my ear and informed him that my firm, Lawson Valentine, had an outstanding reputation; furthermore, as my mom used to say, I was 'félelmetes' which means formidable or something like that in Hungarian. I probably didn't need to add that last bit.

Isabella eyed me curiously. "Signore Calisto. He is a nice man?"

I pretended I hadn't heard her properly and replied, "Signore *Clemente*, Faro, is a very nice man."

Faro was a confident lawyer who met life's challenges with easy grace. He was in his mid thirties, close to my age, and far less judgmental than his older partner. He'd overheard Calisto's 'little nothing girl' comment and announced they'd take me to lunch to make amends. Calisto resisted the idea until Faro reminded him they could expense the lunch to their client, Vesper.

A couple of hours later we were strolling down the shady side of the street to escape the sun blasting off the pavement; it was unseasonably warm for April. Soon we were seated at a small table in a charming little restaurant called Luna's. Calisto snatched the menu out of the waiter's hand, lay it in front of me and pointed to various dishes he thought I should try.

Faro peppered me with questions while Calisto prattled in my ear. Did I ski in the Rocky Mountains (no), did I like the cold winters (no, I barely survived), was it true the birds froze in mid flight and shattered when they hit the ground (yes, and polar bears roam through our backyards).

Eventually the waiter returned, setting our selections in front of us with care. When the pasta slithered off my fork for the third time, I realized bucatini had been a mistake. Calisto raised his arm, loudly demanding a spoon for his guest. This was an insult: only small children eat pasta with a spoon in Italy. I said I was fine, thank you, and made a mental note to eat nothing but gnocchi, penne, or risotto in his presence.

Faro broke the sticky silence that followed by asking Calisto to tell me about his background. Calisto beamed, saying he hailed from the great city of Milan in northern Italy. It was terribly expensive but blessed with rich history, art, and culture. He was expounding on the beauty of the Duomo when Faro interrupted.

"Ah yes," he said, "Milan is a magnificent city, but—"

Faro shot me a mischievous grin. "Piero was born in Bari, in Puglia." His smile widened. "Puglia is about as far south as you can get in Italy."

Calisto turned red as a tomato, and not from the heat.

"Bari is on the sea," Faro continued. "That is why Piero enjoys seafood so much." We all glanced at Calisto's plate, piled high with discarded mussel shells.

Calisto carefully dabbed his lips with a snowy white napkin. "I moved to Milan when I was a young boy—"

"Not so young, a university student," Faro interjected.

"Yes, yes, a university student," Calisto conceded. "And I've lived in Milan ever since."

"You mean until you moved to Rome." Faro patted Calisto's hand gently as if he were a dotty old uncle. "Piero misses the south. At this rate he'll be back in Bari in time to retire."

Calisto snatched his hand away; his face was tight, unamused.

The following day Calisto announced he was much too busy working on a very important matter and Faro would assume conduct of the Vesper file.

"Miss Evie." Isabella brought me back from my reverie. "There is Signore Ray." She hustled off to greet Ray who was standing in the doorway, a vacant look on his face. She pointed him in my direction and he ambled over, blinking in the soft morning sunlight.

"Late night?" I asked.

He grunted, gestured to Isabella for his usual, an Americano, then sat down and stared out the window at the garden. Ray had spent the last two months flying back and forth to Italy for meetings with Matteo Vianelli, Vesper's CEO, and the rest of the Vesper team. He always stayed at this hotel and Isabella knew his preferences better than I did. But even I knew it was pointless trying to talk to Ray before the caffeine kicks in and I pulled up The Guardian on my laptop.

We were in no rush. Vesper's lawyers would not arrive until well past nine. On my first day here, I'd shown up at their office at 8 a.m. It was locked. I knocked and knocked until the hinges creaked and a beady black eye peered out through a tiny crack. It was the coffee lady. I showed her Faro's business card and she led me into a dim alcove outside his office. When I clicked on a lamp she exploded, making it clear in a burst of Italian that under no circumstances was I to touch the light. Later in the day I discovered why: the building was not air conditioned and its occupants did everything they could to stay cool. This meant turning off the lights and flinging open the windows to catch the early morning breeze, then shutting them tight for the rest of the day.

Eventually Ray set down his coffee cup and turned to me. "Okay, counsellor." He always called me that, even though I'd told him many times Canadian lawyers don't use that expression. "Ready to go?"

CHAPTER 4

Thirty minutes later we were meandering along the sidewalk. Ray was chattering like a magpie; I was distracted by shopkeepers sluicing water across the tiny patch of pavement outside their storefronts. Small trucks blocked traffic while wiry men unloaded blue plastic cartons and piled them high in doorways. It was early morning and already the air was thick with heat.

We came to a courtyard protected by a high stone wall. Faro's office was one of several located in an ancient three-storey building that formed a U around a stone terrace edged with skinny cypress trees and scruffy mulberry bushes. Birds flitted among the branches singing songs I'd never heard before.

We climbed the stone steps and let ourselves in. The coffee lady had tired of us banging on the door and would leave it unlocked so we could enter without distracting her from her duties, which as far as I could tell consisted of getting a cranky espresso machine to work properly without scalding everyone within a ten-foot radius.

"Buongiorno," I called out.

"Good morning," a male voice replied. Calisto? He was sitting in his office at the end of a narrow corridor. A shaft of sunlight flickered through wooden shutters onto papers piled high on his desk. A couple of law books lay open on the credenza behind him and a cardboard Banker's Box sat heavily on the floor.

"You're here early," I said.

"I'm always here early," he replied. Ray and I exchanged a glance. Calisto cleared his throat and ran a hand through his thinning hair. Always a fashion plate, today he wore a stone-coloured linen jacket and had a vintage Rolex strapped to his wrist. I wondered what he made of Ray, a professional engineer and business executive, who dressed like a cowboy and had enough hair for the two of them.

Calisto nodded at the Banker's Box. "Matteo's driver delivered this. He said you wanted to see the latest test results."

Matteo and Ray were wrestling with some lingering performance issues which had to be resolved before I was prepared to let Ray sign anything that would commit Phoenix to spending $75 million to upgrade its compressors. This jacked up Ray's stress levels but as I repeatedly told him, net-zero means nothing if it doesn't actually work.

Calisto stood up, flicking a hand toward the door. "You can use the coffee room." He shoved the box forward an inch with the tip of his fine-grained leather shoe.

"Here, let me." Faro Clemente moved effortlessly into the room. He shook his head at Calisto, saying the idea that Ray and I work out of the coffee room was preposterous. There was barely enough room for the coffee lady and the finicky espresso machine. "They radiate so much heat, it's unbearable." He picked up the box. "Come, you can work in the conference room next to my office."

Faro placed the box on the conference room table and

disappeared. Ray flicked through the test results while I pulled up the draft contract on my laptop.

Three hours later we were interrupted by a cacophony of noise. The sound of loud voices, piercing whistles, and rattling drums rolled up from the street. I was peering out the window when Faro popped back into the room and said the racket would continue for a while and this was as good a time as any to break for lunch. Ray waved a hand; we were free to go without him as long as we brought him back a pizza.

"What's all the racket?" I asked Faro.

He grinned. "You'll see." I followed him across the courtyard and onto the sidewalk into what looked like a protest but felt like a party. Hundreds of men and women waving red placards, banners, and balloons marched down the street; traffic was at a complete standstill.

"What are they saying?" I asked.

"They're SI, *Sinistra Italiana*, a left-wing socialist party; democratic socialism and green policies." The crowd was deafening, I could barely hear him.

He bent closer and shouted in my ear. "Come, we'll go to Milvio."

"Milvio?"

"Bakery, pizza, fast food, come on." The wall of protesters appeared impenetrable, but he grabbed my wrist and boldly stepped off the curb. We angled across the street like a sailboat heading into the wind. The marchers slowed down to let us pass and we emerged, safe, on the other side.

"That was exhilarating!" I shouted. "Very different from the protests back home. For some reason ours are characterized by semi-trailers and exhaust fumes." Faro shook his head, saying something about polarization that I didn't catch.

A few minutes later I was perched at a high-top table, eating the best fast food I'd ever tasted. Faro finished his sandwich and slowly sipped his coffee. He looked as comfortable here as he did at Luna's restaurant.

"How did you come to be working with Calisto?" I asked.

His eyes crinkled at the corners. "You think I don't belong with Piero?"

"It's not that." It was exactly that, but I didn't know how to say it without sounding nosy. "It's just that you and Piero are like chalk and cheese." My dad was an Englishman, and this was one of his favourite expressions. Over time many British clichés had become engraved in my vocabulary. Faro tipped his head to one side, not catching the reference. "What I'm saying is you and Piero are so very different."

"How do you mean?"

Faro was going to make me say it. "Well, Piero is what, twenty, twenty-five, years older than you? He seems more uptight, more focused on status and his position in the hierarchy. Whereas you, you're more relaxed; back home we'd say you're comfortable in your skin. You two seem to be an unlikely combination."

"Ah," he said, "like chalk and cheese."

"Precisely."

He rested his elbows on the table, smiled and took another sip of coffee. "Piero and I have very different backgrounds." His expression became thoughtful. "I shouldn't needle him like I do but sometimes he has it coming."

"You mean like when he announced to the entire

restaurant that the uncouth Canadian needed a spoon?" It was silly, but I felt more aggrieved about it now than I did at the time.

"Yes," he said. "Sometimes Piero needs to be put in his place." He paused. "Italy has a class system, just like England." Like everywhere, I thought, except ours is based on money more than genealogy.

"Italians from the north look down on Italians from the south; Italians from the south pretend they don't care, but they resent it. Piero is from the south. I'm from the north, Milan. I went to school there and in England." His shoulders lifted in a shrug. "Piero tries too hard to erase his background. You can't erase where you come from."

I said, "It shouldn't matter where anyone comes from. What matters is who they are, what they've made of themselves. In Canada, successful people boast about their humble beginnings. They're proud they made it to the top without the advantages of money, a private-school education, or their parents' connections."

An odd look, almost sad, flickered across Faro's face.

"No really, I mean it," I said. "I'm not being naïve." Was I?

He said, "Canada is a very young country. The legacy, no, the pedigree, doesn't count for you the same way it counts here. People like Piero who've come from nothing to become successful, they are very rare." He paused. "Unless they play soccer or belong to the Mafia."

It was quieter outside now. The *Sinistra Italiana* protest had moved farther down the block, the sound of banging drums and screeching whistles fading away. I grabbed Ray's takeout bag and slid off the stool.

Ray peered at us as we entered the small conference room. "God, I thought you two had been kidnapped." His sleeves were rolled up and his jacket hung limply on the chair next to him. The air was close and muggy but I didn't dare open the window.

"And yet you didn't text, or offer a ransom, or anything." I handed him the Milvio bag.

He guffawed, sliding the pizza and pastry out of the bag onto a sheet of paper covered with calculations. The coffee lady burst into the room carrying a small plate. She picked up Ray's food, arranged it on the plate, and shyly offered him a napkin. A minute later she returned with a small espresso in one hand and a cold orange soda in the other. When Ray thanked her in choppy Italian, she blushed and whispered something to Faro as she left.

"Francesca thinks you're a real cowboy," Faro said, a playful look in his eye.

I laughed. "Ray *is* a real cowboy — one who happens to live in a posh neighbourhood in the city. He owns two horses, he boards them at a fancy ranch in the countryside." I smiled at Ray. "He's the only guy I know who doesn't look like a dime store cowboy at the Calgary Stampede." Now it was Ray's turn to blush.

Faro's eyes shone with curiosity. "Horses? Are they wild? Broncos? Did you tame them yourself?"

"You mean break them? Hell no," Ray said. "They came to us, um, broken. Gentle as kittens. I got them for my wife and daughter."

"Two horses, not three, none for you?" Faro asked.

"Nope, I didn't need one."

Faro looked at Ray, unsure what to make of this comment. I knew the story and why Ray would not go into it. The horses were a last-ditch effort to save his teenage daughter who'd fallen in with the wrong crowd at her private school. I thought it was insane; if an irresponsible teenager couldn't take care of herself, how could she possibly take care of a horse? But Ray knew his daughter well. The girl turned herself around and was now studying medicine at Trinity College in Dublin. Ray refused to sell the horses after she went away to school. He said she liked to ride when she came home on break. I wondered whether the horses were a kind of talisman: as long as he owned them his daughter would be safe.

"Still," said Faro firmly. "You have horses, you are a cowboy." The matter was settled.

"How's it going?" I nodded at Matteo's files.

Ray took a slow, careful bite of his pizza then grinned. "Counsellor, after two months of back and forth, Matteo and yours truly finally nailed it."

CHAPTER 5

The countryside slid by the windows in a blur of green and yellow squares. The steady rhythm of the train clacking on the tracks was hypnotic, slowing my breathing, rocking me to sleep. I wriggled deeper into the seat cushion, thankful for the air conditioning. We were on our way to the Vesper plant which was located near Salerno, a small town south of Rome. The temperature and humidity were high, even at this early hour.

This promised to be an auspicious day—today we were signing the Vesper compressor contract—but it didn't start that way. Ray, never at his best first thing in the morning, went off the deep end when we discovered the hotel restaurant was closed because of the hospitality workers' strike. It's not as if we didn't have ample notice. There were *sciopero* signs everywhere. We simply hadn't given it much thought. Sure, we could survive with day-old towels and unmade beds, but we'd failed to consider that sciopero also meant no Isabella, no continental breakfast, and most importantly, no Americano for Ray. His face flushed with irritation when he discovered the strike included the coffee shops at the train station. Thumbs flying across his phone he texted Matteo, demanding that a pot of coffee be waiting for him when we arrived at the Vesper plant in a couple of hours.

Now he was sitting kitty corner to me in the facing seat; his head turned slightly away, his eyes half closed. Cranky and even more uncommunicative than usual. I sent Matteo an urgent text: *Make that TWO pots of coffee!*

The Salerno train station was small and deserted but for a shiny black Audi parked close to the entrance. Matteo's driver honked when he saw us and soon we were sailing down a winding country road to the plant. A friendly young woman greeted us in halting English and escorted us down the hall to an office at the end of a long corridor.

Matteo and Faro were all smiles and hearty handshakes, and we made ourselves comfortable at a metal conference table. But for the colourful photos of the manufacturing plant hanging on one beige wall and the safety awards gleaming on top of the filing cabinets, the room had a plain, utilitarian feel about it.

Ray reached for the stainless steel coffee carafe sitting in the centre of the table next to a plate of bombolone, those ubiquitous Italian donuts. He poured me a cup while I pulled a yellow legal pad out of my briefcase. Clients think lawyers write everything down to keep the facts straight, but sometimes it's the only way we can stay awake.

We reviewed the changes Faro made last night and confirmed they accurately reflected the modifications Matteo and Ray had requested. Faro, bless his heart, did not try to slip in any last-minute landmines as some lawyers are prone to do. I nodded at Ray; we were good to go.

The contract was fully executed in quadruplicate within minutes. Matteo threw his arms in the air as if he'd scored the winning goal at a soccer match and ran around the table to give Ray a high five. Ray laughed and pumped Matteo's hand and patted him on the back. Faro and I beamed like indulgent parents and after we all stopped congratulating each other Matteo asked if we had time for a quick tour of the plant.

He gave Ray's shoulder an affectionate squeeze and said, "Now I can show you all the Vespers that didn't make the grade."

"Dammit, Matteo," Ray said with a mock frown, "don't tell me that after you've unloaded twenty-six of the suckers on me."

As we crossed the cement quad it became obvious that unlike the administration building, the six-storey manufacturing plant was a state-of-the-art structure, a massive space intersected by crisp architectural lines and curving spaces.

We passed through another set of doors and entered a large high-ceilinged room. Light slanted across the white walls through tall windows and bounced off the shiny cement floor. Pipes, hoists, and overhead cranes marched across the room in orange, black, and yellow arrays.

Men and women scrambled down from movable staircases and emerged from around corners to gather around Matteo; they'd been waiting for this moment. Matteo clapped Ray on the back and said a few words in Italian. His employees drowned him out with whoops, cheers, and applause. Out came the cell phones, cameras clicking. Matteo and Ray posed in front of a prototype. Matteo beamed and Ray laughed and threw thumbs up at engineers and technicians he recognized in the crowd. I pulled out my cell and caught an image of the two men standing side by side, arms across each other's shoulders, laughing as if nothing could stop them now.

After the hubbub died down Matteo took us over to a prototype Vesper—we all called it Vesper now, the eight-digit model number was too cumbersome to remember. With its 3D carbon fibre blades and titanium shell it looked like a gigantic jet engine or an elongated space capsule.

We toured the test bed area where the Vespers were subjected to extreme stress, pressure, heat, and frigid cold that was well beyond anything they would experience in the field.

I nudged Ray. "Looks like they'll survive our winters."

"That's the idea," he nodded.

It was only when we returned to the Audi, now idling under an umbrella tree to avoid the blistering sun, that I realized the magnitude of the task Ray and Matteo had taken on. Everyone talks a good line about going net-zero; few have accomplished it.

*   *   *   *

The hotel doorman ushered us in with an elegant bow. Bell hops assisted travellers in the lobby and the front desk manager was scolding one of the housekeeping staff who scolded him right back. The hospitality workers' strike was over and everything had returned to normal.

As we crossed the lobby, I asked Ray whether he was interested in dinner on the terrace in the hotel. Normally Ray and I went our separate ways for dinner. He liked a blow-out multi-course meal followed by a raucous night of barhopping with Matteo, while I preferred the terrace where the air was sweet, a mixture of ancient dust and lemon trees, and I could eavesdrop on the lazy chatter of the other guests.

Ray was horrified. "You want to eat in? On our last night in Rome?" Every businessman I've ever travelled with thinks eating at the hotel restaurant is abhorrent and I have no idea why.

"Well, yeah. It will give us a chance to — oh, I don't know, relax. Reminisce about what a great job we've done."

He bugged out his eyes like a child.

I laughed and said, "Okay, fine. But if we're eating out, we have to go early. We're on the seven-twenty flight out of here tomorrow; that's a.m., Ray. We have to be in the cab by four-thirty or we'll never make it through security—"

"Dammit!" Ray cut me off, a scowl on his face. "I promised Linda a souvenir, something from that restoration studio."

"What restoration studio?"

He whipped out his cell phone and squinted at the screen as he scrolled through his emails. "Ah, here it is, Studio something-I-can't-pronounce, specializing in artworks made from glass and ceramic — it's not too far from here. If I go now, I can get it out of the way before dinner." Then he sighed. "Not that we need any more junk in the house."

I knew Linda, but not very well. I'd met her at a couple of industry functions. She was a small, expensively-dressed woman who had Ray scurrying all over the place fetching her drinks and canapés. All it took was a quiet word and a dewy-eyed smile.

Ray was across the lobby and out the door in pursuit of Linda's gift before I finished asking the concierge to book us reservations at a restaurant close by.

CHAPTER 6

The sun was a soft red ball and the rooftops were smudged with a velvety grey light when I arrived at the restaurant and wound my way up a narrow flight of stairs to the rooftop terrace. Candles flickered on the tables and Ray was nowhere to be seen.

A sturdy waiter in a starched white shirt and black tie handed me a menu. He said the chef liked his dishes to reveal their flavours gradually. He called it buio which meant darkness. I thanked him and ordered a tall gin and tonic. If Ray didn't reveal himself to me soon, he'd have to carry me back to the hotel.

I was trying to figure out which of the many domed cathedrals shining on the horizon was the Pantheon when Ray plopped down in the chair opposite me.

We ordered and soon he was plowing his way through the antipasti, the primi course and the secondi course, several cocktails and one and a half bottles of wine while I grazed on my salad and stuffed myself with bread. We always ate well on the company's dime.

His eyes became brighter and his speech more animated as he described his visit to the art studio. At first he was disappointed, nothing sang to him regardless of the price tag. Then the attendant took him into the back and showed him a blown glass sculpture. Ray passed me his phone to show me a photo.

"It looks like a Chihuly," I said. "How big is it?"

He grinned. "Huge, something like five or six feet in diameter."

I looked at the photo again. It was an enormous glass ball of spikes and curly tendrils, glistening blue, green, and red in the fading light of the studio. The gallery had not yet prepared it for display but would be happy to package it up for delivery to Canada if Ray was interested. It would arrive in a month's time without so much as a scratch. Ray gladly handed over his credit card.

"Linda's going to love it," he said. "It looks like a blob right out of a science fiction movie."

"Congratulations, Ray," I said, touching my wine glass to his. "On the glass blob and more importantly on the Vesper deal. I'll bet Bannerman is happy."

He drained his wine, reached for the bottle and refilled his glass. "Bannerman's like all CEOs. He won't be happy until all the Vespers are online. He wants to announce we're at net-zero by September."

"That's only—"

"I know, four months. Less than that, to get the prototype up and running at Elliot Lake and install the remaining twenty-five as they roll off the assembly line. The minute the prototype is cleared for performance the rest will go online."

"Can't you push the go-live date back a couple of months? I mean, this is revolutionary new technology, there are bound to be some glitches along the way."

"Nope." He took a large gulp of wine, then spoke through clenched teeth. "Bannerman's bonus, everyone's bonus, is riding on us going live by September first."

He wiggled the wine bottle at me; I shook my head, he finished it off, then waved a hand at the waiter, indicating he'd like another.

By the time the sun slipped behind the terracotta buildings across the way and a humid darkness crept across the patio, Ray was drunk and feeling nostalgic. He and Matteo were like brothers, he said. They'd met in January when Ray issued the bid for proposals. He'd travelled to Europe, the US, and Asia, visiting companies that made the shortlist. Once Ray selected Vesper as the winning bidder, Matteo invited him back to Rome to celebrate with 'one hell of a booze-up.'

"That's when I found out Matteo was connected."

"To the mob?"

He laughed. "Jeez, Evie, not everyone in Italy belongs to the Cosa Nostra. No, Matteo knows someone who can get his hands on exotic cars at a really good price." Ray described the glorious day he'd spent tearing up the Italian countryside in high-end sports cars before finally settling on a Ferrari something or other.

"If you're ever in the market for a nice car or boat, let me know. Matteo will tee it up so it runs through Italian and Canadian customs without costing you an arm and a leg."

I frowned. "I don't know, Ray. You know what they say about something that's too good to be true..."

"No worries there. I ran it by Dave Bryson, he said when in Rome, do as the Romans do. It's all above board."

Ah yes, Dave Bryson, the second-most senior lawyer at Phoenix after Michelle. Dave and Ray had been friends for years. Dave's 'when in Rome' assertion was exactly what people tell themselves before they're charged with violating the *Corruption of Foreign Public Officials Act.*

A waiter appeared at Ray's elbow, suggesting Ray might like another bottle of wine. Before Ray could respond, I asked for the bill. The waiter raised a skeptical eyebrow at Ray who nodded his assent.

The air was warm and heavy as we strolled back to the hotel. We took our time. Neither of us was in any rush to return to the frigid prairies.

CHAPTER 7

"Pssst, Quincy, wanna go for a run?" It was four-thirty in the morning. I didn't know why I was whispering; my sister Louisa, a nurse, was working the night shift, she wouldn't be home for hours. Meanwhile Quincy, her bull terrier, was out cold and snoring like a band saw on her bed. After Louisa divorced her wretched husband, she and Quincy moved in with me. It was supposed to be a temporary arrangement, just long enough for Louisa to get back on her feet, but five years later they were still here. It caused a bit of a kerfuffle with the neighbours, we have the same dark hair and brown eyes, and in the beginning they couldn't tell us apart.

Quincy raised his head, surveyed me with a bleary eye, then scrambled off the bed sending the pillows flying in all directions. He knows he's not allowed up there, but he's a sneaky little guy.

"Come on you goofus, you wanna go for a run or not?" He wagged his tail tentatively: a run at this hour? Really?

Jet lag is worse coming home than getting there, at least in my experience. I'd been wide awake for a full hour before I decided to put my insomnia to good use and go into the office.

But first, a run. I clipped Quincy into his harness and we headed to the footpath that leads down to the river behind our house. My townhouse is one of six nestled on the banks of the Bow in the Mission District. The front windows face a wide, leafy street, the back overlooks the riverbank lush with wolf willows, birch, and poplar trees. The sound of nesting birds and small animals scurrying through the underbrush competes with the background hum of traffic.

The wind sweeping across the river was cold and the sky, gun-metal grey, did not look promising. It was the end of April. If we were lucky, we might squeak through to spring without a 'gotcha' snowstorm that would freeze the budding branches.

"You should have seen them, Quincy." The dog twitched an ear but didn't look up. He's accustomed to me prattling on like this when we run. "Matteo's people at the Vesper plant, they were so excited, they know they're going to be a part of something big."

Then I slipped on some icy gravel and yanked reflexively on Quincy's leash to regain my balance. He gave me a look that said 'get a grip' and continued to trot along beside me. It might be spring in Rome, but it was still winter here.

*   *   *   *

The parking lot was deserted and I smiled at the prospect that I'd actually made it into the office before Keith. My partner lives in the country with his wife and six-year-old daughter. He arrives at the crack of dawn, puts in a full day, then barrels down the highway to get home in time for dinner and a couple of hours of doing whatever it is people do in their free time on country acreages.

I unlocked the front doors and paused, reveling in the

quiet; no phones ringing or computers binging, just the delicate pink sunrise gleaming softly on the mahogany walls. I was putting the coffee on when Keith came up behind me.

"Hey, Evie, welcome back." The fine lines around his eyes crinkled in a smile. I caught myself before I gave him the classic Roman greeting, kiss-kiss-kiss on both cheeks. The poor man would be mortified.

"We got your email, sounds like it went well. Michelle must be pleased."

"Given that she took a chance on us"—Lawson Valentine was the smallest firm to bid on the file—"it's a damn good thing she's pleased."

He peered into the coffee maker, then gently pried the glass carafe out of my hand. "Coffee tastes better if you put grounds in the filter before you pour in the water and turn it on."

"What, people don't like decaf around here?"

"There's decaf and there's no-caf. No-caf is hot water." He chuckled and reached for the filter box in the cupboard above the sink, then tucked a new filter into the coffee basket and spooned coffee inside.

"You know what we need," I said, "our very own coffee lady. Faro's coffee lady could make their beast of an espresso machine whip up anything you wanted."

We watched the coffee pot burble until there was enough to fill our cups, then wandered into Keith's office. I stepped over a pile of files and made myself comfortable in one of his visitor's chairs. Keith stopped in front of his credenza, picked up an antique clock and cranked the small brass key at the back. It ticked slowly, the clock glass reflecting the sparkling river beyond his windows.

"I assume Ray has settled down," he said. I'd told him

Ray was one of the most mercurial clients I'd ever had, uncommunicative in the morning, voluble, especially when drunk, at night.

"Let's put it this way, Ray was very relaxed on our last night in Rome."

The roar of AJ's MGB roadster, followed by the out-raged cries of crows, blasted through Keith's window. "Does he do that every morning?"

"Only in the spring, summer, and fall. He says the roadster needs an Italian tune-up after being cooped up in the garage all winter. I think he's getting revenge on the crows for crapping on the front seat that time he left the top down."

AJ came to us straight out of law school. He's athletic but not in a muscle-bound way, more like a world class soccer player. With sandy blonde hair, intelligent blue eyes, and an open, friendly face, he charms the clients—especially the female ones. We'd offered him an equity interest in the partnership a couple of months ago and were delighted when he accepted.

"Evie Valentine! You're back!" AJ bounded in the door like an overgrown puppy, his cheeks were red and his black cashmere scarf crackled with static electricity when he pulled it off. It looked expensive and I wondered if it was a gift from his mother.

"Did you drive in with the top down?" I shivered. "It's freezing outside."

"It's refreshing, bracing..." He saw the look of horror on my face and changed the topic. "How was Italy? You guys signed the deal. Did you see the share price this morning?"

"Italy was fantastic, yes we signed the deal, no I didn't see the share price this morning."

Keith's eyes bounced back and forth between AJ and me, trying to keep up. We often communicate this way, like we're batting a ping pong ball back and forth across the table. Keith is more reflective, a slower thinker. He once said he was amazed we accomplished anything at all, given our inability to hold a thought for more than five seconds.

Keith raised his hand and said, "The shares spiked yesterday when Phoenix announced the deal was signed; they're a little lower today. The market is waiting to see whether Phoenix can deliver on its promise to go full net-zero in September."

There was a commotion in the lobby, closets opening and closing, chairs rolling across plastic floor mats. Bridget barged into Keith's office, Madeline strolled in behind her.

"Evie, I thought I heard your voice." Bridget's face lit up and she crushed me in a big, prairie girl hug. Our administrative assistant is taller and stronger than I am, wears very little makeup and sensible shoes. Her 'get 'er done' attitude reminds me of Rosie the Riveter.

Madeline, our paralegal, took a discrete step back to avoid being drawn into a group hug. She's a good two decades older than Bridget and considerably more sophisticated. With her thick auburn hair and penchant for retro clothing, she's glamorous in a 1950s movie star kind of way.

"Welcome home!" Bridget grinned. "You look like you've been to Hawaii. So what'd you bring us?" Eyes bright, she rubbed her palms together in anticipation.

Madeline shook her head. "Bridget," she scolded. "It was a business trip, not a holiday."

Bridget waved her off with a flick of the wrist. "It was a trip to Rome, not Moose Jaw. Well...?"

I laughed. "As a matter of fact, I did pick up a little something for you guys." I went back to my office, scooped up the two paper bags sitting on my desk and returned to Keith's office. With the five of us packed in there it was getting very crowded. "Voila, treats from Roma!"

"'Voila' is French," Keith said. I ignored him as I set one clunky bag on his desk and passed the other to Bridget.

Bridget oohed and ahhed as she ripped open a large foil-wrapped box filled with marzipan, chocolate, and silver candied almonds. AJ grabbed the other bag before Keith could touch it, tossed aside the tissue paper and pulled out an oversized bottle of Limoncello. The golden liqueur gleamed in the morning light.

I said, "Limoncello is one of Ray's favourites. He says you should drink it cold; that doesn't improve the taste, but if you're still drinking when the bottle is warm, there's a damn good chance you're hammered."

After a short debate about whether we should test Ray's theory here and now we decided to save the bottle for a real celebration. Madeline whisked the candies and booze into the coffee room where, under Bridget's watchful eye, she divided the sweets into two serving dishes, one for Bridget's desk and one for her own.

The room became considerably quieter after they left. AJ picked up his cashmere scarf which had fallen to the floor, and said, "You were talking about your trip...?"

"Right. Well, that was about it. You should see those compressors, they're amazing. Like jet engines on steroids." I picked up my cell phone and flicked through the photos I'd taken in the plant.

"You've got too many shots of people and not enough of the factory," AJ complained.

"The people are there for scale," I replied. "That's what my dad used to say when we went on road trips and he made Louisa and me stand next to a big boulder or weird statues like the giant perogy in Glendon."

Keith and AJ were debating which strange giant statue—the pinto bean on Bow Island or the Starship Enterprise in Vulcan—was the most impressive when I left to ask Bridget to draw up the bill. The Vesper file may be a game-changer, but it progressed the same way as all our other files: retainer letter, work in progress, final statement.

Madeline called out as I passed her office. "I've sent you a draft announcement to put into *Lexpert's Big Deals* section." Madeline projects an air of amused detachment but when it comes to the firm, she's a bigger booster of our achievements than we are. "It's time to crow from the rooftops," she said with a smug smile.

I expected the deal would get lots of coverage in the legal and trade publications. And it did. But for all the wrong reasons.

The Day It Happened

November 12, 10:01 A.M.

CHAPTER 8

"Move!" Kirsten's voice was raw in her throat. The twins clawed their way farther up the snowbank. Where's Amy? Kirsten had knocked the little girl over when she shoved the boys onto the shore. There! Amy was sprawled on the ice, face down. Kirsten reached out, grabbing Amy's hood, hauling her closer.

"Up, Amy. Get up. That's my girl." The child was quiet. Kirsten dug her skates into the snow, desperately struggling for purchase as she heaved Amy's limp body a foot closer to the base of a giant fir tree. Tyler reached for Amy's hand. "Grab her!" Kirsten yelled. "Pull her up!"

Kirsten felt it again, this time in her feet and knees. Another deep tremor radiating out from the centre of the lake, like a living creature, sensing them, seeking them.

"Get back!" she screamed at the children. *Where? Nowhere is safe.*

A split second of silence. Then *crack*. The crystalline lake shattered. Ice heaved and splintered. A silver metal spine bucked on the surface, coiling and flailing in a murky black pool. Water, steel, rocks, and mud shot through the air like shrapnel. *The shock wave.*

"Stay down!" Kirsten screamed, spreading her arms, frantically trying to shield the children with her body. "Stay down!"

Shards of metal arced across the sky, biting deep into tree trunks and snowbanks. Dismembered branches, clods of dirt, and ice rained down on them like an airborne avalanche.

Then a splash.

Please God, let it be over.

Five Months Earlier

June

CHAPTER 9

"It is remarkably flat." Faro Clemente, Vesper's lawyer, pivoted in the seat of the SUV, straining against his seat belt as telephone poles flashed past the window. Fields of bright green canola glowed against an intense blue sky. Soon the crop would turn to gold, ready for harvest.

Matteo sat up front next to Ray; Faro, Michelle, and I were jammed into the bench seat behind them. We were on a road trip. Ray was taking us to the Elliot Lake compressor station to check out the Vesper prototype. It had been installed in May and according to Michelle was experiencing what Ray called 'teething problems.' For over a month Matteo and his team of engineers had proposed all sorts of solutions, but nothing worked. And now Matteo was here to see for himself why the Vesper refused to do what it had been designed to do. Since Matteo never went anywhere without Faro, Ray invited me. At the last minute Michelle announced she was coming along for the ride.

Faro lowered his window for a better view. Heat blasted into the car, blowing my hair into my eyes.

Matteo said something in Italian; Faro replied in English. "Yes. Nothing like Tuscany."

"That's why it's called big sky country," I said, peering over Faro's shoulder. Michelle was quiet, staring out the window on the other side, oblivious to the breeze flapping her ruffled silk collar against her chin.

"Sky? No, I'm talking about the earth," Faro said. "It is very flat."

"Yes, I know, but look out to the horizon, where the earth meets the sky." He stuck his head out his window. "If you stepped out of the car right now, assuming you didn't get your head knocked off by that truck," he ducked back into the car, "you could turn a full three-hundred-sixty degrees and see nothing but blue sky, like a crystal bowl hanging over the landscape."

Faro smiled politely and rolled up his window. "Yes, it's very pretty. But it's too big. Where are the hills and the trees?" An image of the Tuscan countryside came to me. Louisa and I toured Tuscany right after I finished law school. We were captivated by the rolling green hills and the tall cylindrical trees; Louisa called them Mona Lisa trees because they reminded her of the painting.

Faro shuddered. "No, it's too much sky. A person is like a tiny mouse out in a field, there's nowhere to hide from the eagles." As if on cue a very large bird flapped down onto a telephone pole, spread its dark wings, and soared back up again, making lazy circles in the air.

"How much farther?" Michelle asked.

"Half an hour." Ray glanced at Matteo. Both men had been unusually quiet on the ninety-minute drive from the city. This was understandable given the Vesper's reliability problems. Michelle said their boss was putting a lot of pressure on Ray to get the prototype up and running. 'Green light Elliot Lake, Ray, then green light the rest.' Michelle mimicked the tense exchange Ray and Bannerman had had outside her office. 'September first is a hard deadline, Ray.'

When I asked what Bannerman would do if the compressors weren't ready, she said Ray would be in a very difficult position. When Bannerman latched onto an idea, it required superhuman effort to change his mind.

The car's indicator ticked loudly as Ray navigated a tight turn onto a two-lane gravel road. We passed through a chain-link fence and parked on the tarmac in front of a building the size of a soccer pitch. We had arrived.

Ray led us into a small room furnished with a metal desk, a couple of chairs and a desiccated plant. Marty, a burly young man wearing a company baseball cap, said he was delighted to be our 'tour guide' but first we had to don protective gear and watch the safety video.

Just as we were about to enter the main part of the building Marty shouted, "Ladies, shoes!" And pointed at Michelle's feet.

Decked out in our yellow hard hats, safety goggles, earmuffs, and Nomex overalls we looked like minions, except I was wearing flats and Michelle was in heels. Marty turned to look at Ray, who wagged his finger at Michelle and said, "Okay, we'll let you through this time... but..." then made a tsking noise.

We followed Marty deeper into the building. Energy crackled in the air. Not a sound really, more like the feeling you get in the pit of your stomach when you stand too close to the amp at a rock concert. Machinery hummed, gauges flicked, lights blinked. Highly flammable natural gas coursed through reinforced steel piping all around us.

Ray and Matteo veered off to a bank of computers where a small group of technicians was waiting to brief them.

Michelle, Faro, and I trailed behind Marty who stopped next to a metal staircase at the base of a platform.

The Vesper compressor was suspended above us, its elongated space capsule body gleaming in the bright overhead lights. As we climbed the metal stairs, we could see a section of its titanium outer shell had been removed, exposing a black tangle of wires; fat cords connected the Vesper's innards to a computer terminal sitting on an upturned metal box on the platform.

Laying a hand gently on the Vesper's titanium sheathing, Marty said, "This little beauty repressurizes the gas entering at one end of the compressor station and pushes it out the other side. Along the way greenhouse gases are extracted to be stored off-site." He gazed at the compressor. "When we get her working right, we'll have the first net-zero pipeline system on the planet."

Michelle ran her fingers along its metal skin. Marty grabbed her hand. "Careful, Michelle. Those blades are razor sharp." I crowded closer to them and said the Italians used explosive bolts at the base of the blades to test the metal shell's integrity.

Marty's eyes grew wide. "Makes sense. The last thing we need is compressor blades flying around because it sucked in a hard hat."

We passed Ray and Matteo as we headed toward the back of the building. They'd moved down the long table and were now standing with a technician who was pointing at a computer screen.

The dull vibration in my chest became heavier as we approached another series of units high up on raised platforms.

"These are the old compressors, right?" Michelle raised her voice to be heard. Marty nodded. These units were larger, duller, and bulkier than the Vesper. In essence they were a series of massive pistons, arranged in banks of eight and ten, surrounded by tubes connecting to pipes that snaked up to the ceiling.

"We'll scrap these, once the Vesper goes online," Marty said.

A line from the safety video popped into my head. *Follow the instructions of company personnel in the unlikely event of an alarm signalling an incident has occurred.*

"Marty? What would happen if a compressor exploded?"

He tugged at the visor of his hard hat, pulling it down over his eyebrows. "Christ, that'll never happen."

"I'm curious too," Michelle said.

He grimaced and said, "You know those movies where a nuke explodes? It's the same thing. The first explosion is a sonic boom. It would flatten everything in the death zone. The second explosion would send a shock wave down the pipe. The sudden increase in pressure would unroll the pipe which then self-evacuates."

Faro bent his head so close to Marty's that their hard hats almost touched. "Self-evacuates? I don't understand."

Marty stepped back. "The pipe throws itself out of the ground. They're laid in trenches, right? The trench is refilled, but the fill is never as hard as the surrounding soil, so when the pipe comes out of the ground it blows everything out of the ditch. Crap flies everywhere. There's a spark, and the natural gas ignites."

"How do you stop it?" I asked.

"Listen," he shook his head. "That will never happen. We know what we're doing."

"But still," Faro glanced at me, then said, "if it did happen, how would the company respond?" We're lawyers, we focus on the worst-case scenario regardless of how unlikely it is.

"The guys in gas control shut the valves, whatever's left in the pipe dissipates, and that's that." Marty smiled again. "Really, there's no need to worry about explosions. We know what we're doing."

That was the second time he'd said that and I wondered whether we'd offended him with our persistent questions. Too bad, I couldn't stop now.

"How much time would people have to get out of the death zone? Would alarms go off?"

"Sure, alarms go off." Marty pointed at the emergency stations positioned at intervals along the walls. "See those big red buttons? They're alarms. You pull them, not push them." He chuckled. "We changed them out after a high school class came through and some yahoo leaned against a button as he was taking a selfie. Caused quite a commotion in gas control until we called to let them know it was a false alarm."

Michelle eyed Marty carefully, then looped her arm through his. She lifted her face and said something about alarms that I couldn't hear over the thrum of the machinery.

Marty glanced over his shoulder—Ray and Matteo had disappeared—and suggested a quick tour of the yard. It wasn't until we'd stepped out into the blazing heat that I realized why Marty hadn't answered my question: *how much time would people have to get out of the death zone?* No time. It was called the death zone because there was no time to get out.

Michelle fell into step with Marty, still clinging to his arm and leaning close to ask questions. At first, I thought she might be unsteady in her heels on the loose gravel, then I remembered the technique she used to ferret out information. She'd disarm people by asking simple questions she already knew the answers to, then go deeper and deeper to get the answers they were reluctant to share. Michelle knew all about explosions and death zones and self-evacuations, she was digging for something else.

By the time Faro and I caught up with them they were standing in the shade of a tall outbuilding. Michelle nodded, fully engaged as Marty waved a hand at the three-storey building on the other side of the gravel pad.

"See those metal cylinders," he was pointing at what looked like a set of giant salt and pepper shakers, "they're mufflers. They keep the noise level down so at the fence line the station is as quiet as a dishwasher." Not my dishwasher, I thought.

Forty-five minutes later, after touring every outbuilding on the site, we returned, flushed and sticky, to the reception area to sign out and join Ray and Matteo in Ray's air-conditioned SUV.

"So what'd you think?" Ray asked as he drove back out through the chain-link fence. Before we could respond he added, "You know what, you guys should visit the Vault." He glanced over at Matteo. "I could arrange a tour the next time you're in town."

The Vault was a high security building located in the northeast quadrant of the city that housed the company's gas control room. I told Ray to count me in. I've never understood the math behind engineering, but I love watching how things are made. The highlight of one family vacation to the Okanagan was a tour of the Sunkist factory where Louisa and I watched peaches roll down the assembly line and emerge out the other side as peach juice in sealed juice boxes. Dad called the boxes 'poppers,' the English have all sorts of weird names for things.

Matteo said that as much as he would like to accept

Ray's invitation, he sincerely hoped that they would resolve the Vesper's 'teething problems' and he could spend the summer with his family at their house on Lake Como.

Ray laughed, "I hear you buddy," and swooped onto a cloverleaf looping us onto the highway back to the city.

"Faro, look." I nudged Faro who was dozing in his seat, his head slowly bobbing up and down with the motion of the car and pointed out his window.

"My God." His eyes shone with excitement. Michelle stirred beside me and peered over my shoulder.

Billowing thunderheads hung heavy over the canola fields to the west. Lightning flashed silently across the darkening sky. Ray met my eyes in the rear-view mirror and grinned. The boys from Italy were in for a show. The car shuddered as the wind picked up and rain lashed the windshield.

"Here's hoping it doesn't hail," I said to Ray.

He nodded. "That's why we're in a fleet car, better this jalopy than the Ferrari." No sooner had he said it than the first hailstone tinked off the roof. Within minutes the car sounded like a popcorn bag inside a microwave. Hailstones battered the roof and hood, bouncing up into the windshield. The road ahead was a writhing white strip.

"Will the windshield hold?" Matteo shouted.

"We'll know soon enough," Michelle said. I could hardly hear her over the drumming on the roof. Ray said he'd pull over at the next underpass.

"You and everyone else on this highway," I yelled back. Ray's eyes narrowed as he scanned the road ahead. Then as quickly as it had started, the hail stopped. By the time we reached the city the sun was glimmering behind the clouds. Trees sparkled with rain and children darted back and forth, scooping up handfuls of hail to fling at each other. Adults trudged through their yards, inspecting the damage to their homes and vehicles.

"Wow, will you look at that." Faro pointed out Michelle's window. An elderly couple was standing beside a demolished hedge in their front garden. Wind whistled through a jagged hole in their living room window and large chunks of siding had been torn away.

"It looks like someone machine-gunned the place," Michelle said softly.

The ferocity of the damage abated by the time we reached the downtown core. Ray dropped Matteo and Faro at their hotel and circled around the ramp into the Phoenix parking garage, stopping in front of the visitor's stall where I'd left the Mini. He grinned broadly when I thanked him for the tour. "My pleasure, counsellor."

Just as I reached for the door handle Michelle touched my arm. "Evie, can you stay for a few more minutes? Ray, I need you too."

Ray glanced at his watch. It was just after 6:30 p.m. on a Friday. He pursed his lips and said, "Sure, I need to make a call. Meet you in your office. Okay?"

CHAPTER 10

The marble and terrazzo lobby was deserted when Michelle and I stepped out of the parking garage elevator. I followed her past the koi pond. The koi were gone and the pond was dry. It was a shame really, the koi were the only thing that distinguished the Phoenix, a nondescript glass and steel tower, from all the other office towers built three decades ago. Employees referred to it as the Girder; unlike its British counterparts the Gherkin and the Shard, there was nothing about the Girder to excite the imagination. Although it's hard to conceive what an architect could do to reflect the identity of the building's occupant short of setting the place on fire.

The security guard looked up and Michelle said, "She's with me." He nodded and let me pass.

There was no one at the executive reception desk when we stepped off the elevator on the thirty-eighth floor. The lights were dimmed and the massive earthenware urns on either side of the glass entryway gave the place a moody, Aladdin's cave feel. Rumour had it that Bannerman's security staff checked the urns every morning for bombs.

Michelle asked if I wanted any water. Although we'd both been cooped up in an SUV for several hours, she was fresh and unruffled, while I felt like a crumpled Kleenex. The sun caught the glass pitcher sitting on the rosewood conference table and the water became a tiny rainbow as it splashed into my glass.

"Long time, no see," Ray said with a grim smile as he ambled into the room. Right behind him was Dave Bryson, Michelle's second in command. "Evie, I believe you and Dave know each other. I asked Dave to join us, seeing as he handles our day-to-day legal work." True, but if Michelle had wanted Dave here, she'd have invited him; she didn't and his unexpected appearance irritated me.

Dave gave me a curt nod and slipped into the chair beside Ray. We've known each other since law school. He was a little rounder and better dressed now, his curly hair nicely trimmed, his trousers neatly pressed, but he still had an air of ingratiating pomposity. We'd competed for the same articling positions after graduation. When I landed a coveted spot at one of the Big Five, he told everyone I'd been offered the position solely to meet the firm's diversity quota.

But karma has a way of making things right. After four years in private practice Dave went in-house with Phoenix. Michelle was already on staff and when their boss retired, she was promoted to the position of Chief Legal Officer. Overnight she went from being Dave's peer to being his boss. Dave grumbled that Michelle's gender and Asian ethnicity gave her an unfair advantage, but over time they settled into an uneasy working relationship. Had I been in Michelle's shoes, I'd have shown him the door but she's a much nicer person than I am.

Michelle said, "It's been a long day so I'll get straight to the point. Ray, I had a disturbing conversation with Marty this afternoon. He says the alarms monitoring the pipe at Elliot Lake kept going off, and you disabled them."

Ray glanced at Dave who studied the carpet as if it

were the Rosetta Stone. Ray rubbed his chin, making a scratchy sound, and said, "Ah, yes. We turned them off. The guys knew they're false alarms so we turned them off."

"What?" Michelle's eyes were round and black.

"We've got bigger problems than the alarms." Ray sounded aggrieved but also a little nervous.

Michelle set her jaw and stared at him. Still and self-contained. No one was leaving this room until she got a satisfactory answer.

Ray's eyes flicked back to Dave. After a very long minute Dave said, "Look, the incessant alarms were distracting; the noise created an unsafe work environment for the operations techs. I told Ray he could turn them off."

Michelle rounded on Dave. "You shut off the health and safety alarms because they were unsafe from a health and safety perspective, is that what you're telling me?"

Dave sat back, arms folded across his chest, and said, "Legal support to Operations is my responsibility, Michelle. I deemed it to be necessary; the lesser of two evils."

Michelle's hand shot up, cutting Dave off. "I don't want to hear it." Her gaze shifted to Ray. "Turn the alarms back on, Ray. Now." Dave opened his mouth, thought better of it, and snapped it shut again.

Ray nodded, then said, "Michelle, we've got bigger problems than the alarms."

"What problems?"

"Today when we reviewed the Vesper data with the technicians, Matteo discovered something he called an anomaly in the AI system. Matteo is something of an AI expert, at least as far as the Vespers go, but neither he nor anyone on his team has the expertise to build a workaround."

"Oh God," Michelle let out a soft breath.

"Wait, wait." Ray held up both hands. "Before you flip out on me, Matteo knows someone who can fix this. He's called her in on past projects."

Eyes bright, Ray reached into his file folder and pulled out a few sheets of paper, passing them around:

"THE UNICORN" — JUDY JANGO, AI ENTREPRENEUR

It was Judy Jango's bio. Her headshot was that of an energetic young woman with light blue eyes, a wide smile, and spikey, bright blue hair. Her achievements were impressive: highly successful entrepreneur; sold her first AI company to Silicon Valley while still a student at Cambridge; divided her time between non-profit and for-profit ventures including projects to mitigate the effects of climate change.

Michelle's face softened. "She looks promising, where can we find her? Silicon Valley?"

"It could be tricky tracking her down on short notice," Ray said. "Matteo says she's always jetting off somewhere. But her home base is London. He's trying to set up a meeting in the next day or two." Ray cleared his throat. "Matteo will be taking Faro; I need to take a lawyer."

Right on cue Dave announced he had nothing pressing and could leave on a moment's notice. Michelle ignored him, turned to me and asked whether I could accompany Ray to London.

"Of course," I said.

Dave glowered at Michelle, then said, "Obviously you don't need me anymore." He glanced at his watch. "It's late, I'm heading out." With exaggerated care he picked Judy Jango's bio off the table and slid it into his file, then wished us a good weekend and marched out the door.

Ray coughed and said he'd get his assistant to contact my office to confirm travel arrangements.

After Ray left, Michelle moved over to the window wall. She was quiet for a few moments, staring at the mountains hidden by the shifting clouds. Then she turned around and leaned against the glass. I felt a flash of vertigo; it took every ounce of willpower I had not to leap up and drag her back to the safety of her desk.

"Unbelievable." The word came out hard as a bullet. "Shut off the alarms. Is he nuts?" I was wondering which one she was referring to, Dave or Ray, when she settled the matter with a resigned sigh. "You know those Continuing Ed courses for in-house counsel where they tell you you'll get ahead if you make yourself indispensable to the business team?" I did. It was a time-worn message that wasn't as simple as it sounded. "Dave thinks he's supposed to tell them what they want to hear, give them what they want, but sometimes we have to say no and force the company to go back to the drawing board to find another solution." She gave her head a little shake, then looked at me gratefully. "Thank you for agreeing to go to London, I know it's really short notice."

"Dave's not going to like it."

Her mood shifted again. "Oh, there's a lot Dave's not going to like by the time I get through with him. But guess what, I'm the Chief Legal Officer, what I say goes."

Perhaps, but I'd known Dave much longer than she had. He held grudges and nursed them hard.

CHAPTER 11

Louisa and I never get up at the crack of dawn on a Saturday, but today was Dinosaur Day, our annual pilgrimage to the Tyrrell Museum, and when I discovered Faro had nothing planned before he flew back to Rome this evening, I invited him to join us.

"Well," Louisa said, as she watched Faro stride out of his hotel and over to the Mini, "at least he's not wearing a brown fedora."

"What?"

She chuckled. "Look at him, he's dressed like Indiana Jones." She hopped out of the front seat, her light blue sun dress swirling around her bare legs, and clambered into the back so Faro could ride up front. He was wearing khaki slacks, a light-grey shirt and low walking boots. A brown bomber jacket was slung loosely over one shoulder. Yep, he did look like Indiana Jones, the younger version, and he was enjoying the view, which at the moment happened to be Louisa.

When I introduced him to Louisa he grinned, and despite her earlier derisive comment, she sparkled in a way I hadn't seen for a long time.

"You won't be needing that jacket," I said as he tossed his coat into the back seat.

"I checked the temperature," he said, "the high today

in Drumheller is twenty-five degrees Celsius. Not hot by Rome standards."

Louisa snorted. "Twenty-five degrees in Drumheller is thirty degrees anywhere else, trust me."

"Ah," Faro said, "you Canadians. A little heat is good for the bones."

Louisa and I exchanged a glance in the rear-view mirror, we'd see about that. Louisa told him since he was riding in the front it was his job to watch for hoodoos. He thought she said voodoos which led to a bizarre and yet entertaining exchange. By the time I pulled up in the museum parking lot I could see that Faro was besotted with my little sister.

Faro chattered excitedly as we approached the entrance to the building, a long flat structure designed to blend in with the rolling yellow hills. The air was hot and still. Prairie grass hissed and grasshoppers creaked as they sunned themselves on the rocks. Then came the quiet stillness of the air-conditioned lobby as we proceeded to the rooms that would eventually lead us to the Mass Extinction exhibits.

Every time we come here this happens: the excited babble of visitors gives way to thoughtful silence. There isn't a human being on the planet who isn't awestruck by the displays of strength and fragility.

* * * *

"Black Beauty was discovered by two schoolboys on a fishing trip, did you know that?" Faro was reading from a card affixed to the front of a large display case. Inside, a T Rex skull, five feet of bone and jagged teeth, gleamed under fairy lights. His eyes flicked from the skull in the case to the T Rex skeleton towering high above us. With its head flung back and its tail whipping in a high arc, it looked like it would leap off the fibreglass rocks and tear us to shreds.

Louisa flashed an indulgent smile. "Yes, I did know that. The kids spotted some strange scratches on a sandstone outcropping and figured they'd found a fossil of some kind." Louisa and I had been visiting the Tyrrell Museum every year since we were children. Between the two of us we knew every discovery story in the place.

Long necked dinosaurs towered overhead, an armoured dinosaur lay at our feet, a nest of baby dinosaurs slumbered in their pure white shells, never to awaken. It was a jumble of strangely shaped skulls, all jaws and eye sockets, fearsome claws, and powerful legs, representing life that existed millions of years ago, then vanished overnight.

We paused in front of a display: seven hominid skulls gleamed white against a shiny grey wall. Each one cast a longer darker shadow than the one before as they progressed through the seven stages of man.

"This is magnificent," Faro said. "Ancient Rome lasted a thousand years, but here, your fossil history goes back millions. Incredible."

Faro was right, it was incredible. Too often we focus on the history of civilization, forgetting that the Earth is over four billion years old, dinosaurs appeared 200 million years ago, and humanity has been around for just six million years. Given the impact our puny little species has had in such a short space of time, we need to shift to a longer time horizon.

He paused in front of the last skull in the display, *Homo sapiens.* "What will come after us?" Then with a curt shake of his head he moved along a blue-grey corridor to the glassed-in room where real paleontologists prepared fossils for display. The sight of museum staff poking at ancient bone fragments with dental picks and tiny mallets depressed me for some reason and I was relieved when Faro announced all this extinction talk had made him hungry.

A wall of heat hit us when we stepped out of the museum and made our way back to the Mini. It was like being inside an Easy-Bake Oven and I rolled down all the windows which didn't do much and waited for the A/C to kick in.

Faro started quizzing Louisa about the place names that flashed by on billboards at the side of the road. What was the nefarious history of Devil's Coulee, or Horsethief Canyon, or the Badlands? Louisa amused Faro with the same mix of fact and fiction we used to tell each other in the backseat of the car when Dad would solemnly declare, 'Girls, we are now leaving the pit of hell'—with his crisp British accent he sounded like a hoity toity tour guide— 'get your shillings ready because there will be hell to pay.' We'd shriek we didn't have any shillings and Mom would say she had enough shillings for the lot of us but she'd leave Dad behind if he didn't stop scaring us half to death.

I glanced at Louisa in the rear-view mirror. Of the three of us she was the only one who looked comfortable in the heat, but then again, she was wearing that little nothing sun dress. "Let's go to Madge's Diner," I said.

She nodded in approval and we both sang in unison, "The home of the mile-high lemon meringue pie!"

Faro grinned and said he couldn't wait to try it.

Soon we were pulling off the highway and sliding into a slot at the far end of the crowded parking lot. Faro stepped out of the car and arched his back, then asked us over to join him in a selfie in front of the ten-foot-high yellow and white neon version of Madge's signature pie. He said he collected photos of vintage neon signs, but I suspected what he really wanted was a snap of Louisa.

Over the years, Madge's had evolved from a gritty truck stop into a retro family restaurant with an interesting menu. Faro wondered whether he could manage a two-patty burger with poutine and pineapple rings—Louisa advised against adding pickled beets and banana peppers—and still have enough room for a pina colada milkshake and pie.

He glanced around the room after we placed our order, taking in the blue walls, the red tables and chairs and the black and white serviettes and placemats. In the back we could see the kitchen. The cook was muttering over a hot grill, oblivious to the magpies squawking on the other side of the screen door. Soon the waiter returned with three heaping plates. "This is nice," Faro said, "it reminds me of uni."

"Where did you go to university?" Louisa asked.

"England."

Faro was being modest. When I was in Italy with Ray, Faro got into a silly argument with Calisto, his partner who refused to retire, about an arcane bit of trivia. Faro shut down the conversation by reminding Calisto he'd received a first from Cambridge whereas Calisto had graduated from the University of Milan, a good university to be sure, but not as prestigious as Cambridge. Calisto didn't speak to Faro for the rest of the day.

"It was Cambridge, wasn't it?" I nudged Faro. He nodded. As he slurped his pina colada milkshake he became loquacious and I began to wonder whether it was spiked with alcohol. "You know what I liked the best?" Faro said in a faraway voice.

I suggested the historic setting and magnificent architecture, Louisa guessed the university's proximity to London.

"No," he smiled. "The Union. In addition to debates, Cambridge Union hosts some amazing speakers. I've seen everyone from the Dalai Lama to Lisa Kudrow."

"The Dalai Lama?" I asked.

"Phoebe from *Friends?*" Louisa interrupted. This was as bad as the conversations we used to have at home around the dinner table. It was impossible to stay on topic.

Louisa pressed Faro for details, what did Kudrow look like, what did she say. It turned out they shared an enduring love for the comedy series and the conversation quickly moved on to an animated version of 'remember the one where...'

On the way home Faro didn't say much until we reached the city limits and the skyline popped up as we crested a ridge. The skyscrapers glittered gold and red in the evening sun. "It's pretty, isn't it," I said. The view from our balcony catches downtown from a different angle. It still takes my breath away.

"It is," Faro said. "Again, very different from Rome, but beautiful nonetheless."

I wheeled up in front of his hotel and he waited while Louisa crawled out of the back seat and slipped in next to me. She reached over her shoulder and pulled out his leather jacket. "I told you, you wouldn't need it," she smiled.

Faro thanked me for inviting him, saying he'd see me next week in London, then turned to Louisa and said it was a real pleasure meeting her. He walked slowly to the lobby, turned again and waved before disappearing inside.

"Louisa, my dear," I said, "I think you have an admirer."

She smiled shyly and smoothed the hem of her sun dress. "Home, Jeeves," she said.

CHAPTER 12

A couple of days later Louisa and I were sitting on the patio at The Bakehouse, enjoying brunch in the mid-morning sun. Louisa didn't have to work today and I was treating her because I was going out of town and leaving her on her own with Quincy again. Although technically he is her dog and I shouldn't feel guilty.

"He's going to mow someone over if he doesn't stop that." I glanced down at Quincy. His plastic cone bashed into the table legs and snagged on people's ankles as he struggled to get comfortable under our tiny table.

Louisa shifted her wobbly wrought iron chair to give Quincy more maneuvering room. He mashed his cone into her thigh and it caught the underside of the table, rattling our cups and plates.

"How long does he have to wear that thing?" I scratched his shoulder, trying to settle him.

"Four more days."

Louisa is a nurse not a vet but when she discovered a tiny lump on Quincy's ear, she insisted it be removed. It turned out to be nothing but Quincy wouldn't leave the stitches alone so now he was stuck in a plastic cone the size of a satellite dish. She finally got his attention by waving a rolled-up ball of croissant in his face. Mesmerized, he froze until she popped it into his mouth.

"So he'll be back to normal by the time I get back." I bit into my mushroom wrap, ignoring the pleading eyes peering up at me through the plastic cone.

Louisa rested her arms on the table. "I can't believe you're going to London, you just got back from Rome. The life you lead, you high-flying lawyer, you."

"That's what everyone at the office said too, but let me remind you, as I reminded them, it's not all glamour and sightseeing. Ray and I will have work to do when we get there." I didn't tell Louisa the rest of my conversation with Keith and AJ. They were concerned about Dave—clearly me going to London with Ray was a serious ego blow, one that Dave would not soon forget. I told them that unlike Michelle, I didn't have to work with Dave day in and day out, if he wanted to throw a hissy fit in the lobby, it was fine with me.

Louisa received my comment with a snort. "Oh yeah, you and Ray stuck in London...with Buckingham Palace, the British Museum, the London Eye. It's enough to break your heart."

I scooped up what was left of the foam on my cappuccino. "I've never met a real AI engineer before. Her bio says she's got a degree in philosophy as well as computer science." People who were comfortable with words as well as numbers always impressed me.

"I wonder if Faro's met Phoebe from *Friends*." Louisa had a faraway look in her eye.

"I'll be sure to say hi to him for you," I said with a smug little smile.

She set down her breakfast croissant and said, "Don't you dare!" They'd exchanged a few texts and emails after our Drumheller trip but when I asked her if she was embarking on a long-distance romance, she said the man was charming but it would never work. And that was that.

"We can drive you to the airport, can't we Quincy?" she said. The dog banged around under the table at the mention of his name.

"That's sweet of you, but Ray is stopping by the house to pick me up."

"What, in his fancy sports car? There won't be enough room for your purse, let alone your luggage."

"God, no, he wouldn't dream of leaving the Ferrari in the airport parkade. Phoenix uses a limo service."

*   *   *   *

Later that day Ray and I were in the back of a sleek town car heading to the airport under a leaden grey sky. A few raindrops splatted on the windshield. Motorists were flying all over the highway as if they'd drown if they didn't reach their destination before the skies opened.

Ray was prattling on about the engineering marvel that is his garage. When he bought the house, he was shocked to discover he couldn't tear down the old garage and replace it with something three times bigger. Undaunted, he is an engineer after all, he designed a structure that looked like a two-car garage from the street but had stacked parking underground. His wife parked her Mercedes at grade while he tucked his Ferrari and two other exotic cars into specially designed stalls on the level below.

He chuckled indulgently. "Did I tell you about the time Linda dinged the hood of my Porsche? She knocked a garden rake off the wall and just left it there in the vee crease for me to find when I came home."

I said I was surprised he hadn't strangled her on the spot. Ray just smiled.

We made a beeline to the first-class lounge when we reached the airport. I don't often travel first class and was delighted to learn that Phoenix bumps its executives into business or first class for any flight lasting longer than three hours.

I nibbled on a snack, some kind of meat wrapped in phyllo pastry, while Ray wandered back and forth in front of the bar before returning with another stiff drink. At this rate he would be very relaxed by the time we reached the gate. He rolled the bottom of his glass around and around on his coaster, the golden liquor slid up and down the sides of the glass, and said, "Dave isn't happy you cut him out of the deal."

"Oh Ray, I didn't cut him out of the deal. Besides, it's Michelle's call. She decides how best to use her in-house and outside lawyers."

Ray pondered that for a moment. "That's not how Dave sees it." For an instant I had an image of Dave holding his breath until he turned blue.

"And how do you see it, Ray?"

The question surprised him. He lifted his glass and took a long swig. "Makes no difference to me," he grinned, "one lawyer's as good as another." Then he turned his attention to the big screen TV in the corner of the room.

Ray snored all the way across the Atlantic. I tossed and turned fitfully. Even tucked up under my blanket, wearing airplane socks, and shut off from the world with ear plugs and an eye mask I was distracted by bells dinging and lights flicking off and on as the plane droned across the inky sky.

Ray awoke just in time for breakfast and a bumpy

descent into Heathrow. We cleared customs and he plunged into the crowd which parted before him like the Red Sea; my rollie bag and I followed in his wake.

Eventually we pulled up in front of the Dukes Hotel in Mayfair. Ray's wife insisted it was the only place to stay in London. It's a very pretty hotel, the white stone accenting the front door and windows gives it a light, frothy appearance. *Well done, Linda.*

Before long I was submerged in a hot, scented bath in the elegant black marble bathroom. Ray and I were meeting Faro and Matteo at the AI unicorn's warehouse apartment in Shad Thames in a couple of hours. I was excited and a little in awe. What does one wear to meet a unicorn?

CHAPTER 13

I folded my umbrella and trundled into the back of the black cab. Rain hammered the roof and sheets of water rippled down the windows, the view reduced to a blurry wash of people, buildings, and cars. Ray muttered as he crawled into the seat beside me, scrolling through his phone looking for The Unicorn's address.

The trip would take less than twenty minutes, a little longer on foot, but Ray refused to walk. He'd almost come to blows with the hotel clerk who innocently offered him an umbrella, snapping he wouldn't be caught dead carrying one back home and he'd be damned if he was going to carry one here—as if that made the logic of his position any clearer. I shot the clerk an apologetic smile, grabbed the proffered umbrella in one hand and my briefcase in the other and waited under the awning while the doorman signaled a cab with an expert flick of the wrist.

Ray was calmer now that we were in the cab out of the rain. He hunched in his damp overcoat and stared at something on his phone. I listened to the *shush* of the tires and the wet wind shuddering against the windows, wondering what Ray would do if The Unicorn couldn't help us. Phoenix had already spent $75 million on the Vespers. Bannerman was determined to go live with the Elliot Lake prototype on September first. It was the middle of June, we were running out of time.

The Unicorn—I really had to start calling her Judy— lived in a converted warehouse apartment in Shad Thames. The cab wound through narrow cobblestone lanes and came to a stop in front of a low brick warehouse. The cab driver tilted his head at the oversized black door. This was the place. Ray paid the fare and the cab zipped off, its tires hissing in the lashing rain.

"Ray, are you sure you've got the right address?"

Before he could reply, the door swung open and a light female voice said "Hello! Come in, come in, before you drown." Judy Jango reached out and hauled us inside. She was about thirty, energetic, and moved with a willowy grace.

"Hello," I said with a bemused smile. How did she know we were there? Did she have CCTV cameras tucked under the eaves?

Ray said, "Wow, your hair is really blue." She laughed and disappeared with our wet coats, heading down the hall to the bathroom. "I'll put them on the heated towel rack, shall I?" she said over her shoulder.

The flat was a large airy space with exposed brick walls and a wooden floor that gleamed in the pearly evening light. A breeze floated in through large evenly-spaced windows facing the river. Matteo and Faro were sitting in the living room at opposite ends of a rich blue sofa. Matteo stood up and clasped Ray's hand in a vigorous handshake, Faro was more subdued and I noticed he and I were dressed alike in slim black slacks and black cashmere sweaters.

Judy clapped her hands. "Right. Shall we begin?" She shooed us into the dining room where we made ourselves comfortable in red upholstered chairs around a heavy wooden table while she zipped back to the kitchen to fetch wine and a bowl of cashews. This was a business meeting—she'd flown in from Kenya last night and was heading to Switzerland tomorrow morning—nevertheless she welcomed us as if we were the first to arrive at a cocktail party.

Judy said she'd reviewed the material Matteo and Ray had provided her in advance of this meeting and had some thoughts. The mood became somber as everyone flipped open their laptops.

She scratched her head vigorously and said, "I will admit, it is a puzzle. I can offer some tweaks that should improve the Vesper's performance, but to be frank, it is a very good system. It should not be having any issues."

Ray set his jaw but didn't say anything.

Judy continued. "I could not find one thing that's out of whack. That leads me to conclude the system is experiencing one or more unanticipated events, which have yet to be identified, that are confusing the AI."

Then she gave Matteo a radiant smile. "I must say, Matteo, your team did a stellar job with the programming. Very nice."

Matteo flushed and sat taller in his chair, the tension in the room easing a little.

Soon the three of them were tapping on their keyboards and scribbling notes in their Moleskine notebooks. Judy walked them through her work like a conductor leading the strings through a thorny patch of music.

With one raised eyebrow and a tilt of my head I signalled to Faro that we should move to the sofa. It could be hours before Ray and Matteo finalized what they wanted to add to the Vesper contract. Faro and I had our laptops.

We would draft the amendments on the fly. We'd been doing a lot of that lately.

I wrapped myself in the fluffy white throw draped over the back of the sleek sofa. Dusk was rising and the air puffing through the gauzy curtains was cool. Faro and I looked up, startled, when Matteo exploded in a belly laugh.

"Matteo seems to be holding up well," I said to Faro.

He glanced at me. "Don't let his demeanor fool you. The Vesper compressor is Matteo's life's work, his legacy. He's put everything on the line for this project: his business, his reputation, his home. It has to work or he's ruined."

I remembered something Ray said in the cab on our way over here: You can't change the laws of physics just because you don't like the result. I shivered and Faro pulled the edge of the soft throw up over my shoulder.

Two hours later, just as I was dozing off, Judy declared they were finished. Ray handed me his notes and printouts. I pounded out the revisions to the contract. Faro approved them. Judy printed a couple of copies that I scanned and sent back to Michelle and just like that we were done.

We had time for one celebratory drink before Judy disappeared down the hall to retrieve our coats, now toasty warm. Ray and Matteo debated about calling one cab or two to take us all back to the Dukes Hotel.

"Look, it's stopped raining," I said. "Let's walk. The fresh air will do us good."

As we tumbled out into the street Matteo offered me his arm. I was lightheaded from jet lag and Judy's wine and accepted it with a grateful sigh. The streets sparkled in the light of a magnificent moon, the streetlamps glowing a buttery yellow. Matteo made silly jokes as we peered in the windows of elegant storefronts displaying designer fashions, handbags, and ridiculously expensive watches. I could hear Ray and Faro talking quietly behind us.

*　*　*　*

Almost an hour later, after getting lost a couple of times, we finally rounded a corner and strolled up the marble steps of the Dukes Hotel. A burst of laughter spilled into the hotel lobby from the pub. Ray perked up and suggested a quick drink. We pressed through the rowdy crowd to a small table crammed into the back corner of the room.

"Did you know," Ray raised his voice to be heard, "Ian Fleming invented James Bond's signature drink right here in this bar?" We scanned the room. The soft overhead light bounced off the cream walls and gleamed on walnut liquor carts.

"No, I didn't," I said. An elderly waiter dressed in a pristine white jacket and black vest slowly approached our table.

"Yep," Ray said, his eyes twinkling. "It was a dry martini. Guess what he called it."

At that moment Matteo chuckled; Faro and I shook our heads.

"The Vesper," Ray said triumphantly.

I laughed and said Vespers seemed to follow him everywhere he went.

"It is destiny," Matteo said as Ray turned to the waiter and announced I'd be having a Vesper. Although I try to avoid hard liquor, I agreed, on the condition we ordered some food as well.

What I'd failed to consider was the Vesper was straight

alcohol, a silky-smooth concoction of gin, vodka, and something called Lillet Blanc. In no time at all the room felt warm and fuzzy and everything Faro said was hilarious. I glanced at Ray and Matteo, Ray's face was drawn, his jaw clenched. Matteo placed a reassuring hand on Ray's arm, as if to calm him.

A cheer went up from the group at the next table and I couldn't hear what Matteo said, but I felt a flutter in my stomach, something was happening.

I asked Ray about it the next morning on our way to the airport. "Counsellor, I have no idea what you're talking about. The Vesper must have gone to your head."

The Day It Happened

November 12, 10:03 A.M.

CHAPTER 14

The twins scrambled up the snowbank like miniature soldiers crawling across a battlefield. Kirsten gripped Amy's parka tightly, dragging her limp body up the bank. The front of Amy's snowsuit snagged on a sharp rock; Kirsten heard it tear as she tugged her free. Amy's hood was twisted to one side, caught on her helmet buckle, obscuring her face. Kirsten was frantic, she had to see Amy's face.

At last the buckle snapped open and Amy's hood slid free. Her cheeks were raw, smudged with dirt and pine needles, but her grey eyes were shining. "Did you see it!" she squealed. "The dragon! Did you see it?"

"Holy shit!" Tyler said. He'd rolled on to his back and was struggling to sit up. His brother Jack wobbled to his feet.

"Watch it!" Jack kicked at Tyler's skate, angry and afraid. Bits of frozen snow and ice drifted down from the treetops, silvering their hair. An enormous cloud of mist billowed white in the centre of the lake, floating on the surface and rising high as it crept closer to shore.

"Holy shit!" Tyler repeated. He shot a sidelong glance at his mother. Kirsten didn't hear him. She spread her arms wide, desperate to pull her children closer, but the boys pushed her away, eyes focused on the gigantic black hole in the middle of the lake. Water bubbled, dark and greasy, the ice was littered with debris. Glittering wisps of mist floated closer, touching the shore. Shining steel arced in the sunlight above the water then slumped back down to rest on the turbulent lakebed.

"We have to—"

Crack! Another explosion, a sonic boom, shattered the air, drowning out Kirsten's words. Then a deafening roar. A massive fireball flashed in the woods on the opposite side of the lake, flames shooting three hundred feet into the air. The ground rolled and bucked beneath them as the fireball obliterated the clear blue sky.

"Is it a bomb?" Jack's voice was small. "Mom?"

Kirsten's thoughts were a chaotic jumble. A phrase from what seemed like a hundred years ago looped through her brain. *Close the valve! For the love of God, close the valve!*

Five Months Earlier

June

CHAPTER 15

They say no news is good news, but what do they know. Have they, whoever they are, spent night after sleepless night staring at the ceiling, wondering whether a blue unicorn fixed an AI problem no one understood so they could save the world from climate change? Okay, that was a bit melodramatic but Ray and I had been home for five days and I had yet to hear from anyone whether Judy Jango's improvements had eliminated the random alarms and shutdowns.

It was 4:00 a.m., I was padding around the kitchen with Quincy padding along behind me.

"You never give up, do you?" I tickled him under the chin. The bull terrier wagged his tail, then looked into the hall. The stairs creaked and Louisa came into the kitchen. She pulled the belt of her housecoat tightly around her waist and yawned. "What are you two doing up at this godforsaken hour?"

"I don't know about him," I said, nodding at the dog, "but I've got jet lag. My stomach says it's lunch time and I haven't even had breakfast. We didn't wake you, did we?"

Louisa slid onto a chair at the kitchen island. "Don't worry about it." She yawned again and Quincy flopped down in a noisy heap at her feet.

I popped two pieces of bread into the toaster and took

some processed cheese slices out of the fridge. "Want some?" I waved a perfectly square piece of yellow cheese at her and put the kettle on. She shook her head; she hates plastic cheese.

"You've been home for days, are you sure it's still jet lag? I thought everyone had the utmost faith in this Judy Jango person." I started to say it wasn't Judy I was worried about when Louisa cocked her head and said, "Either I'm having a stroke or you've incinerated the toast."

Louisa pointed at the smoking toaster. A charred slice of bread was jammed in the slot. I unplugged the toaster and started poking at its innards with a fork. Then the smoke detector went off with a deafening squeal. Quincy started barking and Louisa began flapping around with a tea towel. When the din subsided, I held up a black piece of toast. "Do you think he'll eat this?"

"Are you kidding? He'll eat anything."

I ripped the blackened bread into small pieces, scattering crumbs all over the countertop, and dumped them into Quincy's dish. He bolted to the bowl as if he hadn't eaten for a week.

"This is why he hangs around you, you know." Louisa wiped down the counter with a wet dishcloth. "You're such a horrible cook, he knows it's just a matter of time."

I tipped my chin, acknowledging the truth of her statement, and went back upstairs to have a shower.

*   *   *   *

It was still early, barely 6:00 a.m. when I pulled into the parking lot next to Keith's car. I found him in his office staring at the painting of a mountain hanging over his bookshelf. His wife is an artist, it was the first painting she'd sold. He was slowly winding his ancient clock. It's such a needy thing, that clock. If he misses a day, it throws a hissy fit and dies. Keith jumped when I stuck my head in his door to say hello.

"Jeez, you almost gave me a heart attack." He put his hand to his chest feigning medical distress, then smiled quizzically. "What are you doing here so early? Is this the new you?"

"Can't sleep." I shrugged and dropped into his visitor's chair.

He sat down, leaned back in his chair with his hands clasped behind his head, and waited. That's why I like working with Keith. He knows when to sit back and let me ramble on. When we worked together at Gates, Case and White, a high-billing client insisted his lawyers take a personality test to ensure his 'guys and gals' had complementary skills. The whole thing was ludicrous as far as I was concerned, but if a client wanted to pay us to fill out a quiz that looked like it had been torn from the pages of *Cosmo*, who was I to argue. The survey said I was an intuitive extrovert (surprise) and Keith was the exact opposite. We're nicely matched, kind of like my mom and dad now that I think about it. If our business relationship lasts as long as their marriage did, our law firm would be around forever.

I told him I hadn't heard from Michelle, or Ray, or anyone at Phoenix, and I was getting worried.

"Why? I thought the Judy Jango meeting was a success."

"It was. And yet an hour later in Dukes Bar, Ray was hunched in a corner with Matteo, looking like his dog had died." Ray's sour mood lasted through the next day. On our flight home I ate everything the flight attendants offered and watched endless movies to pass the time because Ray had shut down completely. "Something is off, Keith."

He leaned forward and focused on my face. "Evie, you're doing it again. You feel personally responsible. I understand that this is an extremely important file, but you've done everything you possibly can, including haring all over the world, to put the paper in place. It's up to the engineers now. So stop stressing about it."

My lips twitched in a small smile. "Is this where you quote Kenny Rogers?"

He chuckled. "If you're referring to 'playing the hand you're dealt,' that wasn't Kenny Rogers."

I was about to Google *The Gambler* when Bridget raced down the hall, her blonde hair flying. "Is AJ here yet?" she asked as she flew past Keith's door and disappeared.

Madeline, looking serene in a light green sleeveless sheath and pale pumps, followed at a more leisurely pace. "Has anyone seen AJ?"

"Not yet," Keith said. "What's going on?"

"Meet us in the conference room." Madeline has a way of making a suggestion sound like a command you dare not ignore.

The sound of AJ's MGB roaring into the parking lot announced his arrival.

"Quick, stall him!" Madeline deftly sidestepped Bridget who charged out of the supply room carrying a large brown envelope and ducked into the coffee room. The fridge door opened and closed.

"AJ!" I planted myself squarely in front of him when he opened the front door. He stopped, shifting his messenger bag off his shoulder.

"Hello?" He squinted one blue eye and tried to step around me. "What's going on?"

"Going on? What makes you think something is going on?" I stepped to one side, mirroring his movements. He looked at me as if I'd lost my mind.

Just then Bridget's voice rang down the hall saying we could join them in the conference room. Dutifully, he followed me down the corridor. The large window in the conference room was obscured by an enormous multi-coloured banner spelling out "Congratulations!" A large pink and white sheet cake and a stack of paper plates, plastic forks, and transparent plastic cups sat in the middle of the table. Propped up next to the bottle of Limoncello was a large brown envelope festooned with an elaborate red bow.

AJ's laugh lines deepened in a wide grin. "What's all this?"

Bridget nodded shyly at Keith and me. Keith looked confused. Luckily, Bridget had been my admin assistant for eight years; we'd reached the point where we could read each other's minds.

"AJ," I said, "we'd like to formally welcome you as a full partner of Lawson Valentine, now known as Braxton, Lawson, Valentine." We'd dithered for weeks over our new name until Bridget backed us into a corner by announcing she was running low on stationery supplies and would rename the firm 'Apple' if we didn't make a decision in the next five minutes. We decided to list our names in alphabetical order even though clients would default to our initials and BLV sounded like a sandwich.

AJ tore the bow off the envelope and shook out a few sheets of our new BLV stationery, business cards, and a ruby red USB fob bearing the BLV logo.

"I'm honoured." His voice was low and sincere. "Deeply honoured."

Madeline cut the cake into pieces with a very large, very sharp butcher knife, slid them onto the paper plates and passed them around. We raised our plastic cups—Madeline had poured out generous slugs of limoncello—and formally welcomed AJ to the partnership.

He beamed and said, "I can't tell you how—"

"Excuse me?" A voice called from the reception area. "Is anyone here?"

"Jeez. It's my first client." AJ gulped his drink and dabbed icing off his upper lip, then grinned and raced out into the lobby, his sandy hair flopping into his eyes.

Madeline said, "Wham bam and it's all over."

I shook my head at her. "You made Bridget blush." To make amends Madeline offered to help Bridget carry the cake and the liquor back into the coffee room. I followed and cut myself a second piece of cake. "That was a lovely spontaneous celebration, brilliant. Thank you both." AJ was born into a very wealthy family, he could buy whatever he liked, but we soon learned it was these gestures of appreciation that made his heart sing.

Maybe it was the limoncello, but as I sat at my desk dropping cake crumbs all over my keyboard my mind turned to Ray: his life, his job, his opportunity to make a lasting impression on history. He was exuberant, excited by the challenge, but also moody, bordering on morose. What brought him joy?

The Day It Happened

November 12, 10:19 A.M.

CHAPTER 16

"The truck. Get to the truck!" Kirsten shouted. Tyler wobbled on his skates and turned to the edge of the frozen lake.

"No, no, Tyler, not the ice. It's unstable."

Jack grabbed Tyler's arm and hauled him further up the bank to begin the grim march back to the clearing where Kirsten had left the SUV.

"Amy, look at me, sweetie." The little girl reluctantly tore her eyes away from the fireball high on the ridge on the opposite side of the lake. "Amy, pay attention. We're going. Now!" Amy blinked, gave her mother a quick nod and scrambled farther up the bank.

The four of them picked their way through the debris, a sodden mess of mangled tree limbs, shards of metal, and rocks that slowed their progress. Their skate blades slashed across broken evergreen boughs releasing the crisp scent of pine.

"This is stupid," Tyler muttered. "I'm wrecking my blades."

"Shut up," Jack said.

"Both of you shut up," Kirsten snapped, immediately regretting her harsh tone.

Jack let out a low whistle as they approached the SUV. It was parked nose first facing the lake; dents and gashes pockmarked the hood. Something had smashed through the windscreen on the passenger side creating a jagged baseball-sized hole; pebbles of shattered glass glittered like diamonds on the front seat.

"Everyone get in the back!" Kirsten's voice was shrill. Jack grumbled but fell silent when he caught the look on his mother's face. She climbed awkwardly into the driver's seat while Tyler picked up Amy and stuffed her unceremoniously into the back. Kirsten swung her feet up onto the passenger seat, fumbled with her laces and yanked off her skates. She cranked the seat forward so she could reach the pedals with her stockinged feet.

Amy asked, "What about our boots?" Their boots and Kirsten's backpack were buried in the debris at the edge of the lake.

"We'll get them later," Kirsten muttered as she peered through the windshield. A spiderweb of fractures radiated across the glass, catching the sun, making it hard to see. She had to get her family out of here. The area was criss-crossed with pipelines. Another could explode at any minute.

She fished her keys out of her zip pocket and prayed that the engine would start.

Four Months Earlier

July

CHAPTER 17

It was a brilliant blue morning in mid July. I was standing in the middle of Braxton, Lawson, Valentine's reception area with Madeline pacing in circles around me. "This won't do," she shook her head, her auburn hair bouncing. "This simply won't do."

"Are you talking about the hat or the entire ensemble?" With a sweeping gesture I directed her gaze to my running shoes, slim fit slacks, polo shirt and ball cap. Everything I wore was pale blue or white, even the runners. I'd never been this colour coordinated in my life.

AJ breezed into the lobby, stopping dead in front of Bridget's desk. He looked at me and said, "Nice duds."

Bridget pressed her lips together, biting back a smile. "Evie's going golfing."

AJ grinned. "Well in that case, Evie, this won't do." Madeline crossed her arms and nodded until AJ said, "You're horribly underdressed. Where's your argyle vest and knickers, preferably plaid?"

Madeline and I narrowed our eyes at him. He glanced at Bridget who shrugged. We could hear him chortling all the way down the corridor to his office.

Madeline sighed. "Please tell me you've got golf shoes in the car."

"I hate golf. So no, I don't have golf shoes in the car."

"Will they let you on the course without the proper footwear? It's an exclusive club, you know."

I hadn't seen Madeline this worked up over my attire since last year's Heritage Awards Gala. "Madeline, this is a Phoenix client appreciation event. Bannerman hosts it every year. I'll be fine." Truth be told when Michelle's invitation popped up in my inbox I tried to beg off. I'm a service provider, I said, not a client. Besides, I can't golf.

Michelle refused to take no for an answer. "It's a Texas Scramble, not real golf. It doesn't matter if you can't play, your teammates will carry you."

"I don't want to be carried. I'm going to be sick that day," I said.

She laughed. "It's a non-stress, non-work setting. Besides, I need you there, the ratio of men to women is five to one... Evie, please?"

Eventually I relented. The golf club's website indicated it was indeed a private club, dating all the way back to the late 1800s, with strict anti-cell phone, anti-smoking, anti-cannabis, and anti-lightning policies. When I opened the anti-lightning policy, I was disappointed to discover the club hadn't actually banned lightning but required golfers to head for the clubhouse or a rain shelter when the lightning alarm sounded. As far as I could tell, the dress code prohibited anything that would be remotely comfortable but didn't expressly state female guests could not wear running shoes so I was prepared to risk it. What's the worst they could do, send me home?

"I'll be fine," I said to Madeline as I went out to the parking lot to wait for Michelle. Ten minutes later she roared up in her fancy blue sports car, I think it was a BMW. She looked me up and down but made no comment about my outfit, choosing instead to pass me a sheet of paper outlining the foursomes. "Please say I'm on your team," I said.

"I'm afraid not, there aren't enough women to double up, they've allotted one female to each team. You're in Ray Cook's foursome."

"That's good... wait, he doesn't get competitive at these things, does he?"

"Ray? Nah, he knows it's all in fun, let the client win and all that. Rest assured he won't wrap a nine iron around a tree trunk if you miss a putt."

As it turned out, I'd been fussing for nothing. Ray and my fellow teammates, both executives with mid-sized natural gas companies, carried me through my botched drives and feeble putts. They applauded wildly at my miracle shot: I'd tried to clear a water trap, drove the ball smack into the middle of the pond where it glanced off a submerged rock and ricocheted nicely into position on the lip of the green.

Ray and I were bouncing along the cart path at the edge of a small ridge. The golf cart's wheels kept slipping on the gravel. I tightened my grip on the seat cushions and focused my attention on the Foothills which shone a bucolic grey-green in the distance.

I was about to ask Ray to slow down when an electric horn blared behind us. Ray jumped, our cart skidded closer to the verge, then lurched to a stop. If I fell out now, I'd tumble down the slope.

"Outta the way, Ray!" Bannerman pulled up beside us, his lips pulled back in a smug smile. He was so close that Ray couldn't step out of the cart even if he wanted to. Bannerman's companion, a heavy-set man with a jowly face, rearranged his expression from shock to sardonic amusement. "All right if we play through?" Bannerman asked.

"Given that you've pinned us on the lip of an escarpment we don't have much choice, do we?" I shot back. Ray gave me a sideways look, then waved to Bannerman to go on ahead.

Gravel flew in all directions as Bannerman accelerated away. Ray waited until Bannerman's fire-engine red cart crested a small hummock and disappeared from view before he started ours up.

When he pressed the pedal, the cart hesitated for a moment, then charged back into the centre of the path well away from the edge of the embankment. Ray shifted in his seat, his fingers tight around the steering wheel, his playful mood erased. I'd been waiting for the right time to quiz him about Judy Jango's alterations to the Vesper's AI, and now, thanks to Bannerman's aggressive demonstration of his position in the hierarchy there would be no right time. I had to ask now.

"Ray?"

He lifted his foot off the pedal and we glided into a curve on the path.

"How are we doing with Judy Jango's tweaks? Has the anomaly in the AI been sorted out?"

The cart lurched forward.

"Ray?" I repeated his name.

He lifted his hand to silence me. The two men in our foursome were just ahead, approaching the tee box. They climbed out of their cart and pulled their drivers out of their bags. Ray pulled up behind them and we waited while they took their shots. One of them waved his club in the air after a smooth long drive down the centre of the fairway and they hopped into their cart and drove away.

Ray stepped out of the cart and handed me a club—
we'd reached the point in the game where he was picking
my clubs for me. He said with a touch of impatience, "The
alarms still go off, not as frequently as before, but they're
still going off. They're driving the guys nuts." He shook
his head. "We're working on it."

Then he gave me a rueful smile and said, "You've got
no idea how much is riding on this. To quote my esteemed
boss, 'September first is a hard deadline. The Elliot Lake
prototype better be up and running and one way or
another, and the remaining twenty-five right behind it.'"
Ray turned and picked up his driver. "Or I'm out of a job."

"But you said it yourself, you can't change the laws of
physics just because you don't like the result."

He winced and indicated I should take my shot.

I positioned myself behind my golf ball and tapped
the ground a few times with my club. I looked up at Ray
who stared down the fairway, his eyes tracking our golfing
companions' cart. With a nice clean whack my golf ball
sailed into the bushes on our right.

Ray shook his head. "Looks like you've run out of
miracle shots." He ambled up to the tee box, his driver
swinging loosely by his side. There was something about
the way he moved and then looked down the fairway that
made me drop the subject and I didn't mention the Vespers or Judy Jango again for the rest of the day.

We spent the afternoon racing from one hole to the
next in hair-raising bursts of speed. I had the impression
Ray was trying to catch up with Bannerman, but his boss
was tossing back cold beers on the patio by the time we
returned to the clubhouse.

Bannerman greeted us with a careless wave but didn't
talk to me until the awards ceremony after dinner when

he called out my name as the winner of the prize for the most unusual shot. He handed me a golf shirt with the Phoenix logo emblazoned over the left breast and told me to wear it with pride. I smiled politely. It would be stuffed into the back of my closet for a couple of months, then I'd donate it to charity.

The next morning I told Madeline I was definitely not taking up golf. As far as I was concerned, it was a dangerous sport.

CHAPTER 18

August wound down like a slowly spinning top, clients were taking a breather before gearing up for the round of hearings scheduled for the fall, and the office was quiet. AJ and Madeline were off on vacation and I missed them.

AJ was visiting his family in Saskatoon. When we hired him four years ago, we had no idea his grandfather owned a global agricultural conglomerate. Grandpa thought AJ was wasting his formidable talents practising law with a small green energy firm when he could be working in the family business, making millions selling potash to the world. With every visit, Grandpa upped the pressure—and the money—and I worried it was just a matter of time before AJ cracked.

Normally Madeline, the woman who has everything, would ease my mind with the quiet assurance that 'money isn't everything, darling' but when she flitted out the door last week, she announced she'd be somewhere on the Continent—in Madeline's case that could mean anywhere from Europe to Antarctica—and we were not to contact her under any circumstances.

That left Keith, Bridget, and me to keep the firm ticking over. I poured myself a coffee and returned to my office, preparing to waste what was left of the day rearranging piles of paper on my desk when my phone pinged with a text from Michelle: *Got a moment? Need to talk.*

When I dialed Michelle's number, she surprised me by asking whether I could join her for lunch with one of the Board members. Her tone conveyed a level of urgency I hadn't heard since she bundled me off to London with Ray. When I asked who we were meeting and why, she said she preferred to let the Board member speak for himself and hung up before I could press the point. Dismayed, I went down the hall to Keith's office.

Keith was peering at an engineering drawing precariously balanced on a stack of files on top of his desk. His office was bright in the afternoon light and a slight breeze came through the open window, tugging at the pages anchored by half-empty coffee cups and miscellaneous office supplies.

"How can you work like this?" I asked as I slipped into his visitor's chair.

Keith sat back in his chair and slowly rolled up his sleeves. He was casually dressed, his blue shirt looked nice against his tan. He'd started another project on the acreage, restoring a stone silo—his wife said it kept him out of her hair—and had a weathered, Marlboro man look about him. I watched him for a moment, then said, "Well?"

"You look agitated. What's up?"

"Keith Lawson, you know me too well."

He raised his eyebrows, then grinned. "Evie Valentine, that goes both ways."

I'd met Keith when I joined the regulatory group of Gates, Case and White. When I went through the ringer at Gates, Keith proved himself to be a true friend. We knew each other very well. Other than Louisa, I don't think I trusted anyone as much as I trusted Keith.

I explained Michelle's invitation to join her and a Board member at lunch.

He cocked his head. "That's highly unusual. Board members never bypass the CEO to talk directly to the Chief Legal Officer... unless there's a problem."

"Exactly." I pressed my hands to my face. My cheeks were burning. "But why did Michelle invite me? I'm not Phoenix's Chief Legal Officer, she is."

Keith studied me for a moment, then said, "Obviously it's something to do with the Vespers. The Board member is not comfortable with whatever Bannerman is telling him. How's Ray's AI fix going? Isn't the company going live with the Vespers a couple of weeks from now?"

I shrugged. "That's the plan, Bannerman wants the prototype up and running on September first and the rest of them online as soon as possible after that. When I asked Ray about it at the golf tournament he clammed up and no one's said a word to me since... well, other than Dave's admin assistant, who called to tell me to submit my bill for the London trip. To Dave's attention, no less."

A sardonic smile flitted across Keith's face. "He probably wants it for his 'Evie screwed me again' file."

The corner of Keith's drawing slipped out from under the stapler anchoring it. As he readjusted it, he looked at me more closely. "Are you feeling all right? Your face looks like it's on fire."

Louisa says a red face is my 'tell' and ever since I was a little girl it signaled that my temper was rising. 'That was our cue to clear the room,' she said. But I didn't think I was angry; puzzled maybe or uneasy, but not angry.

I heaved a great sigh as I rose to leave. "Yeah, I'm okay. It just feels like something is going on under the surface and I can't figure out what it is."

CHAPTER 19

"Evie." Michelle's voice rang out across the Phoenix lobby. I was standing by the fishpond, mesmerized by the sunlight rippling across the crystal-clear water. A woman wearing a green polo shirt popped out of a narrow door hidden in the lobby wall. She sprinkled some pellets on the surface of the water and disappeared back to where she came from.

"I see the fish are back." Koi crowded at the edge of the pond, their brilliant jewel-like bodies breaking the surface, mouths bubbling like tiny cups.

"Bannerman decided to spruce up the place," Michelle said as the koi jostled in front of us, demanding to be fed. "He's pretty upbeat these days. Next month when the entire pipeline system is Vesperized, for lack of a better word, he's going to make a splashy press announcement and do the circuit of all the business talk shows. He's driving the public relations group insane with ideas and suggestions."

"I've been meaning to talk to you about that," I said. "How's it going with the AI patch? Is the prototype at Elliot Lake running properly now?"

She pressed her lips together and I fell in step behind her. The revolving doors thwapped as we pushed past the office workers streaming back into the building. It was just after one o'clock, the sun beat down on the pavement and it was very hot. It reminded me of Italy but not as humid. Our reservation wasn't until one-thirty and we had plenty of time for a leisurely stroll.

"Yes, well, that's the question preying on some Board members' minds." Michelle seemed to be choosing her words carefully. "Chris Henzel's mind, to be specific. He's the Board member we're meeting for lunch." She adjusted her French cuffs, her white silk blouse contrasted nicely with her tailored navy suit. Unlike some female executives who switch to light sleeveless dresses in the summer, Michelle maintained an air of elegance all year round. "Chris is the head of the Board's health, safety, and environmental committee. He's been asking some pointed questions about the delays in bringing the Vespers online."

I glanced at her as we stood at an intersection, waiting for the light to change. She squinted at the traffic light in the crosswalk. "Surely the news about the AI upgrades has eased his mind."

"I'll let him explain it," Michelle said, slipping on her sunglasses. They were large and round, she looked like a young Jackie Onassis. "Oh, there he is." She waved at a short, middle-aged man with wiry hair and a ruddy complexion who was pacing back and forth in front of a high-end restaurant. Michelle introduced us and we went inside.

The hostess, a slim young woman with a broad smile, led us past the fieldstone fireplace to a rock terrace overlooking a small, leafy garden. A slight breeze rustled the trees and toyed with the overhead awning as she fiddled with a crank and rolled out a pink tarp to keep the sun out of our eyes. It gave the terrace a rosy glow.

Michelle and I turned to Chris after we'd placed our orders. The small talk was over, it was time for him to tell us why we were here.

Chris shot a wary glance across the room. When he was satisfied no one was lurking within earshot he said he was deeply concerned about the explanations, or lack thereof, Bannerman had given the Board about the repairs to the Vespers.

He spoke with intensity, his eyes never leaving Michelle's face and I realized he was invoking the special relationship between Michelle and the Board. Michelle, as Phoenix's Chief Legal Officer, was the only executive who was directly answerable to the Board as well as Bannerman. She had a duty to tell the Board if Bannerman tried to do something illegal. They would investigate his transgression and, depending on its severity, fire him or give him a slap on the wrist. And that's where it got tricky. If Bannerman was let off with a warning, he'd be gunning for Michelle, the turncoat on his team. Sooner or later he'd fire her on some trumped up excuse. Sure, she'd get a severance package but it was unlikely she'd ever work again.

Michelle rested her elbows on the table and clasped her hands under her chin. "Does the Board have a particular concern?" she asked. She was being cautious, she wanted to understand exactly what Chris was telling her.

He snorted. "It's bloody obvious after months of screwing around that Ray is no closer to fixing the Vespers than he was on day one. Does Bannerman have any idea how serious this is?"

Before either of us could speak a waiter appeared carrying three large plates. I cast a wary glance at Michelle as the waiter set down my mushroom tart.

She stared blankly at her fish while Chris glared at his hamburger. "Um," the waiter cleared his throat, "is everything all right?" Quickly we assured him everything was fine. He ducked his head and retreated to join the hostess by the front door.

Michelle picked up her fork and poked at her fish, carefully, as if it might flip off the plate and land on the floor. She took a small bite before turning back to Chris. "As I understand it, the remedial work on the AI at Elliot Lake is progressing, albeit slowly... and yes, Bannerman knows."

Chris was trying to flatten his hamburger which was too big and sloppy to pick up without making a mess. He sighed and forked the patty out of the bun, sawed off a chunk and popped it into his mouth. He set his knife and fork down beside his plate, staring first at Michelle, then at me, and said, "There's something you two need to know about Bannerman. This is strictly confidential."

The air on the terrace grew still. A small black and white butterfly flitted up to the awning. It clung to the canvas tarp for a few seconds, wings opening and closing, before fluttering away.

Michelle and I nodded but didn't say anything.

Chris took a sip of water then said, "Michelle, as you know, Bannerman was an executive at Meers Co. before he joined Phoenix. He ran Meers' marketing group. I was on the Board at Meers, still am as a matter of fact, and knew him back then. To make a long story short, Bannerman got himself and the company into serious trouble with the Federal Trade Commission."

"What kind of trouble?" Michelle asked.

Chris grimaced. "I can't get into the details; suffice it to say the FTC opened an investigation into Bannerman's marketing practices and subpoenaed him and his lead marketer to a hearing in Washington, DC. They grilled him for three days. Then, out of the blue, the company decided to settle and pay a hefty fine—over a million in American dollars."

Michelle blinked a few times, then said, "Well, some regulatory agencies like the FTC are known for being overzealous."

Chris shook his head impatiently. "And some people make honest mistakes. But that wasn't the case here." The waiter approached our table, took one look at Chris' angry face and returned to the hostess' station to fold napkins.

"Do you know why we settled?" It was clear Chris didn't expect an answer. "Our lawyer said Bannerman lied under oath. She said we should pay up and get the hell out of there before the FTC figured it out. So that's what we did."

My mushroom tart turned to dust in my mouth.

Chris sounded tired. "The Meers Board was going to fire Bannerman, but before we could do it, he announced he was taking the CEO job at Phoenix. I was stuck with him at Meers and now I'm stuck with him at Phoenix."

"Do the other Phoenix Board members know?" I asked.

"No," he said. "I can't say anything without admitting Bannerman, then a Meers executive, lied to the FTC. If that ever got out, Meers would be ruined."

Chris eyed his hamburger which had slumped sideways, the onion jam oozing out onto the dill pickle in a messy heap on the side of his plate. He sawed off another chunk of beef and chewed slowly.

Michelle pushed her plate away. "Chris, am I correct in assuming you're telling us this because you think

Bannerman has been, um, how shall I put it, less than forthright with the Phoenix Board about the Vespers?"

"Bloody right." Chris picked up his fork, then put it down again. His hands were strong and lightly freckled. "I want to be one hundred percent clear here. Bannerman rushed out the press release in April, announcing we'd selected Vesper to replace the old compressors, 'we're going to save the world with a net-zero pipeline', that kind of stuff. The share price moved up. He's planning another big announcement on September first to say the Vespers are going live across the system. The shares will go up again. But"—here Chris paused for a sip of water, his voice was low and raw—"and this is an extremely important but: if the Vespers are a dud, he has to come clean no matter what such negative news will do to the share price. That bugger almost buried Meers, I'll be damned if he's going to bury Phoenix."

Michelle flicked her eyes at me before turning back to Chris. "Evie and I are working the Vesper deal with Ray. You have my word that everything that should be disclosed to the Board is being disclosed to the Board... and to the marketplace. Isn't that right, Evie?"

I nodded with more confidence than I felt.

Chris relaxed for the first time since we'd sat down. "I knew I could count on you ladies." Michelle and I smiled. Sometimes being called a lady is patronizing. Today it was a compliment of the highest order.

The waiter scanned our faces from across the room, wondering whether it was safe to approach our table. Chris waved him over and we ordered coffee. The sound of smoky jazz drifted across the terrace. I hadn't noticed it before. Had the music been playing this whole time? Our conversation shifted to less fraught topics and soon we were back outside on the pavement, shaking hands and promising to stay in touch.

CHAPTER 20

Michelle clipped down the sidewalk so fast I had to take a couple of quick steps to catch up to her. "That bloody bastard!" she fumed. "I knew something was off with Bannerman the minute I met him."

She jammed her Jackie O sunglasses back on her face and threaded her way through the crowd. "From day one, Evie. When he joined the company, we had an all day onboarding session at Lake Louise—making presentations about our departments and what they do, that kind of thing—and I happened to be standing next to him in the lunch buffet line. He was droning on and on about his Harvard MBA, as if up here in the boonies we wouldn't know what that was, and I asked him where he got his undergrad degree."

We stopped at an intersection and I had a chance to catch my breath.

"He mentioned a small private university, I forget the name, he said he played on their football team and I said, 'You're kidding!' Tactless, I know. But you've seen him Evie, he's got spaghetti arms. Heck, even you could take him down in a tackle."

"Gee, thanks. How did he react?"

"He puffed up and said he was much bigger then. That he'd grown up in a rough neighbourhood in Boston and joined a gang." She pulled off her sunglasses and stuffed them back into her purse. "One minute he's bragging about running with a gang, the next he's boasting about his vacation home in the Hamptons."

"Well, both could be true, Michelle. The American Dream and all."

"College football!" She snorted. "Give me a break!"

As we approached the Phoenix building, she took my arm. "Have you got a minute? I'd like to regroup." I nodded and we rode up to the executive floor in silence. When the doors whispered open, we came face to face with Bannerman and another man, a lean, wiry figure with a narrow face and close-cropped red hair.

"Ladies," Bannerman acknowledged us with a cool smile. The other man nodded and waited for us to step out of the elevator car. The doors closed and they disappeared.

"Who was that guy?" I whispered.

"Bannerman's bodyguard," she replied.

"The football player needs a bodyguard? Is he getting death threats or something?"

Her shoulders lifted in a helpless shrug. "Technically he's the head of security. Reports directly to Bannerman. Rumour has it he's ex Special Forces or something."

Given the look of him, grim and icy, I could understand why Michelle was reluctant to ask too many questions.

She told her assistant to hold her calls and shut the door firmly behind her with instructions we were not to be disturbed. The sun bounced off the Rockies making the room very bright. Michelle tilted the blinds to soften the glare. I reached for the pen and notepad in the middle of the conference table but she stopped me with a gentle hand.

"No notes please, Evie. This is just background." We sat side by side in the partially shaded room, slats of sunlight illuminated the dust motes floating in the air. It felt quiet and intimate. "What I'm about to tell you is not relevant to your brief, nevertheless I'd ask you to keep it confidential."

"Of course."

And it all tumbled out. Bannerman was in serious financial trouble. A couple of months back, Beth, the Vice President of Human Resources, came to Michelle in a panic. Bannerman wanted to borrow $900,000 from the company and instructed Beth to prepare the paperwork. Beth told him such a loan was prohibited under securities laws, and even if it wasn't it would require Board approval. He assured her that the Board had cleared the loan, verbally of course, and then demanded she stop throwing up roadblocks and just do her job. That's when Beth came to Michelle.

I sat back, stunned. "What did you do?"

"What do you think I did? I marched straight down to Bannerman's office and told him what he wanted Beth to do was illegal. He argued that he intended to repay the loan by the end of the month, consequently it would never show up on the books and no one, least of all the Board, need ever know. Obviously that story about the Board giving him verbal approval was a lie." The colour drained from Michelle's face, making her eyes even blacker. "I said the auditors and VPs for Human Resources and Finance would know; and I, as the company's Chief Legal Officer, had a duty to report it to the Board. And if for some insane reason they went along with it, I would report it to the securities commission myself."

"God. What did he say?"

"He changed his story. He said he was simply trying to cash in some stock options—something that's handled by the legal group, by the way, not Beth—and it was all a silly misunderstanding."

I couldn't fathom the arrogance of the man. Did he think she was stupid? "Michelle, you didn't mention any of this to Chris Henzel at lunch..."

"No, I didn't. Bannerman dropped the whole thing, nothing came of it." She took a deep breath. "But maybe I should have... I... I don't know anymore."

*   *   *   *

Later that evening as I walked Quincy along the river I replayed our conversation. Bannerman was a multi-millionaire. His annual compensation, including shares and stock options, was well over $14 million. The Vesper announcement in April boosted the share price by fifteen percent, the announcement in September would boost it even more. His stock options alone would be worth a fortune.

And yet he tried to trick Beth into giving him $900,000 of the company's money. For a month? Who needs that kind of money for so short a space of time?

The Day It Happened

November 12, 10:44 A.M.

CHAPTER 21

Kirsten's battered SUV roared to life. She slammed the gears into reverse, plowing recklessly over the broken branches and debris littering the clearing before yanking hard on the steering wheel and careening onto the road.

"Slow down, you're going too fast!" Jack's frantic voice rose from the back seat. Kirsten glanced over her shoulder. He was straining against his seat belt, peering over the front seat into the windshield. The SUV skittered across the road. It was a rough ride at the best of times, now their path was an obstacle course carpeted with jagged rocks and shattered tree limbs.

"Jack, I need you to shut up for once," Kirsten yelled. "Can you do that for me?"

Stung by her tone he slumped back into his seat.

"Watch out!" Tyler shouted. Three deer bolted out of the woods and bounced into the middle of the road. Kirsten slammed on the brakes and the SUV skidded to a stop. The deer stood stock-still, dazed brown eyes blinking at the vehicle.

She leaned on the horn. "Move, move, move!" The deer snorted and wheezed; finally one bounded away and the other two quickly followed.

"I told you to slow down," Jack grumbled, his body hunched and arms folded across his chest.

"Yes, I know Jack," Kirsten snapped back at him. Their eyes met in the rear-view mirror. He was wearing that defiant expression that drove her crazy. Tyler was pointing out the side window, Amy wanted to see the deer but they'd melted back into the forest.

How can two kids be so different? When the twins were around five, they dressed up as Sith warriors for Halloween. They paraded around the living room in matching red costumes, helmets pulled down over their faces; one flapped his hands trying to get Kirsten's attention. "What?" she said. "You want me to guess which is Jack and which is Tyler?"

Both Siths nodded so hard their helmets almost fell off.

"Right. Let's make this interesting. If I lose, you get to stay up an extra hour on the weekend. But if I'm right, you load the dishwasher for a week." The Sith on the left grabbed the other Sith's arm. The second Sith shook him off. Right there she had them. "The Sith on the left is Tyler, the Sith on the right is Jack."

Jack ripped off his helmet in disgust. "How did you know?"

"Mommy magic."

Tyler moaned. "I told you this was a stupid idea."

Kevin walked in as the boys huffed out of the room, heads down and acting very un-warriorlike. He said, "You don't really trust those two to load the dishwasher, do you?"

She replied, "I wouldn't trust them to feed the gerbil. Don't worry, I'll keep an eye on them."

The image of Kevin's smile faded as Kirsten focused her attention on the road. They were almost at the main highway, they'd be home soon. One year after the Sith contest, Kevin was gone and she was heavily pregnant with Amy. She'd fled California and the life they'd known to settle in the woods near a tiny prairie town in the middle of nowhere.

"We're home," she said as she turned down the lane to their little house.

"What are we supposed to do?" Jack muttered. "Wreck our skates on the gravel?"

"Jack, it's that or take them off and walk to the house in your socks." She glanced at her own skates which were lying in a pile of pebbled glass on the passenger seat. "The ground won't kill you."

The kids slid out of the back of the SUV and wobbled down the driveway in their skates. The ground won't kill you, she thought, but the pipeline might. Her hand trembled as she reached for the doorknob and stepped inside. Fear rose in her chest, choking her. She breathed slowly, in and out, in and out. She didn't have the strength to go through this again.

Two Months Earlier

September

CHAPTER 22

"Where did you get that?" AJ strolled into my office, casting a ravenous eye at my chicken pita.

"Goodness, you've been gone, what, ten days, and already Vasili's is but a distant memory." I inclined my head in a vague 'out there' gesture to suggest the blue and white food truck parked across the street. We'd been Vasili's customers for so long we knew the names of the proprietor's kids; his oldest was heading to Queen's this fall. I told AJ to grab a seat while I continued to peel the damp paper wrapping off my chicken pita. I'd finally learned to eat the sandwich over a plate to avoid getting tzatziki sauce all over myself.

Eyes fixed on my pita, he eased into my visitor's chair. "You know how it is when you spend your entire holiday with your folks," he said.

AJ was using the term 'folks' in the extended family sense. The only one left in Saskatoon was his grandfather. His parents were divorced. His mother dragged AJ around the Prairies before decamping to Vancouver and his father hightailed it to a tiny town in Nova Scotia. Neither parent wanted anything to do with AJ's grandfather, the scion of a potash conglomerate, which was why AJ was under pressure to take over the family business. He was the only one left.

AJ sighed. "Time loses all meaning when you're vacationing with my Granddad. A day feels like a week, a week feels like a month, and so on, and so on..."

I laughed. "Louisa and I were lucky, our folks lived here. We could pop over for dinner and pop out again. We didn't have to hang out at their place for days on end." My parents died seven years ago and sometimes I still catch myself thinking I'll just drop in for a cup of coffee and an animated game of cribbage.

"Here." I rifled through a stack of files on my desk and found what I was looking for. "Phoenix made the 'big announcement' while you were gone."

I handed him the press release:

FIRST NET-ZERO PIPELINE LAUNCHED
Phoenix Corporation (TSX:NYSE:PHX), a leading North American energy infrastructure company, kicked off a green initiative to install twenty-six Vesper net-zero compressors on its intercontinental natural gas transportation pipeline system.

AJ furrowed his brow in concentration. "The headline is a little misleading, isn't it?"

"What, in the sense that only one Vesper's been installed, the entire pipeline won't be 'Vesperized' for months?"

He nodded as he plowed through what he called the bumf. "Ah," he said, "here it is, the CEO's quote: '...a major step in making the planet greener...embrace our role in leading the way to a net-zero future...optimizing our existing pipeline in a safe and sustainable manner.'" He glanced up at me. "Interesting that there's no quote from Ray."

"Could be they didn't want to clutter up the press release. That said, it's packed with extraneous details you'd need a Ph.D in mechanical engineering or computer science to understand."

AJ glanced up and said, "So Ray's happy? The Unicorn's AI fix did the trick?"

"It appears so. The share price skyrocketed the minute the news of the launch hit the stock market. Bannerman's been giving interviews all over...The Wall Street Journal, CNBC, Bloomberg...Word on the street is the stock will stay high for the next few months."

"Good for Ray." AJ stood, holding the announcement in front of him like a placard. "You know, we should frame this. BLV played a role, however minor"—here he winked and quoted from the release—"in 'leading the way to a net-zero future.' Now, I've got to catch Vasili before he moves the truck."

As AJ ambled down the corridor my mind went back to the morning of the announcement. Ray had called to say he was sending me an advance copy of the press release. He stayed on the line while I opened the email.

"Wow! Ray, congratulations!" I'd said as I read it over. I was jubilant and also greatly relieved. The last six months had been a rollercoaster not just for Ray—who on the scale of one to ten for capricious clients scored an eleven—but also for me. Despite Keith's sage advice, I hadn't stopped feeling responsible for a file that was never in my control. "I'm so glad the Unicorn's fixes worked."

There was a tiny hesitation before he said, "Right," suggested we get together for golf sometime, and rang off.

Just Before It Happened

November 12

CHAPTER 23

Sometimes being outside counsel is like being an actor on a movie set. You're brought in for a project, you play your part, you get paid, and poof, you're gone. Everyone forgets you exist until the next time they need someone with your skill set. I hadn't spoken to Ray, or Michelle for that matter, since September and was caught by surprise when Ray rang me out of the blue on a frosty November afternoon.

He'd barely said hello before I started pelting him with questions. "What's happening? Are the Vespers all right? Is the pipeline running?" Why did I instantly assume he was calling to convey bad news?

He laughed. "Slow down, counsellor, slow down. We're good. Hell, we're golden. The Vesper's purring like a kitten." The image of a large titanium cat with blue razor-sharp claws came to mind. "We're bringing the rest on one at a time, slowly, to make sure they run fine in local conditions. But that's not why I'm calling. Are you up for a tour of the Vault?"

"The Vault?" Oh yes, the high-security building that houses Phoenix's gas control group in the northeast quadrant of the city.

"Yes, the Vault. If I don't take you through now, I won't get a chance until the spring."

*   *   *   *

The following day, just after sunrise, he picked me up at the office and we set off. The sky was clear, the sun redder and the air softer than it would be later in the day.

"Where did the summer go?" I asked, smothering a yawn with the back of a gloved hand. Poplar trees rimed with frost flashed by the window. "I wish we were in Rome."

"Rome is wet this time of year," Ray said.

"Oh. Have you been there in November?"

"No, because the weather is crappy."

Ray, normally uncommunicative this early in the morning, wouldn't stop talking about how sad he was to say goodbye, temporarily, to his Ferrari. It was parked in the hydraulic marvel that is his garage, safe from what the *Farmer's Almanac* predicted would be a harsh and miserable winter. The company fleet car, a clunky white SUV, lumbered down the road like a sofa on wheels. Ray didn't like it one bit.

"On the upside," his tone brightened, "the Vespers sailed through September and October. Looks like sub-zero temperatures won't be a problem."

"I'm sure the Board is relieved."

He glanced at me out of the corner of his eye. "Them and me both. My bonus would have gone kaput if I gave them anything but good news." He scowled into the rear-view mirror. "Bannerman made that crystal clear."

I pulled my coat more tightly around my knees. The SUV's heater was blowing cold air across my legs and I flipped the air circulation slats shut. "So, tell me about the Vault."

The Vault—Ray said the word with reverence—was the

gas control centre. Encased in a fortified building on the outskirts of the city was a system of computers that ran the network of pipelines stretching from the northwestern tip of British Columbia across Alberta and Saskatchewan before sliding across the border and plunging deep into the American Midwest. "Think of it as the beating heart of the system," Ray said.

We pulled up in front of a grey metal structure that looked like a futuristic three-storey office building. Instead of a ribbon of glass windows marching across its façade, sunlight shimmered off random triangular windows that floated up one corner of the building like glass leaves drifting in the wind.

Ray's face was flush with pride when we stepped out of the car. "An Italian architectural firm designed the building. Made quite a splash in its day." He pointed to the only corner of the building with windows. "That's where the managers' offices and conference rooms are."

"Seriously? Natural light for the managers and no light for anyone else?"

He smiled. "Don't judge until you've seen it."

The parking lot was crusted with snow that crunched under our boots as we made our way to the lobby, a warm stone space illuminated by three topsy-turvy triangular windows. Ray flashed his card key in front of the card reader and a shiny metal door bearing the company's logo clicked open. The security guard beamed at Ray and handed me a temporary pass. Ray led the way down a narrow corridor into a sprawling space filled with moody blue light.

"Still no windows, Ray."

"Too bright for the computer screens," he said as he

called for someone named Samir. A slim middle-aged man stood up from his console, grinning as he approached us.

"You're early," Samir extended his hand.

"Wanted to catch you before you got up to no good, Samir." Ray told Samir to give us the full-meal-deal tour.

"With pleasure," Samir said. We followed him into the centre of the cavernous room. Dozens of operations techs sat at oversized desks, their eyes flying across banks of flashing computer screens. Some spoke softly into their headsets, others huddled in twos and threes pointing at screens or scribbling calculations on scraps of paper.

One long wall was filled with massive computer screens blinking and flashing like a NASA control room. Samir said the data wall showed the op techs what was happening across the system in real time. He chattered excitedly about telecom status, RTUs and system clearances.

"Whoa, Samir," Ray said, "she's a lawyer, not an engineer."

Samir hesitated, unsure how to respond. Ray patted him on the shoulder and said, "Data on flow, temperature, pressure, everything that's happening in and around the pipeline, goes to sensors, bounces off satellites to our servers that interpret it before sending it onto our computers. So we know what's going on across the system, in real time."

Ray scanned the room. "Twenty-eight thousand kilometres of pipe, carrying pressurized natural gas. And we know what's happening in every square centimetre. But, it's not enough to respond to alarm events after the fact. This"—with a broad sweep of his arm he encompassed the entire room—"allows us to predict problems *before* they happen."

"Makes perfect sense to me," I said. "Better to fix a small problem before it becomes a big one, right?"

Ray and Samir continued to talk about things I really didn't understand then moved on to trading barbs about their favourite football teams when we heard it.

A small ping sounded from one of the sixteen computers arrayed at the console next to us. The op tech leaned forward to peer at her screen. "I've got an anomaly," she said calmly. She moved her mouse and her cursor floated over the computer screen and settled on a box flashing red. "We've got an unplanned event, tracking it."

Another small ping. Then a series of pings echoing back and forth across the room. I glanced up at the data wall. The computer screen on the far-left side of the array was flashing red.

A different alarm sounded.

"Loss of containment," someone said.

When I turned back from the data wall, Samir and Ray were hunched over the op tech. "Loss of containment," she repeated more urgently. Other op techs glanced up from their screens, some confirmed they too had an 'unplanned event.' An alarm wailed, then a second and a third.

Ray looked at the op tech's screen, then the data wall. Red lights were inching north and south along the pipeline from a point in central Alberta. "Shut down Elliot Lake."

"Elliot Lake. Shut down," an op tech confirmed.

The alarms continued to ping, bouncing off the windowless walls. "Not enough," Ray said. "It's getting ahead of us. Keep going." All op techs focused on their screens, supervisors at their backs.

That's when I understood. *Loss of containment.*

Pressurized natural gas—explosive, flammable—was escaping. Ray was shutting valves to cut the gas flow. To contain it.

"Ray?" The urgent voice of a young op tech. "Just blew through C/X 57. Rosalie is twenty minutes south-east." I knew Rosalie. It's a small, picturesque town, a tourist attraction year-round. "Jeezus, it blew...it blew at C/X 60. Still coming like a bow wave."

"Shut down the northeast leg," Ray said. "Right down to Regal." A few operators stared helplessly at their screens. The rest fixed their eyes on Ray.

"Thirty valves? All of them?" someone asked.

"Do it," Ray said, still calm. Then he looked at me. "We've got to get the pipe back."

We waited in the twilight room. Digital clocks on the wall ticked down the minutes and finally the bleating alarms and flashing lights stopped. A moment of silence, then a collective sigh of relief. I exhaled, unaware I'd been holding my breath.

A phone chirped. An op tech slipped on her headset. Phones on either side of her began to ring. People were calling the control room reporting explosions and blinding flashes of light, frantically seeking reassurance.

Ray looked at the clock: 10:06:22. His face was grey. "What the fuck just happened?"

CHAPTER 24

Ray stood at the front of the room, his back to the data wall which still flashed yellow warning lights across a great swath of pipeline. He thanked the staff for their cool heads as they restored containment and stressed that from this point forward emergency protocols were in effect. "Everyone back on task, please. You know what to do."

He asked Samir and a middle-aged woman named Bernadette to join him in the incident room, which was tucked behind the control room, but first he needed to touch base with Bannerman. Ray punched Bannerman's number into his cell, then looked up. "Sorry Evie, the tour's over."

"I gathered that."

"Listen, do you want to stick around for a while?"

"Absolutely, if you don't think I'll be in the way." I had been trying to fade into the woodwork since the first alarm rang out.

He gave me a thumbs up. Bannerman did not pick up. Ray left a message, pocketed his phone and beckoned Samir, Bernadette, and me to join him in the incident room. Unlike the dim blue bubble of the control room, the incident room was brightly lit. The glare of overhead lights reflected off the whiteboards ringing three walls.

Two large computer screens and a flat screen TV were embedded on the fourth wall.

Samir touched a small remote on the table and the computer screens flared to life. He clicked the TV remote and a commercial for a donut shop played soundlessly while he adjusted the volume.

As we focused on the computer screens, Ray explained that one, the SCADA screen, let him see what was happening on the pipe in real time. He shot me a rueful smile. "That way I won't get underfoot while they're"—he tipped his head in the direction of the control room— "trying to do their jobs."

Samir and Bernadette outlined the incident response process. Ray listened, nodding occasionally. The jargon was incomprehensible until Ray asked whether there were any fatalities or injuries. No news yet.

A helicopter had been dispatched to assess the damage and operators would soon be on their way to secure the blast site at the Elliot Lake compressor station and check for ruptures further down the line. Bernadette confirmed that staff from all key departments were already reporting to the command centre at Phoenix's head office. They would have a preliminary status report ready for Ray to share with senior management soon. Samir said the company's emergency response teams would liaise with the RCMP, the regulators, landowners, media, and the general public as soon as they knew more.

"And our customers feeding gas onto the pipe?" Ray asked.

"They're getting outage notices as we speak. The connecting pipes downstream have been notified, industrial customers will be cut off, gas to residentials only."

"Local emergency response centres?"

"We're pulling the field techs; they'll be redeployed to local ER centres as soon as we figure out where to set them up."

Ray nodded. "No word yet on loss of life? Injuries?" That was the second time he'd asked the question.

Samir's face was grave. "Nothing yet. But given the magnitude of the blast..." He stopped, not daring to continue. "We've called in the locals, firefighting, EMT. We'll evacuate anyone who may be impacted." Samir rubbed his brow. His hand trembled slightly. "We'll know more soon."

Ray's cell phone buzzed. He glanced at the screen. "It's Bannerman." He walked over to the corner of the room, said a few words, nodded, then hung up and returned to the table. "Right," he said. "I'm heading to the office to update Bannerman and the executive team."

"I'll catch a cab back into town," I said.

Neither of us said anything on our way out to the parking lot. Ray gave me a curt nod, then slipped behind the wheel of his fleet car and sped away. The wind whistled across the lot, tearing at my hair and making my eyes water. I pulled my coat more tightly around me and waited for the cab to arrive.

CHAPTER 25

Bridget leapt up from her desk before I made it through the front door and crushed me in a tight embrace. "Thank goodness you're all right!" She held me out in front of her as if to confirm I was indeed alive. "It's all over the news. Were you there? How awful!"

"No. No, Ray took me to the Vault, the gas control building. Here in town. We were hundreds of kilometres away from the blast."

Keith hurried down the hall. "I thought I heard your voice. You all right?" He raked his fingers through his hair and gave me a small, worried smile. "We're in the conference room, following it on TV."

I tossed my coat on the corner of Bridget's desk and followed him into the room where AJ and Madeline were perched on the edge of the walnut table, eyes glued to the screen. The blinds were partially closed and the room was filled with shadows. AJ squeezed my shoulder almost absentmindedly. Madeline grabbed my hand and patted it twice. No one spoke.

A newscaster was narrating the images that flashed up on the screen. A helicopter edged closer and closer to a plume of thick black smoke. It looked like a small drag-onfly. Flames roiled the sky and flared in the surrounding woods. A large structure, perhaps a house or a barn, slumped to the ground, sending sparks high into the air.

Keith said, "They think a compressor station exploded. Everything is on fire."

"How do they know this already?" I asked. "Has the company issued a statement?"

AJ stopped flicking through his Twitter feed and looked up. "No, nothing yet. They'd better get on it fast or the conspiracy theorists will have a field day." AJ was right. As environmental lawyers, we've run into our share of kooks who swear wind farms created the polar vortex. Any change in the status quo brings the weirdos out of the woodwork.

The image of the helicopter tilting across the terrain gave way to a solemn looking reporter in a puffy jacket standing in the middle of a frozen field. Next to him was a heavy-set man. Pillars of grey smoke curled up on the horizon behind them. The reporter thrust the microphone in the beefy man's face and asked a question. Has anyone been injured or killed? The man stammered and shrugged, saying he had no idea. The reporter asked more questions that the man could not answer.

"God, I hope that's not the company's spokesman," Madeline said. "He's pathetic."

I said, "They shut down the northeast leg of the line, closed thirty valves." Keith let out a low whistle.

AJ looked dismayed. "That's miles and miles of pipe."

"And miles and miles of people along the route," I replied. Hundreds of tiny towns and hamlets sit on top of a spiderweb of pipelines running all over the province.

We were startled by a rap at the conference room door. Bridget appeared, her face drawn. "Evie, I've got Ray on the phone, he says it's urgent."

She transferred the call to my office; the red light on my phone flashed and I hesitated for a fraction of a second before picking it up.

"Evie?" Ray said my name in a measured tone.

"This is Evie Valentine... I mean, yes, Ray, it's me."

"I have some news. It may be nothing or it may be something. Either way I just wanted to give you a heads-up." He inhaled slowly. "Michelle was out on the line. At Elliot Lake." I closed my eyes, waiting. "Evie, she's unaccounted for, missing."

Missing? Not dead? A sliver of hope.

Ray pressed on. "Listen, we don't know anything for certain yet. It's too soon. They could be somewhere without cell service; the fires took out some towers."

"They? Who's they?"

"She had a meeting with Marty at the Elliot Lake station."

"Marty? That guy we met when you took Faro and Matteo to the plant?" The image of jovial Marty, face shiny in the summer heat, proudly showing us the Vesper prototype, floated into my mind. God, that was such a long time ago.

Ray's voice was momentarily muffled, as if he'd covered the receiver with his hand and was speaking to someone else. Then he came back on the line. "Look, I've got to go. Just wanted you to know about Michelle. She's missing. So's Marty, two firefighters, and a compressor tech from Elliot Lake. Five in total."

"Uh huh." My mind skittered back to Michelle. "I don't get it, Ray. What the hell was Michelle doing out there with Marty in the middle of November?"

"I don't know, Evie. I'm sorry."

The pen I was clutching slipped from my fingers. It

rolled slowly across the desk and fell to the floor. "She can't be there... she has no reason to be there." My voice had dropped to an insistent whisper. I had to stop. Ray didn't know anything.

I straightened my spine; I'd been slumped over my desk, head hanging down, phone pressed to my ear. "Ray, thank you for letting me know. You must be very busy, thank you. I really appreciate it."

When he hung up, I paused to consider this strange feeling. The interregnum between knowing and not knowing. In this very moment Michelle could be dead or alive. I chose to believe she was alive. Freezing her ass off with Marty on the pipeline right-of-way, waving her phone in the air, looking for cell service.

Right now Michelle was alive.

CHAPTER 26

"Your phone." Madeline nodded apologetically at the phone ringing on my desk.

"What?" I felt like I was emerging from a drugged sleep, struggling to orient myself. "Pardon. What?" It had been hours since I'd spoken with Ray and then told Keith and the others that Michelle was one of five Phoenix employees unaccounted for.

"Your phone is ringing," she repeated. "It might be important." She gave me a gentle smile and retreated to her office.

I glanced at the red light flashing like a tiny siren and picked up the receiver.

"Evie, it's Dave Bryson, got a minute?" Oh God, Michelle's second in command.

"Any news on Michelle?" I asked.

"Ahh, no, nothing yet. It's terrible, simply awful." A long pause. What did he want?

"So listen, Evie. The Board is getting antsy—"

"The Board? The pipe blew up at ten this morning. It's been six hours, haven't you updated them yet?"

"Give me a moment to shut my door." The phone clattered when he set it down and then again when he picked it up. "They've been calling all day. We've been updating them piecemeal, but it's hit and miss: some want a blow-by-blow description of what happened, others are satisfied with the broad strokes."

"Dave, they understand they're not supposed to talk about the explosion to anyone, right? All communications must go through Phoenix's spokesperson." Michelle would have sent a confidential memo to the Board setting out the emergency protocol and promising updates as the day wore on.

"Relax, will you? Bannerman's called an emergency board meeting tomorrow morning, nine o'clock. That's why I'm calling. He wants you there."

My shoulders sagged. Suddenly I was very tired. "Why? I don't know any more about the blast or its implications than you do, probably less."

"I *know* that." Now he was peeved. "Ray will speak to the incident. Bannerman wants you to discuss the implications for the Vesper agreement."

"What implications? No one knows what caused the explosion." Madeline walked slowly by my door and peeked in. I rolled my eyes in exasperation. "For God's sake, Dave, five people are missing, they could be dead. Who knows how many more have been injured... and the property damage, insurance claims, reputational damage. Is the Transportation Safety Board even on site yet?"

"There is no need for histrionics." Lovely, now he's chiding me. "The purpose of the meeting is to update the Board on the rupture—"

I rose and started pacing in front of the window, my temper rising. The light from the townhouses on the other side of the bank reflected off the water in sheets like gold foil. They had to find Michelle and Marty before nightfall, it gets so cold when the temperature drops.

Dave was now babbling about recouping damages from Vesper.

"Damages? Dave, did you not hear me? No one knows what caused the explosion. If we don't know the cause then we can't say it's Vesper's fault."

"It's true we don't know the precise cause of the rupture, but the preliminary view is that the blast originated at Elliot Lake, where we installed the Vesper prototype."

"So what? Unless you've got evidence connecting the explosion with a Vesper malfunction you can't blame Vesper."

For a few seconds all I could hear was Dave breathing heavily into the receiver. I was about to hang up when he said, "Look, maybe I didn't express myself properly. Bannerman's intention is to reassure the Board—"

"Dave, how can you 'reassure' them if you don't know what happened?"

We went around and around like a dog chasing its tail for a few more minutes, then Dave changed tack. I didn't have to attend the Board meeting. All he wanted was a quick pre-meeting so he could bounce a few ideas off me, then I'd be free to leave. Would I be so kind as to stop by his office around eight a.m. tomorrow? Like a fool I agreed.

CHAPTER 27

My body zinged with restless energy. It was nine p.m. and still no word about Michelle. To make things worse Louisa was working the late shift and it was blizzarding outside. The storm started around dinner time with a couple of lazy snowflakes drifting out of the dark sky. Now it was pelting down so hard the office towers on the other side of the river were shrouded in mist. Louisa is an excellent driver but this town is full of idiots. Either they forget how to drive in winter conditions or they can't be bothered with snow tires.

"Quincy, stop looking at me like that." The dog was watching me place kindling into the fireplace in our TV room. He's got an expressive face for a bull terrier and right now he looked skeptical. The two of us were leaning over the hearth, staring at a sloppy triangle of sticks and a couple of logs that kept sliding off a wad of balled up newspaper. "This is how Google says to do it."

I flicked the barbeque lighter a couple of times and the newspapers ignited with a *whoosh*. Something made a hissing sound. Quincy looked at the small stack of wood, then back at me. "Yes, I know, not dry enough,"

He snuffled around in his toy box and deposited a plush warthog at my feet. It was missing a tusk and one leg. I was about to toss it across the room when my cell phone buzzed on the coffee table. It was Ray.

"Do you have news?" My heart fluttered. "Have you found her?"

"We found her," he said. "Evie, it's not good."

"But she's going to be all right, yes? With medical attention, she'll be fine." I started pacing in front of the fireplace, a log slipped off the pile and a burst of sparks floated up the flue.

"Evie. Evie, listen to me." He spoke even slower. He said the search crews found Marty on the right-of-way about two hundred yards south of the compressor station. "He was in the blast zone... he didn't have a chance."

"Michelle, where's—"

He talked over me, determined to finish what he had to say. "Once they recovered Marty's body, the searchers fanned out. They found Michelle's body at the base of a rock outcropping. She may have been struck by flying debris, a hunk of steel or rock, who knows what was flying around after the explosion."

He cleared his throat quietly. "She was untouched by the flame, if, well, if that's any comfort."

Blood pounded in my temples. Suddenly I was furious. "She's dead, Ray, how can that possibly be of any comfort?" Then I stopped. It was wrong to lash out at him. "I'm so sorry, Ray, I shouldn't have said that."

He continued talking. I think I registered every second word. Something about blast zones and secondary explosions and helicopters flying through the night searching for chunks of pipe, hot spots that could start a forest fire.

"What about the others?" Had he mentioned them? I couldn't recall. "Did you find the other three? Did they make it?"

"Yeah, they're all fine. The two guys in the firetruck had to abandon their vehicle. It got trapped behind the blaze. They walked out of the forest a couple of hours ago. The compressor tech left the plant just before the explosion to check on his dog. It was sick or something and he decided to take it to the vet. Then the pipe blew up and in all the confusion he forgot to let anyone know where he was."

It was beginning to sink in. Five were missing, three survived, two didn't. Michelle and Marty were gone. I stopped pacing. In my mind's eye I could see it all, the bleak right-of-way, the dark outcropping in the distance, speckled rock pushing through scruffy snow-covered grass. At its base, Michelle's crumpled body. It must have been very cold out there in the open. She hates the cold.

Ray's voice came down the line, small and thin; I'd let the phone drift away, now I pressed it back against my ear. He asked whether he could send someone over to be with me. I said it wasn't necessary, Louisa would be home soon.

I set the phone on the mantle and sank to the floor, tears trickling down my cheeks. Quincy dropped his toy and nuzzled my face. I put my arms around his strong shoulders and sobbed. "What was she doing out there, Quincy? What the hell was she doing out there?" He dropped his head into my lap and I stroked his velvety ear. He didn't leave my side, not even when he heard Louisa's key in the lock. She found the two of us huddled on the floor, staring at the embers of a fire that had gone cold hours ago.

CHAPTER 28

The next morning I was standing in the Phoenix lobby watching the koi fish bobbing along the surface of the fishpond. I'd slept poorly after Ray's phone call, was fuzzy minded, and somehow managed to arrive at the building forty-five minutes early for my meeting with Dave. "Well, hello." The fish was solid bronze, its scales gleamed metallic in the dappled sunlight. It gulped and bubbled, ignoring the blue and orange fish churning beside it. "I don't think I've seen you before. You look like a little Hindenburg, hanging there."

"Evie?" I looked up into the concerned face of Michelle's assistant, Sarah.

"Oh, hi," I said, "You caught me talking to the fish."

"They are beautiful, aren't they?" The lines on Sarah's face softened a little as she stared into the shallow blue water. She was in her mid fifties, formally dressed in a dark blue suit with a large sparkly broach high on one shoulder. She'd been Michelle's admin assistant for decades.

A young woman emerged from a door set flush in the wall on the other side of the fishpond. She stuck a small scoop into a plastic bucket and sprinkled pellets onto the surface of the water. Hindenburg dismissed me with a swish of his tail and muscled his way past the other koi jostling into position, waiting to be fed.

"Sarah," I said softly, "Ray called me last night... about Michelle... I am so sorry." Her eyes became misty, I swallowed hard and gave her a moment before asking the question that had kept me awake last night. "Sarah, what the hell was she doing out there?"

"I have no idea." Sarah stepped closer. "I caught a glimpse of her yesterday morning when her husband dropped her off at the curb. She waved at me, hustled across the lobby and went straight down to the parking garage for her fleet car."

"And you didn't get a chance to talk to her?"

"No." Sarah pulled a Kleenex out of her sleeve and carefully dabbed the corner of her eye. By the time we got off the elevator on the executive floor, she was in full control, head held high and back ramrod straight. I followed her past the two large terracotta urns that stood guard outside the executive sanctum.

Dave's office was three floors down with the other senior managers, but he'd instructed me to meet him up here on the executive floor. When Sarah ushered me into Michelle's office I understood why. He'd moved in, claiming her space as his own. He asked Sarah to bring him a cup of tea. Did I want anything? I shook my head.

He strolled over to Michelle's conference table, waving his hand to indicate I should follow, then sat down and flipped open a leather portfolio case. His name was embossed in gold lettering across the bottom. He leaned back in his chair and said he was devastated by the news about Michelle and Marty, it was terrible, simply terrible. Before I could reply his face changed, now he was all business. He explained he'd moved upstairs "temporarily, of course" to be closer to Bannerman should the CEO need urgent legal advice or any other kind of support. Sarah returned with a cup of tea, placed it on a coaster just out of Dave's reach, then shut the door quietly as she left.

I resisted the urge to tell Dave not to get too comfortable in his 'new' office and waited for him to get to the point. Patience is not my strong suit, but I've learned the hard way that some situations are best approached slowly and with caution, the way you'd corner a scorpion in your bathroom. Dave studied me for a few seconds then said he wanted to make sure we 'had our ducks in a row' and 'were both on the same page.'

I stared at him, nonplussed. "I have no idea what you're talking about."

With an agitated grimace he said, "I don't need to tell you this is a critical board meeting. Everything has to go off without a hitch."

"Yes, I understand that, but I don't know what you want from me. I don't know what's on the Board agenda… other than what you told me yesterday."

"Exactly." Now he looked triumphant.

"Hold on." I raised one hand. "Just so we're crystal clear here. If you're asking me to say Vesper is on the hook for our damages, I can't do that. Vesper is only responsible for compressor failures—"

"Yes, but if a compressor failure causes a pipeline failure and—"

"Dave, don't go there. You know as well as I do the only way Vesper would be responsible for our damages is if we can prove that the compressors, directly or indirectly, caused the explosion. At this point we don't know what caused the explosion, so there's no legal basis for saying it was Vesper's fault."

He glowered at me. "Well, that won't do."

"Well, that's what the contract says, like it or not."

There was a light tap at the door. Sarah appeared in the doorway. "Dave, Bannerman is heading down to the boardroom, he's looking for you." Dave snapped his portfolio case shut. I followed him into the hall and turned to go back out to the reception area to pick up my coat when Sarah stopped me. "Evie, Bannerman expects you to be there as well."

"What?" I looked at Dave who was hustling down the hall in the other direction.

"Let's go," he called over his shoulder. "The Board is waiting."

"That's just peachy, Dave, thanks." He ignored me, greeting Ray who emerged with the Chief Financial Officer from the hallway. The rest of the executives trailed after them; Beth, the VP of Human Resources, looked haggard, with dark circles under her eyes. Bannerman was waiting for us in the small anteroom adjacent to the boardroom. We could hear the sound of coffee cups rattling in saucers and Board members talking to each other in hushed tones.

Bannerman nodded at me then looked at Dave. "Everything squared away?" Dave nodded energetically.

Bannerman jutted out his chin, then adjusted his cufflinks. They were studded with diamonds and sparkled in the sunlight streaming in from a small side window. He ran his fingers through his thinning hair, then swept into the boardroom issuing a hearty greeting to everyone. Dave and the executives fanned out to claim their chairs at the bottom end of a long rosewood table. Bannerman made himself comfortable at the head of the table.

The Board members settled in their chairs. Did they

always sit in the same place? If status was conferred by proximity to Bannerman, then the Chairman of the Board, a round bald man who had been the CEO before Bannerman took his job, was the second most important person in the room. He sat on Bannerman's right. Chris Henzel, the Board member Michelle had introduced me to over lunch, was seated at the middle of the table in the transition zone between the Board members and the executives.

Bannerman introduced me as I took my place next to Ray. Twelve pairs of eyes pivoted in my direction then flicked back to Bannerman, anxious to get on with the business at hand. Michelle once said the Board's decision-making process was a mystery. Momentous decisions to spend millions of dollars were made on the strength of a two-minute slide presentation while a decision to purchase a couple of Alex Janvier paintings for the reception area spurred hours of debate. Everyone had an opinion on art, but not many understood the intricacies of a credit swap arrangement. Today the tension in the room hung like a miasma, choking us all.

Bannerman said this was not a real Board meeting, just an update on the tragic incident that had taken the lives of two Phoenix employees.

The Board members shifted, uneasy in their chairs. Sad business, very sad, someone said. Chris Henzel cast a troubled eye at me, then turned to Bannerman and asked why Michelle and the team leader were out on the line in the first place. Bannerman said it was a routine visit which unfortunately ended in tragedy. Chris puckered his brow. Why would the company's Chief Legal Officer choose to walk the line on a bitterly cold November morning? Was she there with a specific purpose? Bannerman looked at

Dave who responded right on cue, saying Michelle loved getting out into the field. Something drifted into my mind, niggling for a moment before curling away like a wisp of smoke.

Bannerman turned the meeting over to Ray who tapped a few buttons on his laptop, picked up a remote and walked to the front of the room. The lights dimmed, the mechanical blinds whirred down, and the large flat screen at the end of the room brightened. We waited in the gloom until the company's logo, a stylized Phoenix, appeared, followed by a map of the pipeline system marred by a pulsating red dot. It transformed into the Elliot Lake compressor station surrounded by billowing black smoke and columns of flame. Aerial footage showed a wide, deep crater scarring the surface of the frozen ground below.

Ray explained he was in the Vault when the alarms started beeping and panicked calls from residents flooded the phone lines. "It was huge. You could see the fireball from forty kilometres away."

Over the next hour Ray walked the Board members through all the actions the company had taken to mitigate the disaster, coordinating with the local EMT, firefighters, and RCMP to secure the site and evacuating residents and school children to the local arena.

His voice was soothing and the Board members nodded along—the company had done everything it could—it was only when Ray got to the part about the dog that they fussed with concern. A house had been completely incinerated. "Luckily, the homeowner was out walking his dog. The damn dog took off when it heard the explosion, but the owner found it a couple of hours later."

A murmur of relief washed over the room. *Michelle and Marty were dead and they're upset about a dog?*

"What about our customers and connecting shippers?" a Board member asked. Everyone swung their attention from Ray to Bannerman. This was the big money question.

Bannerman assured them that alternative gas supplies had been redirected downstream. "No worries, Granny won't freeze to death in the dark." Someone chuckled.

At this point Bannerman told Ray to wrap it up. Ray hesitated, then clicked on to the next slide.

"Only a few more to go," he said.

Bannerman, who'd been sitting at the corner of the table, rose to his feet as if to sidle Ray out of the way. Just then the Chairman of the Board stirred in his chair like a sleepy old bear. When the lights dimmed and the blinds closed, his chin had dropped on to his chest and I thought he'd fallen asleep, but now he was animated, saying he wanted to hear what Ray had to say.

Bannerman raised an eyebrow. "Fine," he flipped a hand at Ray, "tell them about the podunk media requests PR's been getting." It was a very condescending comment which Ray immediately contradicted by saying the company was working with all the major media outlets to ensure the public was informed.

"What about the regulator?" Chris Henzel again. An agitated murmur washed over the table. The Transportation Safety Board had the power to shut down the pipeline indefinitely.

"You mean the TSB? They're on site and have started their investigation. Expect it to be exhaustive and time-consuming. It will be months before the TSB is satisfied it knows what happened and why."

"What *did* happen?" Chris' question was directed at Bannerman.

"Sir," Ray said deferentially, "we're investigating the root cause, our best people will work hand-in-glove with the TSB to get to the bottom of this as soon as we can."

Chris pressed his lips together but said nothing.

When Ray returned to his chair he whispered to me, "Thank God, that's over."

In fact, it was just the beginning.

CHAPTER 29

Bannerman scooped the remote off the table, cranked open the mechanical blinds and raised the lights. We blinked in the harsh light like schoolchildren after an in-class movie.

"Thank you, Ray, for that fulsome presentation." Bannerman shot the Chairman an aggrieved look and crossed the floor to stand next to the big screen. "It's time to shift our focus. It will come as no surprise that this unfortunate event has negatively impacted our share price."

An interactive chart appeared on the screen. Even in the reflected glare of the windows we could see the thick red line tracking the company's share price move up at the end of April when Phoenix announced the purchase of the Vespers, then shoot even higher on September 1 when Bannerman announced the first Vesper at Elliot Lake had gone live, only to nosedive yesterday.

"The share price is lower now than it was before we announced this deal." Bannerman paused. His cold blue eyes swept across the room. "We owe it to our investors to do whatever it takes to push the share price back to where it belongs." A dotted line appeared and flew up to match the trajectory of the September 1 line.

The room became hushed. Were they thinking what

I was thinking: How was Bannerman going to pull off this miracle?

"Gentlemen... and ladies," Bannerman nodded to acknowledge the two female Board members, "this flutter in the market will reverse itself eventually, but the drag on our share price makes it hard for us to carry on business in the meantime."

I glanced around the room. If ever there was a statement that cried out for a follow up, it was that one. Why? Why was it harder? How much harder was it?

But no one said a word. They didn't want to challenge Bannerman—heaven forbid they look uninformed—and just like the CEO of Enron, Bannerman carried them along.

"Christ, Alastair, just get on with it, will you." That was the Chairman.

Bannerman raised his hands in a placating manner and said, "The TSB doesn't have the resources to run this investigation without help from Ray's team. Ray tells me there was no negligence on our part, and at the end of the day the TSB will concur. So the problem must be with Vesper. The sooner the market knows this, the sooner our shares will bounce back to the September 1 price."

His eyes glittered hard and black as he unveiled his plan. "With your concurrence, Ray will call Matteo Vianelli, Vesper's CEO, and tell him that unless Vesper publicly admits liability for the explosion, Phoenix will launch a lawsuit that will destroy Vesper."

What? I turned to look at Ray. His eyes were fixed on the pen clutched in his fist, his knuckles were white and the pen looked like it might snap in two.

Bannerman continued. "Matteo is a smart man. He'll cooperate."

I glanced across the table at Dave who nodded sagely. And that's when the penny dropped. Dave and Bannerman wanted me at this meeting because I'd drafted the Vesper agreement. My mere presence here created the impression I supported Bannerman's plan.

"Excuse me," I said.

Bannerman narrowed his eyes at me, I narrowed my eyes right back and continued. "With all due respect, suing Vesper and threatening to kill their company would expose Phoenix to an expensive countersuit and untold damages." Lawyers use phrases like 'with all due respect' when they're telling someone they're an idiot. "No one knows what caused the explosion. Consequently, it is inadvisable, indeed foolhardy, to threaten such a lawsuit, let alone make any public accusations that the explosion was Vesper's fault."

An uncomfortable silence filled the room. Perhaps I shouldn't have used the word 'foolhardy.'

All eyes turned back to Bannerman. Two red spots appeared high on his cheekbones.

Chris glanced at me, then at Dave, then back at me again. "So which is it? Can we sue Vesper for damages, or can't we?"

"No, you're jumping the gun," I said.

"Yes, we know enough already," Dave said.

Bannerman snorted in disgust and said, "Gentlemen, you know how it is with lawyers, ask them if the sun sets in the west and they'll argue about it all day long if you pay them enough."

I bit my lip, refusing to let him goad me into saying something rash.

Chris leaned forward in his chair, his arms resting lightly on the edge of the table as he addressed

Bannerman. "Alastair," he said Bannerman's first name slowly, with a hiss. "Given the gravity of the risk I think a formal legal opinion would be in order, don't you?"

"Good suggestion, Chris." Bannerman recovered quickly. "Dave will prepare a legal opinion and circulate it to the Board ASAP." Dave's head bobbed up and down like a yo-yo on a string.

The Chairman of the Board coughed a great phlegmy cough and said, "Alastair, in an abundance of caution I'd prefer a joint legal opinion, penned by Dave with our... our outside counsel." He waved vaguely in my direction. He'd forgotten my name.

On paper Bannerman reports to the Board, but in reality, he calls the shots. The only person in that room he couldn't push around was the man he'd replaced; the Chairman. This was likely one of the few times they didn't see eye to eye. Everyone waited. Did Bannerman have the guts to buck the Chairman? Bannerman inhaled, then smiled a thin smile. "Of course. Evie," he flicked his eyes at me, "and Dave will deliver a joint opinion to me, er, the Board in two days' time. Agreed?"

Before Dave could respond I said, "Provided the Board understands that Dave and I may not agree." A joint opinion that was a mass of contradictions was worse than useless, but if Bannerman wanted to go there, fine. I would not be bullied into saying something I didn't believe to be true.

With an impatient nod Bannerman declared the meeting over and strode out of the room. Dave bolted after him. The Board members filed out to the reception area and formed dissolute groups of twos and threes, waiting for the receptionist to retrieve their coats and summon their town cars. The executives who typically hung around making self-serving small talk with the Board members, fled.

Sarah met me in reception and handed me my coat. "You left it in Michelle's office." She glanced around the empty reception area. "Everyone certainly cleared out in a hurry. How did it go?"

I shuddered as I slipped my arms into my coat sleeves and wrapped my scarf around my neck. "Remember that movie, The Defiant Ones, where two prisoners escape but are handcuffed together. They hate each other in the beginning but grow to respect each other by the end?"

She nodded.

"Yeah, well that's Dave and me, except we hate each other now and we're going to kill each other before this movie is over." Sarah glanced over my shoulder and put her finger to her lips, shhhh. "Oh great, he's right behind me, isn't he?"

A quick nod, then, "Never mind, he just steamed into Michelle's office and slammed the door."

CHAPTER 30

That evening it was so cold the air hurt our lungs. The Garrison Pub parking lot was packed and Louisa and I had to leave the car a half a block away. We pulled our woolly toques down over our ears, our scarves up over our noses and crunched through snow with the blind determination of a heat-seeking missile. Someone stepped out of the pub just as we neared the door which slammed shut in a blast of frigid wind. Louisa grabbed the door handle with a mittened fist and strained to hold it open while I staggered inside, scanning the noisy mob in search of a table.

"Evie!" My name floated across a sea of puffy jackets and soggy boots. The pub was jammed, the floor was gritty with tracked-in road salt. The smell of burger grease mingled with the musty odour of damp wool. AJ was waving his arms like a windmill, trying to catch my attention. Madeline was sitting next to him, pretending he did not exist.

Louisa and I rarely go out on a weeknight, but when I got home she announced we were going to the Garrison.

"What? Why?" I'd said, using my knees to stop Quincy from shoulder checking me into the hall closet. He had the bull terrier advantage, all muscle and low to the ground.

"Settle down, you silly dog," I muttered. "I've had a lousy day, Louisa, I'm fine with tea and toast."

"No can do. The water's off."

"Why?"

"Because some guy in a fluorescent vest showed up on the doorstep this afternoon and said so. There's a water main break somewhere. Must be the cold."

I groaned. "Did you fill the kettle or something?"

"Nope, no warning. So unless you want to boil what's left in Quincy's water dish, we're going out."

I groaned and she grabbed my shoulders and spun me around. "Go upstairs, put on your jeans, and let's get out of here. I'm starving."

As we inched through the pub crowd, I realized that I too was starving. AJ and Madeline wiggled their chairs around and Louisa and I squeezed in beside them at the end of a long table packed with people celebrating Wednesday. Soon we were hoisting beer mugs and shouting over the racket, trying to decide what to order for dinner.

"So, what brings you two here? Is Bridget coming?" I asked.

AJ said, "To answer your questions, (A), it's been one of those days, and (B), Bridget's not coming." That wasn't surprising. Bridget usually heads straight home after work to feed Coconut, her pudgy little puppy who was getting pudgier with each passing day.

We placed our orders and Madeline asked, "Have you settled down yet?" She turned to AJ. "Evie was in serious gripe mode after the Phoenix Board meeting."

I rolled my eyes and told AJ about Bannerman's ridiculous plan to boost the share price and how I got trapped into drafting a joint legal opinion with Dave. "I'm guessing Bannerman thinks Dave will bludgeon me into submission."

AJ laughed. "As if that would ever happen." His face was flushed despite his jacket being unzipped and his scarf hanging loosely around his neck. He flexed his shoulders the way athletes do before they go onto the field and I realized once again how good looking he was. The fact he appeared to be completely unaware of it didn't hurt either.

The server leaned over our group, placing a gigantic plate of nachos on the table and we set upon them like a pack of wild dogs.

I was picking at a nacho, trying to free it from the cheesy pile without losing all the olives and jalapenos when a stranger's voice penetrated our conversation. "Well, will you look at that, it's Charlie's Angels." At the other end of our table a well-dressed man in a camel overcoat stared at me over the top of his beer glass. He winked slowly. His friends glanced at us and then back at the man in the camel coat and smirked.

One of his buddies chortled and said, "Tell me Frank, how does a guy like that get that much ass?" Frank threw back his head and laughed so hard the people behind him turned around to see what was so funny.

Louisa shot me a warning glance. I turned back to focus on AJ. "I'm sorry, AJ, you were saying...?"

Frank waved his arm at the server behind the bar. This caught my attention. Frank's eyes locked onto mine. He puckered his lips and made a loud, sticky, kissing sound. The hair on the nape of my neck prickled. Louisa squeezed my hand. Frank took another swig of beer, wiping his moist mouth with the back of his hand.

Then I heard the buzzing in my ears, like the hissing of

snakes. The British call it the red mist. Louisa calls it the fury. I don't call it anything at all. It just happens.

"That's it." I stood up abruptly, my chair banging against Louisa's leg.

"Here we go," said Louisa softly.

AJ scrambled to his feet, but Louisa lay a hand on his arm to stop him. He sat down slowly, bewildered.

I walked down to Frank's end of the table. "Do I know you?"

"Not yet, sweetheart." Frank leered at his friends; he was better dressed and older than they were, likely a businessman taking his subordinates out for drinks. They sniggered on cue.

"Then why are you doing disgusting things with your mouth?"

"Hey, no offence, honey. Just being friendly." Frank arched an eyebrow.

I glanced back at AJ. His jaw was clenched. Louisa's hand was still resting on his arm. "See my friend there, the guy with the blue scarf, why don't you blow him a friendly kiss?"

His buddies snorted derisively. Frank's cheeks became blotchy. "Fuck off," he said.

"Oh I get it, what you did just now wasn't a sign of friendship, it was sexual, right?"

He shook his head at his friend on the right. "They just can't take a joke." Then he looked up at me. "You stupid bitch, it was a compliment." At this point in the pantomime I was supposed to slink away, having been put firmly in my place.

I said, "So we've established you made a lewd sexual gesture."

He glowered. "What are you going to do about it... sue me?"

I raised my voice so it could be heard by those sitting nearby. "No, Frank, I'm not going to sue you. I'm going to ask the people in this bar whether they think you're complimenting me or harassing me." The patrons on both sides of us stopped pretending they weren't eavesdropping.

"Come on Frank, stand up," I said it even louder. "Show everyone how you complimented me." The silence at our table rippled out, washing over the tables around us. At least a dozen people were paying close attention to the small dark-haired woman standing over a large angry man. He glowered at his friends; one winced, uncertain what to do next. The other looked away.

"Oh for Christ's sake," Frank said as he flipped up his collar and yanked his leather gloves out of his pockets.

"What's the matter, Frank? You don't like unwanted attention?" I asked loudly.

He glared at his friends. It was clear he was leaving. Were they coming? They looked across the table at each other. *What to do?* They could share their buddy's humiliation by storming out with him or stay put. It didn't take long for them to decide. One complained that he hadn't finished his sandwich yet, the other said he'd just ordered another beer.

Frank stood up so fast his chair toppled backward, striking the woman sitting behind him. She caught it before it hit the floor. Then he stalked toward the door; the crowd watched him every step of the way. He yanked on the door latch, it took him a moment to realize it opened out, not in. The wind slammed it shut behind him when he left.

There was silence in the bar as everyone turned to

stare at Frank's buddies who were now engrossed in whatever was happening on the TV screen hanging on the opposite wall. A beat of silence and the chatter started up. Everything returned to normal.

I returned to my chair next to Louisa. She rubbed my arm. "Nacho?" she said brightly, offering me a chip. I laughed.

"Evie," AJ leaned closer, whispering in my ear, "I could have handled it."

"It wasn't about you, AJ."

He opened his mouth to say more but Madeline stopped him. "Eat your dinner, AJ, it's getting cold." She took a slow sip of her gin and tonic—who but Madeline orders a G&T in the dead of winter—and looked at me. "Tell me Evie, do you make a habit of confronting strangers in bars?"

"Only the bullies," I replied, prying a nacho off the bottom of the dish.

Three Weeks After It Happened

Early December

CHAPTER 31

Kirsten awoke with a start just after four in the morning. It would be hours before the sun broke through the evergreens and brightened the glade where her house stood. She groaned and dragged herself out of bed. There was no point in staying under the warm blankets, she wouldn't fall asleep again. Every time she closed her eyes, she could see it. "Oh Kevin," she whispered quietly, "what am I going to do?"

She splashed warm water on her face and ran a brush through her hair. She may feel like a tormented soul but she needn't look like one. She refused to burden the children with her precarious state of mind. She went into the kitchen and made a pot of coffee before padding into the den to turn on her computer and scan her news feed. Since the pipeline explosion three weeks ago she'd meticulously tracked Phoenix's community relations campaign and the TSB website to see whether the regulator had reached any preliminary conclusions.

Aside from that disastrous initial interview, Phoenix had done a decent job of crisis management. The company's spokeswoman was all over the media. Every word that came out of her mouth would have been vetted by Phoenix's crisis management consultants and legal team. And true to form, the fatal explosion that took two lives morphed from a 'disaster' to a 'rupture' to an 'incident' to an 'interruption of service.' The dead were no longer mentioned, certainly not by name. Their deaths would disappear in the memories of all but the few who mourned them... and Kirsten. Kirsten thought about them every day.

She knew from experience that the company's engineers and lawyers were working hand-in-glove with the Transportation Safety Board to identify the cause of the 'interruption' to ensure it would never happen again. The thought filled her with disgust. *Never happen again?* Pipeline explosions happened with heart-stopping regularity. At this very moment the earth supporting a pipeline could be shifting, an infinitesimally small crack could be forming, a micro switch could be stuck, a pressure surge, and boom, everything would be blown to kingdom come.

A small cold hand touched her cheek. Kirsten started, splashing coffee onto her notepad.

"Mommy?" Kirsten looked into Amy's round grey eyes. "I'm hungry." The little girl stifled a yawn.

"Honey, it's not even six o'clock yet. What are you doing up?"

Amy yawned again and snuggled into her mother's side. She was wearing Jack's hand-me-down housecoat, bunny slippers, and mismatched socks. "Couldn't sleep."

"You look pretty sleepy to me." Kirsten tucked a silky lock of hair behind Amy's ear, hoisted her up on her hip and carried her into the kitchen. "Pancakes okay?"

Amy's eyes sparkled. Pancakes were a weekend treat; today was a school day, for her brothers at any rate. She nodded, her blonde curls bouncing. She'd inherited her hair from Kevin, wonderful blue-eyed Kevin. Kirsten blinked a couple of times to clear the memory and handed

Amy a fresh sheet of paper and some stubby pencil cray-ons from the junk drawer to keep her occupied until breakfast was ready.

Jack and Tyler charged into the kitchen just as their mother slid two piping hot pancakes—lots of butter, no syrup please—onto Amy's plate. Jack was outraged, Amy was getting a special treat, it wasn't fair. Kirsten nodded in the direction of Jack's chair and told him to relax, his would be ready soon. Tyler scrambled into the chair next to his brother, while Kirsten stacked pancakes on their plates and set the syrup and butter down between them. As soon as their mother's back was turned, Jack elbowed Tyler and the syrup bottle tipped over, dribbling syrup all over Tyler's placemat. Tyler let out an anguished wail, Jack put on his 'nothing to see here' face and Amy narrowed her eyes at him and continued to draw.

The kitchen table was a sticky mess by the time the boys left for school. Kirsten wiped down the placemats and the smooth wooden tabletop and Amy returned to her room to get dressed. Kirsten tossed the dishcloth into the sink and picked up Amy's drawing.

It was a dragon. It was always a dragon. Amy had been drawing dragons since the day it happened.

At first the dragons were huge, hideous, scaly crea-tures with blood red eyes and lasers shooting out of their mouths. They stampeded over packs of tiny furry crea-tures that scattered beneath the dragons' birdlike feet. But over time the dragons became smaller, gentler. Their fiery breath softened into wispy puffs of flame that curled through tiny triangular teeth, the small animals were no longer frightened; instead of fleeing they clustered around the dragon's feet, like children gathering for a story.

Amy and the boys were coping with the aftermath of

the explosion much better than Kirsten was. All too often she awoke with a start in the dead of night, drenched in sweat, overwhelmed with a sense of dread. Images of the explosion played on a loop in her brain. She'd managed to navigate her way back the last time. Could she do it again? Everything hinged on the TSB report. Surely the regulator would get it right this time and force Phoenix to clean up its act; either that or shut down the bloody company for good.

A shiver rippled through her body despite the heat pumping out of the Swedish woodburning stove. It radiated enough warmth to augment the solar panels even on the coldest days of the year. Kirsten smiled. Kevin would have liked this place.

Then her eyes filled with tears. "Stop it!" She hissed under her breath, brushing away the tears with the heel of her hand. She had to find a way to cope. Christmas was coming. She owed it to the children.

Two Months After It Happened

January

CHAPTER 32

"Is this a private meeting?" Bridget barrelled into my office, not waiting for a response and joined Keith, Madeline, and me at my tiny conference table. We were catching up on what everyone had done over the Christmas break.

Bridget settled in next to Madeline, who had just returned from an exotic holiday in the Caribbean where she'd had a disastrous encounter with a spotted gecko in the hotel bathroom. "I don't see how they can charge those ridiculous prices when they have wild animals hanging off the shower heads," she said with a shudder. No one dared point out that it was her travelling companion, not Madeline, who'd paid the bill.

The first day back in the office after a long break, well, even a three-day weekend, always feels like the first day back at school after the summer holidays. We're always pleased to see each other and like to spend a few minutes catching up on each others' news.

I was in an exceptionally fine mood. I'd expected to be stuck here over the holidays fighting with Dave over Bannerman's joint legal opinion. But after numerous missed deadlines and two weeks of rancorous phone calls and snotty emails, Bannerman told Dave to drop it. He was prepared to wait for the TSB's preliminary report; Ray assured him it would be issued soon, and it would be favourable: two people were dead but it wasn't Phoenix's fault, they'd simply been in the wrong place at the wrong time.

"Evie," Bridget said, "how was your Christmas?"

"It was wonderfully quiet," I said. Louisa had picked up a few extra shifts, covering for nurses with young families, and the job of Christmas prep fell to me. After our parents died, Louisa and I resolved to continue the oddball Hungarian-English Christmas traditions we'd grown up with: the shopping, the Hungarian baking, the fat Christmas turkey roasting in the oven. I loved it all... except for the tinsel.

Tinsel was a long-standing tradition in our house. Mom insisted on a real tree. Dad refused to buy one until the middle of December. "Get it too early and it will dry out and burn the house down." The tree lots were barren by the time he rolled up to the gate and year after year he'd return with a sad little tree, so wobbly we had to tie it to the wall with eye hooks and twine. Mom spent hours covering the bare spots with ornaments and her secret weapon, packets of tinsel which she insisted had to be hung one shiny strand at a time.

The first Christmas after they died, Louisa declared the tinsel tradition would continue. I flung great silvery wads at the tree, she picked them off, and we never spoke of it again.

Madeline and I were debating the virtues of Brussels sprouts when AJ appeared in the doorway, toque in hand, his sandy blonde hair a cloud of static electricity. "The front switchboard's ringing," he said. Bridget darted out and returned to say Ray was on my line. Everyone scattered like startled rabbits as I picked up the receiver.

"Howdy counsellor," Ray's cheerful voice boomed down the line. "Did you have a good break?"

"I did indeed, how about you?"

Ray said Christmas, always a major production in their household, was even more of a spectacle this year. His wife's parents were visiting from Saskatchewan and 'Linda, the little farm girl' was determined to show them just how glamourous a big city Christmas could be. The house had been professionally decorated and sported so many outdoor lights he was convinced you could see the place from the International Space Station.

"Did your daughter—um, Olivia—make it home from Trinity College?"

"Yeah," his voice softened. "She flew in on the twenty-second. Poor kid was exhausted."

"I'm sure you all had a fantastic time."

"Yeah, Olivia and I got in a couple of hours of riding when she wasn't being monopolized by her mom and grandparents."

Horseback riding in the snow. It sounded like something you'd see in a Hallmark commercial; the mere thought of it was enough to stop my heart. December had been brutally cold. Louisa and I refused to leave the house unless we absolutely had to. Our lives were reduced to working, grocery shopping, and walking the dog. Even Quincy balked at the sub-zero temperatures, although his reluctance to venture outside may have been an aversion to the silly plaid coat and booties we made him wear.

"So, what can I do for you, Ray?"

"We got good news today." The sound of a clicking keyboard reached my ear. "The Transportation Safety Board is releasing its report on the incident this week."

I pulled a yellow notepad closer to me, ready to take notes. "Good news? You've seen the report?"

"Well, no, not yet, but based on what my guys are telling me—hell, we worked so closely with the TSB we practically wrote the report—it's going to be good." I could hear his smile over the phone line. "We'll have a number of deficiencies to correct for sure, but overall the report will be positive."

"Ray, that *is* good news. Bannerman must be delighted." The thought of that pointy-faced little man crowing in victory made my skin crawl.

Ray let out a belly laugh. "I swear if he dropped by my office one more time to tell me to light a fire under their asses, I'd have decked him."

"Based on what he said at the Board meeting, the company had a lot riding on it."

"We *all* had a lot riding on it." Ray said emphatically. "Our STIP took a real hit—"

"STIP?"

"Short term incentive payment, 'at risk' pay, the amount depends on how well I've met my short-term goals. It's got a safety component. Two deaths and the safety payout went to zero." Ray paused, perhaps remembering that these deaths were not a soft and gentle demise at the end of a long and happy life. "But that's how it should be, right. The line was out of service for weeks, the outage impacted other performance indicators—share price, project execution and so on."

He sighed. "Getting the Vespers up and running was a major headache, as you well know..." I imagined him shaking his head slowly. "...Let's just say, my bonus won't be as generous as I expected and my lovely Linda will have to rethink her Mediterranean cruise this spring."

I am always mystified when executives complain about their pay. I'd reviewed Phoenix's securities filings when Michelle retained me and knew exactly how much the company's top five executives, including Ray, pulled down last year. His $600,000 base pay plus his 'at risk' payouts totalled more than five million dollars. Even with the hit to his safety payout, he could still afford a fleet of luxury cars and a specially designed garage to put them in.

I was about to sign off when Ray said, "Oh, before I forget, Bannerman appointed Dave Bryson to act as interim Chief Legal Officer until he finds a replacement for Michelle."

"I'm not surprised. Someone has to hold down the fort now that she's gone." I bit my lip before I could add it was unfortunate it had to be that toady Dave.

As I hung up, something caught my eye. There was movement deep in the dense shrubs that lined the riverbank. At first, I thought it was a duck waddling toward the skim of ice that was building up along the river's edge, but it was a bobcat, all tasseled ears and mutton chops. It looked like a grumpy tabby, but twice as big. There had been a few bobcat sightings in the suburbs, but none this close to the city core, or my house. I'd have to warn Louisa to be careful when we walked Quincy. He's a tough dog, but the bobcat is an ambush predator, all teeth and claws. If it were hungry enough it could be dangerous.

CHAPTER 33

Later that week I was hunched over my laptop, swaddled in my long black coat and scarf, my fingers in pink cashmere gloves sliding all over the keyboard trying to open the Transportation Safety Board website. *Where the hell are Keith and AJ,* I thought for the fiftieth time.

The TSB site appeared. With three clumsy clicks I found the regulator's report on the Phoenix pipeline explosion.

It was so bloody cold in here it was hard to concentrate. Braxton, Lawson, Valentine had had its own emergency and I was on the verge of a meltdown. The boiler blew up, well, out. Again! Last night, on the coldest night of the year, a tiny puff of air whispered down an intake pipe and snuffed out the pilot light. It was minus thirty-one Celsius outside, the inside thermostat was not registering a reading at all. Where the hell are the guys when you really need them? Keith and AJ were the only two people in the office who were willing to lie down on the boiler room floor and twist the pilot light knob with one hand while poking a barbeque lighter into a small round hole in the boiler with the other, again and again until they finally heard the satisfying *whoosh* of ignition.

Madeline stopped at my door. "This is intolerable." She was wearing a beautiful navy designer coat and expensive black leather boots. A nubby green and orange scarf was wrapped around her neck. She tapped her foot impatiently.

"Nice scarf," I said. "Bridget's?"

She nodded. "I hate winter."

"You and me both." My breath puffed out in a small white cloud.

"I don't think you're allowed to make us work under these appalling conditions." She narrowed her eyes and pulled her scarf over her nose. I laughed.

"The guys will be here soon... unless you want to give it a try."

She turned on her heel and stalked off. I called out after her, "If it's not fixed in thirty minutes, we'll call it a day." Her scarf muffled her reply, which was probably a good thing. I sighed and returned to the TSB report.

Every organization has its own unique way of communicating. Tech company reports are stuffed with giddy predictions of game-changing innovations that will create once-in-a-lifetime opportunities. The TSB report, in comparison, was bland, packed with engineering jargon and schematics so devoid of emotion it could be describing why water boils when it's heated.

In a few matter-of-fact paragraphs the TSB set out its findings: The compressor at Elliot Lake experienced a pressure surge that ruptured the downstream pipeline, resulting in numerous fires, the worst of which 'affected' trees and 'baked' 0.5 hectares to a depth of 24 millimetres. I pulled out my phone to punch in the conversion— one inch of soil spread across six square city blocks had burned to ash. Ray said the explosion scoured the earth like a sandblaster.

I was deep into the report when a commotion erupted

in the reception area. Keith had arrived and Bridget and Madeline set upon him with the zeal of someone who'd won the lottery. One stripped off his coat, the other propelled him past my office into the boiler room. A few minutes later I heard a jubilant cheer and my floor radiator moaned and ticked back to life.

Keith entered my office, brushing the dust off the knees of his trousers. "How are you doing?" he asked with a wide grin.

"A whole lot better now that the heat's back on. It's a good thing you got here when you did. We were this close"—I held my thumb and forefinger one inch apart—"to a mutiny. I swear we'll come in one morning and Madeline will have dismembered the boiler and sold it for parts."

"Is that the TSB report?" He nodded at my computer. "Do they know what happened?"

"As far as I can tell, Phoenix hot tapped that section of pipe ten years ago. And that was the start of it."

"Ten years ago?" He raised an eyebrow and slipped into my visitor's chair. He rubbed his hands together to warm them and nodded at me to continue. I stripped off my gloves but was not ready to part with my coat and scarf.

Keith and I had worked on major pipeline files at Gates, Case and White before we set up our own firm. We were familiar with hot tapping: welding a smaller pipe onto a larger pipe without shutting off the gas flow so the larger pipe runs 'hot.' The welders use special valves to ensure they, and the pipe, aren't blown to smithereens. It's a routine procedure.

"The TSB thinks the pipe cracked, either when the hot tap was installed or later as the ground settled." My finger traced the sentence on my computer screen. "It wasn't a problem in the past because the pipe never ran at maximum pressure. Then Phoenix installed the Vespers, cranked the pressure up to the max allowable, gas escaped through the crack, ignited, and boom."

I turned the computer screen around to show Keith an aerial photograph. "It looks like someone gutted the field with a giant switchblade." The meadow, once covered with pristine white snow, was scarred by an ugly black gash; shards of broken pipe poked through the charred debris.

Keith whistled softly. "Good thing it didn't explode farther south, in one of the small towns along the route." He looked thoughtful. "So was Bannerman right? Was the rupture Vesper's fault after all?"

"The TSB doesn't go that far." I scrolled down the screen to the section outlining the regulator's conclusions. "It can't identify the precise cause of the explosion because the pipe segment containing the 'initiating fracture surface' disappeared. It's probably buried deep in a hillside twenty miles away. They've made a number of safety recommendations..."

"Oh my God." My eye caught the paragraph addressing the two who had died, Michelle and Marty. I read it out loud:

There were 2 fatalities involving Phoenix employees: Senior electrical and instrument technician (PE-1), a certified station operator and team lead at CS-N 24, and Chief Legal Officer (PE-2), a senior executive at Phoenix corporate headquarters. Their bodies were discovered 10.5 hours after the occurrence. PE-1 was found on the right-of-way 60.8 metres (200 feet) south of the initial ignition site. PE-2 was found 68.3 metres (224 feet) to the south-east of the ignition site. Neither employee was wearing fire-retardant NOMEX overalls. PE-1 sustained injuries to the head and torso, likely from debris ejected by the force of the ignition and second degree burns to the head and upper body. PE-2 sustained multiple injuries to the head and neck, likely from debris. Such debris was not located. The TSB has referred its findings to the medical examiner for further review.

I inhaled sharply. "Keith, what does this mean, 'referred its findings to the medical examiner for further review'?"

Keith shook his head slowly. "I don't know," he said. "These guys are transportation accident investigators: air, marine, pipeline, rail. They can't assign liability, criminal or civil. All they can do is make recommendations for improvement. You know, I've never seen—"

I finished his sentence for him. "It sounds like the TSB wants the medical examiner to take another look at how Michelle and Marty died." Suddenly I was angry and frustrated. "It will take months before the ME finishes its examination and files its report."

What the hell was Michelle doing out there on the right-of-way with Marty? Why couldn't she just stay in the Phoenix head office where she belonged?

CHAPTER 34

The sky was a dingy grey and the road a mix of dirty snow and gravel as I sailed across three lanes of traffic toward the off ramp. Maybe Louisa was right, maybe driving all the way out to Crisscross first thing in the morning wasn't such a good idea after all. I assured her my weather app predicted a cold clear day. She snorted and returned to reading the morning paper while I went back upstairs and changed into a heavier sweater. I was going to an out of office meeting in the boonies.

Yesterday Bridget received a strange phone call. The caller insisted on speaking to me but refused to give her name. Bridget is a fierce gatekeeper, she doesn't let anyone through unless they provide their name and their reason for calling. But this time she relented. "There's just something about her voice," Bridget said. "I think you should talk to her."

I don't know what I expected when I lifted the receiver, but it certainly wasn't the quietly determined person asking if I represented Phoenix. I explained that Dave Bryson was the company's lawyer. She brushed that aside, saying she would not talk to Dave or any other in-house lawyer at Phoenix. She identified herself as Kirsten Gula and said she needed to talk to someone urgently about the pipeline explosion. Her words tumbled out one on top of the other.

"Please," she begged. "If you'd just meet with me. I'd come to you, but well, the kids... look, this is really important." Then she delivered the kicker. "Lives are at stake. Please."

People say melodramatic things all the time and I tried to fob her off. "Have you talked to the lead investigator at the Transportation Safety Board? They've just completed their report. Perhaps they—"

"Forget it. I've seen the TSB report. It's too late for that. Please hear me out." Her voice became even more forceful. "Look, I found your name in that legal magazine."

"Lexpert?" Madeline had posted a notice about the Vesper deal in the magazine's 'big deals' section. The only people who read Lexpert are other lawyers. She'd gone to great lengths to track me down. Curious, I agreed to meet with her.

"You'll never find my place," she said, "we're off the grid. Let's meet at the Cozy Coyote Café in Crisscross."

Crisscross, population one thousand four hundred give or take a baby or two, wasn't exactly a burgeoning metropolis; if Kirsten was off the grid in Crisscross, she must be way off the grid. As I sped down the highway, I wondered, not for the first time, whether I was about to meet a nutbar keen to enlighten me about the effects of gamma rays on marigolds or something.

The dirty clouds had lifted by the time I reached the Cozy Coyote Café, a square beige building squatting on a corner lot at one end of Main Street. The sunlight drifted across the parking lot, melting the snow one shiny crystal at a time. A woman slipped out from behind the wheel of a silver SUV parked next to the trash bins. She said something to someone sitting in the front seat, shut the door, then walked purposefully toward me. Her jet-black hair cascaded out from under her navy toque. Her leather hiking boots squeaked across the snow. She waited patiently while my window whirred down.

"You're Evie Valentine, right?" She didn't wait for an answer before asking me to join her in her SUV. "You can leave your car here. We'll come back for it."

"Aren't we going into the café?"

"No, I want to show you the site first, then you're coming back to my house for a hot lunch."

Okay, then. I followed her back to the SUV. She opened the passenger side door and I came face to face with a small child wearing a puffy red snowsuit who was busily pulling off her toque. Her silky hair crackled with electricity and fanned out this way and that when she turned her head. She looked like a little dandelion.

Kirsten said, "Amy, this is Evie Valentine. Ms. Valentine, this is my daughter, Amy." The little girl looked at me with solemn grey eyes, then a wide grin spread across her face and she reached over and shook my hand.

"Hello Amy," I said, "you can call me Evie if you like."

"Evie Valentine," she said slowly, "like hearts, you're the Heart Lady."

"Yes, I guess I am." I climbed up into the front seat while Amy scrambled into the back.

Kirsten shifted gears and smoothly pulled out of the parking lot onto a secondary road which quickly turned into a narrow lane squeezed between two high snowbanks.

"Amy knows where we're going, don't you sweetie," Kirsten said.

The little girl nodded. "The glass lake with the dragons."

Kirsten kept the SUV in the icy tire tracks made by those who had come before us. Periodically she glanced up into the rear-view mirror at Amy who was engaged in an intense conversation with an orange dinosaur and a Lego man with no hair.

Kirsten looked over at me and smiled. "You have no idea how much this means to me." Suddenly her eyes filled with tears. She blinked rapidly and focused on the road ahead. The lane was narrowing and it was more difficult to stay centered in the frozen ruts. Sunlight flickered through the dense evergreen canopy, light and dark, light and dark. The experience was dizzying.

Eventually she stopped the car in the middle of the road. There was nowhere to pull off. Amy set her toys down on the seat next to her and pulled on her toque and mittens. Kirsten zipped up her parka, and I slipped into my gloves and hat and eased out the door. The road was icy and I had to cling to the SUV to avoid sliding under its wheels. We walked in the tire ruts for a few feet before Kirsten cut down a narrow path that meandered deeper into the glittering forest.

A crow trumpeted loudly, announcing our presence. I'd read somewhere they were clever birds who could recognize faces and wondered whether he'd remember me if I ever came back.

"Amy, wait." Kirsten yelled. The little girl had run ahead. She stopped and Kirsten lifted her by one arm over what appeared to be a jagged grey rock half hidden in a pillow of sparkling snow. "It's not far now," she said, looking back at me.

We emerged beside a snow-covered lake. At first it looked placid, almost serene, but something was wrong.

"We're on the opposite side of the lake from where the kids and I were the day it happened." Kirsten pointed to what appeared to be a cutline running from the water's edge back up into the dark forest. "The blast was so intense, it cracked the sky, or at least it felt that way. Broken pipe, rocks, and tree limbs flying everywhere. The company cleared away the worst of it, but you still have to watch your footing, so much was buried in the last snowfall."

She glanced at Amy whose grey eyes were focused on the water shimmering in the sunlight on the surface of the frozen lake.

That's what was wrong.

In the centre of the lake, where there should be ice covered in snow was a large, gaping, black hole. Water rippled. It may have been a trick of the light, but it looked like the lake was breathing, in and out, through a gigantic blowhole.

Kirsten followed my gaze. "The lake is wide but shallow. It was frozen clear across to the other side. That hole, the pipe came up through the ice when it blew out of the water. I doubt it'll freeze over again before spring thaw."

Amy teetered on a snowy hummock, moving her arms slowly to stay upright. "Watch your step, Amy," Kirsten said, then leaned closer to me. "She was supposed to be at the sitter, but—"

"I'll be careful." Amy looked up at her mother. "Don't worry about me."

Kirsten nodded and we walked to the edge of the lake. The wind was bitterly cold, coming in ragged bursts, trying to blow us back the way we came, magnifying the sound of birds and the sudden swoosh of snow sliding off a branch and falling in a sparkling heap to the ground. My eyes followed the ring of trees along the lakeshore back to the cutline, the gap in the trees looked like a missing slat in a picket fence.

Kirsten pointed. "That's the right-of-way. The

company brought in earthmovers to clear a path for the boring machines and other equipment it needed to fix the damaged pipe." She pinned me with her dark brown eyes. "I wanted you see the site, to get a feel for it." She pointed back to the trail next to the right-of-way. "That's where we were when the lake blew up. It was like standing in a minefield, debris flying everywhere. Sheer hell."

"Mommy!" Amy shot her mother a disapproving look.

"Sorry, sweetie."

Kirsten laid a hand on my arm. "Did you want to take any photos, this is as good a vantage point as any." This struck me as a strange suggestion until she added that she was a pipeline engineer and would talk me through what had happened in greater detail back at the house. "Photos will give you a good reference point."

As I pulled my phone out of my pocket Amy said, "Mommy, can we call the dragon?" She stared at the hole in the middle of the lake where the water trembled gently.

"I don't think so, darling. She's probably sleeping."

Amy grinned. "I'm glad she's back home."

I was about to ask how one went about calling a dragon when Kirsten announced it was time for lunch. "Are you hungry, little girl?"

"Um hmmm." Amy beamed and slipped her small hand into mine. "We're having lunch with the Heart Lady."

Amy was asleep in the backseat before Kirsten finished turning the car around. The heater was going full bore and the sun flashed across the windshield. Kirsten and I talked quietly. We were roughly the same age, in our mid thirties, worked in the energy sector. She'd been an engineer, I was a lawyer and yet our experiences in this male-dominated world were remarkably similar.

CHAPTER 35

Amy awoke just before we pulled up in front of Kirsten's place. "Slow down!" her mother yelled when Amy bolted out of the backseat. "That girl, she's getting as bad as the twins." We crunched down the gravel driveway, the thin skim of ice snapping under foot like splintering glass. Amy jumped up and down on a desiccated snow ledge; it snapped in two just as her mother told her to go inside. The child didn't have a key, but she didn't need one, the door was unlocked.

Kirsten's home was not what I'd expected. Instead of a rustic log cabin buried deep in the woods she welcomed me into a modern A-frame set in the middle of a small glade. Amy clattered into the mud room, kicking off her boots and flinging her coat onto a small red hook positioned low on the wall. Kirsten led the way through to a sleek open space, pretty enough to be featured in a Swedish design magazine. Light flooded through large windows, bouncing off the whitewashed floors and built-in cabinetry. The kitchen flowed into the living space which was dominated by a pale blue sofa strewn with navy and white striped pillows. Two small bedrooms and a bathroom were tucked under a sleeping loft. The space would have been austere but for the kids' toys scattered all over the floor.

"Sorry about the mess," Kirsten said. I said my bull terrier could do more damage in fifteen minutes than what I was witnessing here. That piqued Amy's interest and I showed her pictures of Quincy and Louisa on my phone while Kirsten set a large pot of vegetable soup on the stove top and popped cheddar biscuits into the oven. Soon the room was filled with the comforting aroma of a home-cooked meal.

After lunch, Amy announced she was going to draw a picture for the Heart Lady. Within minutes she was busily arranging coloured pencils, longest to shortest, at the far end of the kitchen table, chattering to herself like a chickadee. Kirsten poured me a second cup of coffee and nodded indulgently at her daughter. "She lives in her own little world." Then Kirsten's face stiffened. She pulled her chair closer to mine and said, "We have to talk about Phoenix."

She took a deep breath, squared her shoulders, and began. "Twelve years ago I worked for Phoenix in its engineering group. That's where I met Kevin, my husband, he was a financial analyst. We hit it off right away and were married within five months." Her eyes softened with the memory. "We were doing very well in our careers, then I got pregnant with the twins and decided to take some time off."

It was a familiar story, jumping off the career track to the mommy track and never quite making it back again.

"Phoenix offered Kev a transfer to California, as director of operations at its San Remo facility—"

"I thought Kevin was in finance, not operations."

"That's right, Kev was a CPA, not an engineer. But that's how Phoenix does things. Employees who show promise are put on the fast track and moved all around the company to broaden their experience. They assured Kev he'd have all the engineering and tech support he needed to keep the operations side of things ticking along while he focused on improving efficiency."

"By 'efficiency' you mean reducing costs, cutting staff, right?"

She nodded and glanced at Amy who was frowning at the blank page in front of her. "At first, Kev loved it. Learning new things, getting a feel for the operational side of the business, and he was great at dealing with the regulators. There are so many of them down there at the state and federal levels."

She looked down into her coffee cup which was now empty. "We were happy. So very happy. The boys were five then, they'd just started elementary school. We lived in a blue ribbon school district. They were really busy with sports and cub scouts..."

She trailed off. Amy, hunched over her drawing, continued to scribble on the page. A large lumpy creature was taking shape, iridescent pink and yellow against a purple background. I accepted Kirsten's offer of a refill. My nerves would be shot on the drive home.

She talked quietly while she tucked a new filter in the coffee maker and spooned grounds into the paper cone. "Phoenix was losing a lot of money by then, especially in its American operations. They went on a drastic downsizing spree, they called it 'right-sizing' and 'working smarter.' It decimated his department. Kev complained to his boss—Ray Cook, you met him on the Vesper deal, right?" I nodded. "Kev said he didn't have enough staff to do their jobs properly. Ray told Kev to focus on fixing the balance sheet, he'd take care of the staffing problems. But it only got worse."

The coffee burbled. Our mugs clunked when Kirsten set them down on the granite countertop. "Poor Kev. He worked ridiculous hours. I was pregnant with Amy by then. I knew it was getting to him." She filled our cups and returned to the table. "I told him the stress wasn't worth it, we should come back to Canada, but he refused to quit until he had a job lined up back here, he worried about making ends meet with a baby on the way."

Kirsten propped her elbows on the table, holding her cup with both hands. "God, I wish I'd forced him to change his mind."

I stole a peek at Amy, now frowning with concentration as her coloured pencil scribbled back and forth across the page. Kirsten looked at Amy almost as if she'd forgotten the little girl was in here and asked her to finish her drawing in her bedroom. Without a word the little girl stuffed her coloured pencils back into the battered leather pouch and trotted off to her room.

"Then," Kirsten sounded strained, her voice reedy, "one night, just after dinner...I was griping about the heat, I was six months pregnant, it was September and incredibly hot. And boom! The plates flew off the kitchen table and pictures fell off the walls. At first I thought it was an earthquake or a sonic boom. Kev's cell went off. All he said was, 'Turn on the TV, turn on the TV.'

"It was all over the news. A commercial jetliner had crashed in a residential neighbourhood in San Remo... our neighbourhood. You could see the fireball for miles. A couple of minutes later they issued a correction. It wasn't a plane crash but a gas pipeline explosion. Dozens of houses were on fire, people running through the streets screaming, searching for their children. It was early evening, very warm, the kids...our kids...would play outside until the streetlights came on." She let out a ragged sigh. "Thankfully Tyler is such a slowpoke the twins hadn't left the house yet. The explosion was blocks and blocks away but Jack, he likes to wander... I sent them to their rooms. I didn't want them to see it."

She blinked rapidly. "People came from everywhere to help the EMT and firefighters. Helicopters, air tankers, planes. They couldn't extinguish the blaze. They couldn't go in to rescue the injured let alone retrieve the dead. They couldn't shut the valve. It took them an hour and a half! An hour and a half it was feeding the flames."

I realized what she was telling me was a combination of what she'd witnessed firsthand and what she'd learned later from the investigations and lawsuits that followed.

"Then the wind came up. You see, the pipeline was at the bottom of the valley, wedged between two banks of woods. The flames were so hot the eucalyptus trees exploded. I didn't know they did that. The fire burned through the night, flames over a hundred feet high, sparks drifting across the night sky... Those poor, poor families..."

Tears glittered in her eyelashes. She flicked them away with an impatient hand, never taking her eyes off my face. "It's happening again, Evie. There's something horribly wrong with that company."

CHAPTER 36

"Mommy, don't be sad." Amy's clear voice drew our attention to the living room. "Please don't be sad like Daddy." She was sitting on the floor wedged between the sofa and the coffee table, her purple pencil crayon suspended over her page. Neither of us knew how long she'd been sitting there.

Kirsten extended her arm. "I'm okay. Come here, sweetie."

Amy picked up her picture and crawled up into her mother's lap. Kirsten stroked Amy's hair and smiled at me. "Kevin never had a chance to meet Amy." She bent over the little girl, "But you have lots of photos of Daddy, don't you, Amy."

Amy bobbed her head and wiggled onto the chair between us. She unzipped her leather pouch and lay her drawing on the table, carefully flattening a crumpled corner. She beamed at her mother. "Don't be sad, Mommy. I'll make you a picture too. This one is for the Heart Lady."

Kirsten smiled. "I can't wait."

Amy turned the drawing to face me while she shook her coloured pencils out of the pouch and lined them up in a tidy row next to the drawing. Dead centre in the middle of the page was a rainbow-coloured dragon with ribbed pink wings. Its claws were sharp, each talon a different colour. A circle of small cat-like creatures rolled around at its feet.

"It's not breathing fire," I said.

"No, not today. Jezebel is happy today."

"Jezebel?" I shot a glance at Kirsten. She shrugged.

"Yes, that's her name, Jezebel the Pink Dragon."

"Why does Jezebel have curly teeth?"

She looked up at me, surprised by the question. "All dragons have curly teeth."

"Does she go to the dentist?" After the intensity of the last half an hour, this conversation was a refreshing diversion.

"Oh no," Amy said. "She doesn't have to go to the dentist. Her teeth are very strong. She can chew up anything, rocks and trees..." she paused, a thoughtful look crossed her face. "But not people, she likes people. And animals, she likes them too."

Kirsten frowned in mock displeasure. "Amy, is this a 'think-so' fact or 'know-so' fact?" I was reminded of Louisa who went through a phase where her stuffed toys were as real to her as I was. Mom would ask a similar question, is this real or make-believe, to ensure Louisa understood the difference.

Amy put down her coloured pencil and crossed her thin arms in front of her chest. "This is a 'know-so' fact."

"Really? And how do you know-so?"

"I'll show you." Amy hopped off her chair and raced into the mud room where she pulled on her boots.

"Amy? Wait," her mother called out, not that it did any good.

Amy was tearing open the door to the garage by the time we caught up to her. She flew to the back of the garage, shifted a couple of empty cardboard cartons away from the back wall, then stood back and said "See!"

There, in the gloom of the garage, was an old wooden toboggan. On it was something large and lumpy covered by a floral sheet. "I wondered where that went," Kirsten muttered as she yanked aside the fabric, dust motes rising as it fluttered to one side.

She inhaled sharply. "Oh my God, where did you get this?"

"Look!" Amy squealed with excitement. "Teeth marks."

Kirsten grabbed the yellow nylon rope with both hands and dragged the toboggan into the centre of the garage, its bottom scraping painfully across the concrete floor. She dropped the rope and went to the side door where she pressed the button on the garage door opener. As the dove grey metal door creaked open, sunlight revealed a jagged piece of pipe. It looked like an oversized plumbing joint.

Kirsten slowly dropped to her knees while Amy bounced up and down beside her. She pointed triumphantly to a wavy line etched in the metal. "See? Bite marks."

"Amy! Settle down. Where did you get this?" Her tone was sharp.

Amy lowered her eyes. "I didn't steal it."

"No, of course not, but this is a pipe fragment from the explosion. It could be an important piece of evidence. Where did you get it?"

Amy rocked uncomfortably on her feet. "Jack made me promise not to tell."

Kirsten sat back on her heels. "Amy," she said sternly, in a voice that made it clear that her authority as a mother trumped that of her brother.

Eyes dancing, hands waving, Amy told her story. She

reminded me of Louisa who couldn't keep a secret if you paid her. "It's Jack's. He won't let me touch it." Her bottom lip protruded in a small pout. Then she pointed to a line of chevron-shaped markings that stretched along a jagged section of pipe. "Look," she said again. "Bite marks. Jezebel can chew anything."

Kirsten traced her fingertip along the line of chevrons. Just then we heard the crunch of the boys' boots on the gravel lane. "Mom?" The boys ricocheted into the garage. One flung his backpack off his shoulders, it dropped onto the cement floor with a thud. The other stopped dead in his tracks, eyes wide with horror.

They were identical. The first boy scowled. "You can't touch that, it's mine." This must be Jack. He lunged at the chunk of pipe, arms wide as if he wanted to shield it from his mother's gaze. Kirsten popped up an elbow, blocking him.

"This doesn't belong to you, Jack."

"Does so!" he insisted. "I found it. Finders keepers!" He tried to squirm under her arm but she grabbed his shoulder and rose to her feet, meeting his glare with her own.

Hands on hips, Kirsten said, "I want you to tell me exactly how that hunk of metal ended up in my garage."

"I already told you," Amy said.

"You snitched?" Jack rounded on Amy, then stopped, finally registering that a stranger was standing by his mother's side. He glanced up at me, blinked, and said, "Am I in trouble? Are you a cop?"

I bit back a smile as Kirsten explained I was a friend, then instructed them to pick up their backpacks and go into the house.

They were sitting at the kitchen island by the time we

got inside, their elbows on the counter, chins on their hands. Amy was sitting between them, her heels banging a steady rhythm against the chair legs.

Kirsten stared at them for a minute, then folded her arms across her chest and said, "No one is in trouble here. But you need to tell me how you got your hands on that piece of pipe...Jack? From the top, please."

Jack pursed his lips, rolling his eyes upward. Tyler cast a side glance at his brother. "Tell her," he pleaded. Jack let out a melodramatic huff and said, "When you screamed at us to get off the lake—"

"I didn't scream," Kirsten said calmly. "Continue."

Jack's face shifted from defiance to pride—this kid was as mercurial as Ray—he saw a chunk of shredded steel fly over his head and bury itself in the snow about 300 metres away. While Kirsten, Amy, and Tyler watched the fireball and thick black smoke curling into the sky, Jack was triangulating where the fragment was in relation to the fir trees so he could retrieve it later. He and Tyler returned that weekend and dragged it home on the toboggan.

"It was heavy," he said.

"Took us all day," Tyler said.

"I'm sure," his mother replied dryly. "You dragged it for miles. But Jack, you shouldn't have taken it. This isn't a bat skeleton or something weird you found in the bush and stashed in your closet. It's evidence the Transportation Safety Board needed to figure out why the pipe blew up in the first place." She glanced at the chevron markings. "To ensure it never happens again."

Jack's face fell. We could all see where this was heading. "But they didn't find it. I found it. It's mine now." He hopped off his chair and circled behind it, as if to shield himself from what was about to happen.

Kirsten put her hands flat on the kitchen counter, leaned forward, and in a very firm voice said, "The TSB has to examine the pipe, Jack. I'm sure they'll give it back when they've finished with it." He opened his mouth to complain, she tilted her chin downward, and he turned on his heel and stormed off to his bedroom. Tyler followed, slamming the door with a mighty bang.

Amy looked at her mother and grinned. "Dragon's teeth."

"Yes, dragon's teeth," Kirsten said softly. She turned to me and said, "Evie, you saw those chevron markings etched in the steel. That's a down-hand weld. Not as strong as an up-hand weld. Given the pressure and external load, it could be that a stress fracture—"

I raised my hand. "Whoa, you lost me at 'down-hand weld.'"

She shook her head slightly. "Sorry, just thinking out loud. If the contractor improperly welded the hot tap tee, he may have created a seam that would burst if the pressure increased beyond a certain point."

Amy picked up her drawing from the kitchen table and said she was going to show it to the boys. That little girl was spunky if nothing else. I watched her disappear into the boys' room where she was met by a chorus of moans.

An idea came to me. I turned to Kirsten and said, "We agree Jack's pipe should go to the regulator, but I'd like to show it to Ray first. He's been helping the TSB all along. If we can get him onside, he can put extra pressure on the TSB to reopen the investigation."

She bit her lip. "Ray Cook? I don't know if that's a good idea. Can't we just give it to the TSB and leave Ray out of it altogether?"

"I understand your concern, really I do, but even if I

take it straight to the TSB, they'll just turn around and bring Ray in to look at it anyway."

She still looked apprehensive. I leaned forward and touched her hand. "Kirsten, I was there with Ray in the Vault when Elliot Lake exploded. He was devastated. He's lost a colleague and a team leader in that blast. Trust me, he wants answers as badly as we do."

She considered that for a moment and acquiesced. She trusted me, I trusted Ray. We all trusted the Transportation Safety Board. That's all the trust you need, right?

CHAPTER 37

A couple of hours later I was rolling down the ramp into the Phoenix underground parkade. It was well past seven o'clock; Ray said he'd wait for me in the visitor's stall next to the service elevator. I'd called ahead to tell him Kirsten's son had discovered a pipe fragment and we hoped the TSB would reopen its investigation once they'd had a chance to examine it.

Ray trundled over to my car with a dolly he'd caged from the mailroom. It was as erratic as a grocery cart with a wobbly wheel, constantly pulling off to the left.

I popped the trunk. Jack's pipe, swaddled in Kirsten's sheet, filled the cramped space like a gigantic, lumpy Easter egg.

Ray let out a low whistle. "It's bigger than I thought it would be." He fumbled with the sheet until he found the edge and flipped it open, then leaned into the car to peer at the jagged edges of the pipe.

"Kirsten said something about up-hand and down-hand welds—"

"Yes," he said very quietly. "Yes, I can see that." He snapped the sheet back over the pipe and stood back. For a moment he just stood there staring at the lump of pipe, then he clapped his hands together. The sound was sharp in the deserted parkade. "Right, let's get this baby onto the dolly." Grunting and straining, he wiggled it back and forth until he could grasp it firmly without slicing his hands to ribbons. "How the hell did you two get it into the car?"

"A toboggan." We'd used the sled as a ramp to roll the pipe up into the trunk. We almost broke the sled in half and were ready to throttle Jack who wouldn't stop shouting instructions at us until we were done.

Ray and I wrestled the pipe onto the dolly. I steadied the wobbly wheel while he secured the pipe with a sturdy piece of twine. He'd just turned the dolly to face the service elevator when he called out to me.

"Evie, refresh my memory, how do you know Kirsten?"

"I don't know her. She found my name in a law magazine and wanted to talk about the pipeline explosion."

He pivoted the dolly, wedged it next to an insulated utility pipe, and came back to where I was standing next to my car. In the overhead florescent lights his face was sallow.

"How's she doing? Did she mention she worked for Phoenix once?"

"She said she and her husband Kevin both worked for Phoenix and that she left her job when the twins were born."

Ray eyed me carefully. The elevator door behind him opened and a cyclist clad in a helmet, a light orange jacket and water resistant pants walked over to the utility pipe and unlocked his bike. Its studded tires clattered across the cement as he disappeared up the ramp.

"Yes," Ray said. "They both worked for me. First her, then him. That was years ago." He looked down at his watch but made no effort to leave and it occurred to me that Ray wasn't engaged in idle curiosity. He wanted to know what we talked about. "Did she tell you about San Remo?" he asked, glancing over my head and throwing a distracted wave at a car that tooted at us as it approached the ramp.

"As a matter of fact, she did. It sounded horrific."

"It was. Kevin was consumed by that file...and the aftermath. He spent the next year and a half working with the lawyers. The company paid out millions in damages and fines. And lawyers' fees." He made a rueful face. "You guys don't come cheap."

"So what happened to him? To Kevin, I mean." I was pretty sure I knew the answer. Daddy was sad, Amy's voice echoed in my ear.

Ray winced. "He committed suicide. Kirsten went into a tailspin and eventually packed up the kids and moved into that cabin in the woods."

The way he said it made Kirsten sound unhinged. "Ray, it's not exactly a shack, and she's not a hermit. She's made a lovely home for herself and her children."

He shrugged. "Look, all I'm saying is Kirsten's been through a lot. She may be off the grid in more ways than one." He glanced back at Jack's pipe which was sitting heavily on the dolly. "I wouldn't put much stock in anything she says."

I slammed the trunk closed and walked around the car to the driver's side. "Before we get into a debate about whether Kirsten knows what she's talking about, let's see what the TSB has to say about the pipe, shall we? You'll keep me posted, right? Jack was none too happy about giving it up. I promised him the TSB would give it back."

Ray's mood lightened at the mention of Jack's name. He said the kid sounded like quite the character, then he wished me good night and manhandled the dolly into the service elevator.

CHAPTER 38

Government agencies like the TSB move at their own pace and I put Jack's pipe out of my mind for a couple of weeks. It was time to focus on other things, which at this particular moment included trying to make it across the parking lot and into the office without being blown off my feet. A nasty wind was coming across the river, I had my head down and my eyes almost closed when Bridget ripped the door open from the other side and hustled me in.

"What's this, a new BLV service?" I gave her a grateful smile.

Her cheeks were flushed and she looked overheated in her thick Shetland sweater and wool blend slacks. Clearly, her faith in our boiler was not yet restored.

"Something came for you yesterday, last night." She hurried me down to my office.

Sitting in the middle of my desk was a large manila envelope, a little crumpled along one edge but otherwise intact. "It was jammed through the overnight delivery slot. It's marked 'personal and confidential.'" She handed me a pair of scissors. "You'll never get it open with a letter opener." She was right, it was sealed with layers of moving tape.

Madeline appeared in my doorway. Her office is

directly across from mine. "What are you two whispering about?" she asked. Bridget pointed to the mysterious package while I hacked at one corner.

"Maybe it's a secret admirer," Madeline said.

"Stuffing a bundle of love letters through the office mail chute? I don't think so." By then I'd managed to tear open one side and slide its contents out onto my desk.

Madeline said, "Wow, I haven't seen a file like that in a long time." Back in the old days most law firms and inhouse law departments used long, legal-sized cardboard files with coloured tabs and numbers running along one side. This one was constructed of sturdy green cardboard, its spine reinforced with cracked sticky tape. A large metal brad pierced the back panel, pinning a thick wad of hole-punched pages in place.

The minute I flipped it open my heart lurched. *Michelle's file.* It took a moment for me to regain the presence of mind to snap it shut.

Madeline leaned forward. "Well?"

"I need to make a call. Privately. Would you mind closing the door on your way out?" It sounded abrupt, but they were too professional to argue.

A pink Post-it note was stuck on the first page of a stack of correspondence and memos an inch and a half thick. On it someone with a neat hand had written a phone number. I dialed. The phone rang, once, twice, six times before the voicemail clicked in asking me to leave a message. This was her home phone. She didn't want me to call her office number. Under the circumstances, that made sense. I didn't leave a message.

The day unwound with infuriating slowness. It was difficult to focus. If I was this edgy, she would be doubly so. She'd taken an enormous risk in sending me that file. She'd lose her job, or worse, if she was discovered.

*   *   *   *

That evening, around eight o'clock, I finally reached her at home. "Sarah, it's Evie."

"Oh, thank God." Michelle's assistant sighed into the phone. "I didn't know what else to do."

"Sarah, I—"

"Please, not on the phone."

I thought she was being overly paranoid but she sounded too fragile to debate the point and I agreed to meet her at her place within the hour.

Quincy was warming his belly by the fire and barely lifted his head when I grabbed my heavy parka, scooped up my briefcase and clomped downstairs to our heated garage.

It was just past nine when I pulled up in front of Sarah's condo. She was immaculately dressed in a white cashmere turtleneck and crisply pressed black slacks. I slouched in, very aware I was wearing worn jeans and a baggy blue fleece. I followed her through to the small dining room which was crowded with photos and bric-a-brac.

"Oh, Sarah, you shouldn't have gone to all this trouble." A Royal Doulton tea set and teacups were set on the polished table. She blushed and fluttered her hands, thanking me for making the trip at such a late hour, then slipped into the chair opposite me. I drew the file out of my briefcase.

"I see you got...oh—" She leapt to her feet and darted back into the kitchen. Cupboard doors opened and closed, she spoke sternly to someone under her breath; it turned

out to be a fluffy grey and white cat which meowed pitifully and trailed her back into the dining room. Her hand
trembled as she set a plate of shortbread cookies on the
table and I gave her a moment to compose herself. She
nodded at the file open before me and said with a sad
smile, "Michelle's cover-your-ass file."

Years ago I'd become aware of Michelle's CYA file, she
was talking about it over drinks—*that's another one for
the CYA file*. At first, I didn't think she was serious, but I
soon discovered she always created a paper trail to protect
herself in case Bannerman plowed ahead with a shady
scheme against her legal advice.

Why, I asked, would you continue to work for someone
you don't trust? She had leveled her gaze at me and said,
"I have a duty to protect the Board and more importantly
the public. It's easier to be inside the tent where I can have
an impact, than outside where it will be too late."

And now she was gone. Dave Bryson was acting Chief
Legal Officer, ensconced in her well-appointed executive
office, rubberstamping everything Bannerman dreamed
up and hoping, no doubt, that Bannerman would reward
him with Michelle's job on a permanent basis.

"Does Dave know about this file?" I asked Sarah.

She shook her head. "I pulled it out of the drawer at the
back of her desk the day she went missing."

I marvelled at her presence of mind. She must have
been sick with worry when Michelle was reported missing
but still she remembered to protect Michelle's private file.

In the kitchen there was a soft thump. A second cat,
this one a small tabby, appeared at Sarah's feet. "No," she
said, "I'm not picking you up." She turned her attention
back to me. "Did you read Michelle's last memo to file?
The one she wrote the day before she died?"

"I did."

She pushed her teacup away, tears welled up in her eyes. "I worked with Michelle for eighteen years. She was an outstanding lawyer; she always did the right thing." Sarah reached down and scooped up the tabby who purred loudly and curled up into a ball in her lap. "The day before she died, Michelle had a meeting with Bannerman. Her face was like thunder when she returned to her office. A few minutes later Ray showed up. I could hear them shouting through her closed door. He stormed out and headed for Bannerman's office. That's when she told me to clear her calendar and book a fleet vehicle. She was going to Elliot Lake the next day." Sarah jerked her head as if to shake the memory. "It's all there in the file."

"I'll take care of it," I said. Empty words. I had no idea what I was going to do.

Quincy was still stretched out in front of the fire when I returned home. I gave his warm belly a pat and curled up on the teddy bear velvet sofa to reread Michelle's last memo to file.

MTF: November 11

T/C Marty Tkachuk: Marty expressed concerns about pipeline safety/integrity. Very worried re: integrating Vesper compressor into pipeline system. "AI patch" promising but reliability is sporadic. I advised him to speak with his supervisor, Ray Cook. Marty refused; "waste of time," already raised safety concerns on numerous occasions, Ray dismissed them. I said I'd take it up with Bannerman.

A/W Bannerman: Explained Marty's concerns. Was dismissed out of hand. "I trust Ray's judgment over that of a team lead any day."

A/W Ray Cook: 10 minutes after Bannerman meeting, Ray stormed into my office. We argued. Why did I go behind his back to Bannerman? Explained Marty said it was pointless talking to Ray. Ray said Marty is not an engineer, just a tech who's overreacting to things he doesn't understand. I said I was going to Elliot Lake tomorrow to speak with Marty.

CONCERN: Safety issues? Vespers have been unreliable since installation. Ray (on Dave's legal advice) silenced alarms. I reversed that decision. Ray installed "AI patch." Told the Board it fixed the problem. Marty said not true. Marty very worried about safety going forward.

ACTION: Need firsthand information. Meeting w Marty in Red Deer Nov 12.

True to her word, Michelle went to Elliot Lake. She never came back.

CHAPTER 39

A J was standing on the sidewalk outside his house when I picked him up. It was Saturday, shortly before sunrise and the roads were quiet. His black toque was pulled down over his ears and his hands were jammed into his pockets. Given the wind chill it was extremely cold and the Mini filled with a blast of frigid air when he opened the door and settled in beside me.

He fiddled with his seat belt and asked with a stifled yawn, "Tell me again why we're taking a road trip to Red Deer at the crack of dawn?" I turned on the rear window defogger and put the Mini in gear. "God this is a small car," he muttered to himself. He's almost six feet tall and well built. In his puffy grey jacket he looked like the Michelin Man folded double in the front seat.

"I'm not sure three hundred kilometres there and back qualifies as a road trip," I smiled. "I want to retrace Michelle's steps on the day she died and you're coming along as my second set of eyes. You're from this neck of the woods, right?"

That satisfied him and he didn't pursue it further, which was a good thing because I really didn't want to tell him about my meeting with Sarah the night before, let alone divulge the contents of Michelle's CYA file. The only way I could justify keeping it was by classifying it as

Michelle's personal property rather than something that belonged to Phoenix, and that was a stretch.

Two people, Sarah and Kirsten, had reached out to me with the same fear: something bad was happening at Phoenix. After the San Remo explosion, Phoenix should have transformed itself into a stellar corporate citizen; investors won't put money into a company if its pipelines keep exploding. But instead of taking fewer risks to prevent a second San Remo, Michelle's CYA files showed Bannerman continued to dance on the edge. She was so worried about the Vesper deal that she hired me, an outsider, to ferret out any problems with the compressors. She trusted me and I'd failed her. I had to make things right.

AJ and I made good time to Red Deer. The roads were deserted; the only signs of life were the fragile lights of isolated farmhouses flickering in the distance. Our destination was the Tim Hortons just south of town at the turnoff to the Elliot Lake compressor station. Michelle's fleet car had been recovered from the coffee shop's parking lot and I hoped some of the regulars might remember seeing her there.

"Well, son of a gun." AJ interrupted my thoughts.

"You sound like my dad," I said.

"Your dad sounds like my granddad."

"The granddad who runs the potash business in Saskatchewan?"

"Um hum, Granddad would blow into town to visit my folks, before the divorce. He'd take me with him to check out the farm machinery shops. There used to be a John Deere dealership"—he tracked a densely packed subdivision rushing by on our left—"right there. He'd shoot the breeze with the salesmen and I'd sneak out back to the lot and climb all over the combines."

"Were you nuts? You could have been run over by a tractor or chopped to bits by a harvester or something."

He shrugged. "I was eight, at eight you're invincible."

I turned to look at AJ as I prepared to enter the off-ramp. He'd pulled off his toque and his sandy hair was sticking up on one side in a cowlick. The eight-year-old boy was never far from the surface.

"There it is," he said, pointing to the Tim Hortons sign a block away. I had just enough time to squeeze between two semis and take a hard right into the parking lot.

The café was warm and crowded with hefty men in work boots clomping around and talking loudly to each other. I grabbed a table along the back wall while AJ placed our order. He rubbed his hands together after he set our coffees and my donut on the table. "Careful, these are super hot and the paper thing keeps slipping off."

"Thanks," I said as I took a bite of my chocolate glazed donut. "Don't look now," I mumbled, "but the lady in the kitchen has been watching you through that cubby window since we came in." He twisted around and looked over his shoulder. "AJ! I said *don't* look."

He laughed and waved at the woman who was now striding toward us. When she reached our table, he stood up and enveloped her in a big hug. "Crystal!" he said, "how the heck are you!"

She was small and delicate with large blue eyes and a bright smile. She smacked him on the chest a couple of times and said, "Braxton, Braxton, how long has it been?"

"Too long, can you spare a few minutes?"

Crystal glanced at the customers lining up at the cash register. Satisfied that the freckle-faced teenager at the till had everything under control, she slipped into the plastic bench next to me. AJ introduced me and said he and Crystal had gone to high school together. "Yeah," she said, "back in the day before you ditched us for the big city." They caught up on what had happened in their lives over the last fifteen years—she was divorced with teenaged kids and owned two Timmies coffee shops, he was single (such a shame!), a lawyer (impressive!), and worked with Keith and me at Braxton, Lawson, Valentine (nice!).

Finally, AJ took a sip of coffee and I asked Crystal whether she knew much about the Phoenix pipeline explosion.

She nodded and moved closer. "What a terrible thing. Such a shock. It caused so much damage." For a moment she withdrew, lost in the memory. "You know, you live here all your life and you forget there's a bloody big pipeline running right under your feet just waiting for an excuse to blow up."

We talked about the news footage which she said didn't do the explosion justice. "You had to be here," she said. "The fireball, Jesus, it roared like a freight train. I've never heard anything like it."

I said I'd been close to one of the people who died in the explosion.

"Marty?" She asked. "He used to stop in here every morning on his way to work."

"No, not Marty." I pulled out my phone and showed her Michelle's picture from the company website. "This was my friend, Michelle. Do you remember seeing her?"

"Oh, yes." Crystal became very animated. "What a beautiful woman, but..." here she hesitated, reluctant to criticize the dead. She glanced quickly at AJ who raised an inquisitive eyebrow and continued. "Well, she was way under-dressed to be traipsing off to the plant."

I set my donut down on the serviette and wiped the tips of my chocolatey fingers. "How do you mean?"

Crystal's cheeks reddened. "I can see everything from there." She waved vaguely toward the cubby window. "When she came through the door, the whole place got real quiet. These guys are a pretty rowdy bunch, you know, especially first thing in the morning, but when she came through those doors, well, their jaws dropped."

I nodded, willing her to continue.

With a small smile she said, "You'd think they'd never seen a..." she hesitated and I wondered if she was looking for a word to describe Michelle's ethnicity, "...a well-dressed, professional woman before." Then she pursed her lips. "But those clothes, the high-heeled leather boots, the thin coat, even with her leather gloves and her hat, a soft squishy thing, she'd freeze to death if she had to get out of the truck."

Everyone who lives on the prairies knows how to dress for the cold. We bundle up in fat, puffy coats and thick-soled boots, our cars are equipped with emergency rations, lighters, and candles. One Christmas my dad gave Louisa and me emergency kits complete with a folding shovel and a blanket in case we broke down on the highway in the middle of a blizzard.

I said, "She came in a company car though, right? It probably had everything she'd need if she broke down."

She nodded and glanced back out the wide windows. "Maybe, but she left her car in the parking lot, I spotted it the next day and told one of the plant guys. Maybe they caught a lift with that other guy."

"What other guy?" AJ and I said it at the same time.

Crystal straightened in her chair, this was her café and nothing escaped her watchful eye. "Well, Michelle got here first and ordered a coffee. Marty arrived a few minutes later. I saw him come in and brought him his usual, coffee and a cronut. He loved his coffee and cronut. They talked for ten, twenty minutes, then left. When they got outside, they bumped into that other guy."

AJ continued, "Crystal, this could be important. Did you recognize the guy, do you know who he is?"

She shook her head.

He leaned closer to her. "Can you describe him? Was he a plant guy?"

She frowned and shook her head again. "I don't think so. I only caught a glimpse of him. They were huddled together outside, blocking the front door, then someone came in and they disappeared. He was wearing one of those heavy fur-trimmed parkas with a big floppy hood, now he was dressed for the cold."

"You're sure he wasn't a plant guy? Did you see him again? What was he driving?" Her face stiffened and I realized I was pushing too hard.

Crystal pulled back in her chair and raised her hands. "Whoa, you guys sure you're not cops?" She didn't look at me, only at AJ.

He shot me a look that said 'cool it, this is not a cross-examination,' then flashed his most endearing grin. "You got that right, Crystal, not cops. We're just trying to piece together what happened to our friend the day she died."

Her shoulders relaxed a little and she glanced out the window into the parking lot. "You know, I think he came back later, after the explosion. The place was packed with reporters, EMT, lots of people, all milling around yakking on their phones."

"Did he come inside?"

"No, I spotted him in the parking lot. I didn't pay much attention to tell you the truth. This place was a gong show."

"Did you see where he went?" AJ asked.

Before she could respond, something loud and metallic crashed to the floor in the kitchen. Silence fell over the room as all eyes turned toward the back of the café, a brief pause, then the hubbub started up again.

"Look, I've got to get back to work before the kids wreck the place."

We thanked Crystal for her help, tossed our paper cups in a large plastic trash bin and stepped back outside. The air was sharp in our lungs after the overheated warmth of the café, and all I could muster were short, quick breaths as we hustled back to the car.

I turned on the ignition and waited for the heater to kick in while AJ yanked a couple of times on his seat belt. "You and Crystal seem close." I watched AJ out of the corner of my eye. "She got a little jumpy there, that business about us being cops...anything I should know about?" He just laughed and told me to get a move on.

As I pulled through the cloverleaf back onto the highway it came to me, the thing that had been niggling at me ever since that Board meeting in November. "AJ, the story about Michelle and Marty touring the pipeline right-of-way doesn't hang together."

"Why?" He tugged at his seat belt which appeared to be strangling him.

"Because she wasn't dressed for it. Michelle hated winter, but she's not an idiot, she would have dressed for the cold if she was planning to walk the right-of-way at thirty below."

"Maybe she changed her mind. Maybe Marty told her something and she decided to go see for herself."

I squinted at the road ahead. The sun was high, bouncing off the snow-covered fields, and I wished I'd remembered to bring my sunglasses. "Fair enough, but how did she get out there?"

He looked at me as if it was a stupid question. "In Marty's truck."

"No, you read the TSB report. There's no mention of a burned-out vehicle." I'd read that damned report so many times I could repeat its findings from memory. "Just two bodies. Discovered ten and a half hours after the explosion. Marty had injuries, likely from flying debris, and second degree burns to his head and upper body, he was found two hundred feet south of the Elliot Lake compressor station. Michelle, untouched by the flames, was found twenty-four feet further away. Killed by flying debris. Nothing about a truck. So how did they get there?" I glanced at him to see if he'd come to the same conclusion as I had.

His face lit up. "Parka Guy!"

"Yep, he drove them out to the right-of-way, God knows why, and left them there to die."

He was fiddling with the zipper on his parka now, trying to unzip it without tangling his hood strings in the seat belt. "Not necessarily. Let's assume you're right and Parka Guy drove them out there, he couldn't have known that Elliot Lake was going to explode."

"True, but he could see Michelle wasn't dressed for the cold and he left her there. A man wearing a heavy parka with a fur-lined hood left a small woman dressed in, how did Crystal describe it, high-heeled leather boots and a thin coat, in the middle of nowhere. She'd die from exposure in a matter of hours."

The hum of the heater filled the air. It was making a clicking noise that wasn't there before.

"AJ, her death was foreseeable. That makes it manslaughter, maybe even murder. We have to find Marty's truck. That could give us a lead on Parka Guy."

He wrinkled his brow, considering the gravity of what I'd just said. "You're making a lot of assumptions here."

AJ was right. Sometimes I made leaps of logic that baffle the people around me, but I'd learned from bitter experience that when an alarm bell rings, I should pay attention to it.

He pulled off his scarf and stuffed it into a large pocket. "And I don't see the connection between Marty's truck and Parka Guy."

"Frankly, neither do I. But think about it. If Marty's car wasn't on the right-of-way, it should have been in the Timmies' parking lot. But if that's the case, why didn't Crystal report it to the plant at the same time she reported Michelle's car?" I flipped off the heater and cracked my window open an inch. The roar of the tires on the highway rushed in. "It's just strange, like a piece of a puzzle that doesn't fit anywhere."

Other than AJ telling me to watch my speed—I was rushing to drop him off so I could make a phone call in private—we didn't say much more on the drive home.

CHAPTER 40

According to Louisa one of my most irritating character flaws is impatience. As much as it pains me to say it, she's right. I paced around the house for almost an hour, picking up my phone and putting it down before I made the decision: It could wait until Monday morning. I did not have to ruin Sarah's weekend by sending her on what could be a wild goose chase trying to track down Marty's truck.

To put it out of my mind I stuffed Quincy into his little plaid coat and dragged him around the block. The temperature had dropped to minus twelve Celsius and the wind cut like razor blades; we were both relieved to get back inside.

He was lolling in his usual spot in front of the fire and I was watching back-to-back episodes of a bake-off show when Louisa came home from work and announced she'd scored tickets to the new Warhol exhibit.

"Tonight? Are you kidding?" I complained pitifully that the last thing I wanted to do on a freezing cold Saturday night was go to an art gallery to see a bunch of floating pillows. "They're forecasting a blizzard tonight. If we can't get into an underground parkade, the car will freeze solid and we'll never get home."

"Oh, stop being such a drama queen," Louisa said.

"Madeline isn't complaining and she's more of a diva than you are."

"You invited Madeline? I didn't even know you had her number."

She laughed and said someone had given her three free tickets to Warhol's Silver Clouds exhibit and she thought that of all our friends, Madeline would appreciate it the most. The gallery touted it as a major milestone, the critics raved that it showed Warhol could produce art that pushed the fourth dimension, whatever that meant, and everyone who'd seen it said it was pure magic.

We picked up Madeline at her house. She looked every inch the diva in her navy Audrey Hepburn coat and tiny black leather ankle boots. When I pointed out she'd get frostbite in her extremities, she sniffed disdainfully, saying she'd rather go out looking like a model than a lumberjack. I wasn't sure whether she meant "out" in the sense of a social outing or "out" as in to die, but decided not to pursue it further.

We found one of the last remaining spots in an underground parkade and crowded into a dank elevator that clanked and creaked as it hauled us up to street level. Then we plunged into the bitter wind to reach the gallery two long and miserable blocks away.

We joined a short line and were soon pushing back a black velvet curtain to stand awestruck in the centre of a large white room. All around us, oversized silver pillows floated lazily through the air, glittering and twirling slowly in the bright lights. Young people, old people, businesspeople, construction workers, everyone reached out, mesmerized, to bounce the shiny pillows up to the ceiling or across the room. The pillows made a soft *bouf* sound when they collided before rolling away on gentle puffs of air flowing from hidden vents.

"Amy would love this place," I whispered, thinking of Kirsten's little girl, as a silver pillow tumbled over my shoulder and floated into Louisa's face. It felt like we were weightless, floating underwater. Even Madeline, the epitome of worldly sophistication, surrendered to the hypnotic, lyrical mood. Our allotted forty-five minutes expired much too quickly and we decided to prolong what had, much to my surprise, turned into a magical evening by stopping for a quick drink at the bar in the Hyatt a block away.

The bar was quiet for a Saturday evening, the blizzard was coming in hard and fast. We debated whether to scrap the idea but we'd come all this way and the high-backed blue velvet chairs tucked in front of the flickering fireplace were so inviting that we agreed to stay for one drink, two at the most. I swirled my brandy around my glass, watching the firelight glitter red and amber in its depths, while Madeline and Louisa weighed the merits of a trip to Croatia as compared to Madagascar.

The snow was blowing hard by the time we emerged on the sidewalk. With our heads down and our collars up, we braced ourselves for the miserable trek back to the underground parkade. We were hunched together at the cross light, almost three-quarters of the way there when a shiver raced down my spine. *He was still there.* When we'd left the Hyatt, a man followed us out through the revolving doors. He tracked us step by step as we staggered down the sidewalk, buffeted along like rag dolls in the fierce wind. I glanced over my shoulder. He was on the opposite side of the street, peering in the window of a dimly lit souvenir shop. Who goes window shopping in a blizzard? I pulled Madeline and Louisa closer. The wind tore the breath out of my lungs and whipped my hair into my eyes. "We have to go back."

"Are you crazy?" Madeline said. "We're almost there." She shuddered as the wind ripped at the hem of her pretty blue coat, her tiny boots did nothing to protect her legs.

"No, seriously, we have to go back to the hotel. We're being followed."

Louisa gripped my arm. "All the more reason to hurry and get back to the car."

"No, we can't go down there." The wind scooped up my words and I shouted even louder. "The parkade will be deserted at this hour. We're safer in the street."

"Jesus, Evie." That was Madeline. "We'll freeze to death in the street." Her arms were wrapped around her body and she stamped her boots on the icy pavement.

I looked over her shoulder. There he was, fur-trimmed hood up, tightly wound scarf obscuring his face. Still as a rock. The shops and art galleries on both sides of the road were closed, their lights low, their doors firmly locked. Ahead, the feeble light of a coffee shop flickered through gusts of snow blown up from the street. The café was half a block past the parkade, the Hyatt two blocks behind us. "Dammit, you guys, there's someone there, following us. We can't duck into a shop to wait him out. Nothing's open between here and the parkade."

Louisa yanked off her mittens, cradled my face in her cold hands and said, "Evie, are you absolutely sure? It's not your imagination? One too many drinks, perhaps?" Her eyes searched the street. "I don't see anyone."

"He's on the other side of the road, in front of the Tower Gift Shop." I was shaking harder now; I leaned close, touching my forehead to hers. "Trust me on this, Louisa. Please."

She nodded and turned to Madeline. "That's it. Back to the Hyatt. We'll call a cab from there." Madeline stared at us, incredulous and rigid with cold. Louisa grabbed her by the arm and gently tugged her back from the curb. I took Madeline's other arm and we started back the way we came. A car horn honked loudly; its headlights raked across the man loping across the street. Now he was thirty feet behind us on our sidewalk.

We hustled past gloomy, shuttered shops, struggling to breathe against the wind. Head down I spotted a broken piece of paving stone lying next to a spindly naked tree. I stooped to pick it up, almost yanking Madeline down with me.

She said through clenched teeth, "What are you going to do, bash his head in?"

"No, but if he gets any closer, I'm firing this through a plate glass window." Louisa nodded, her breath coming in ragged gasps. She and I had taken a self-defence course after I'd been attacked by a deranged lawyer at Gates, Case and White. We'd learned to trust our instincts. The instructor's voice rang in my ear: "If you feel unsafe in a deserted street, throw a rock through a shop window. That will set off the security alarms which will immediately alert the police and security guards. The racket should be enough to frighten the predator away."

Finally we'd reached the intersection. The lights of the Hyatt glittered in the cold air just a half a block ahead. The traffic signal counted down the seconds before it would turn red: nine, eight, seven. "We're going for it." I tugged Madeline into the crosswalk. She lost her balance and twisted her ankle in those ridiculous designer boots.

She stumbled and I caught her, hoisting her up by the armpit. Without a word Louisa did the same on Madeline's other side and the three of us stumbled across the crosswalk and into the parking apron in front of the hotel. Our stalker broke into a run and was gaining on us. *He's not even pretending anymore.*

"Oh, thank God." Madeline sagged with relief as we dragged her through the oversized revolving door into the hotel lobby. Just then a yellow cab pulled up and three boisterous businessmen rolled out. Louisa darted past them to claim the cab while I shoved Madeline back through the revolving door and into the backseat.

The cabbie sized us up and laughed. "Looks like you ladies had a fun evening."

"You don't know the half of it," I replied as he accelerated out of the layby and the bright lights of the Hyatt receded in the rear window. Madeline patted my hand and I realized I was still clutching the broken paving stone in my fist. The snow swirled in our wake; the man who'd been stalking us had disappeared.

"Who was that?" She whispered. "What did he want?"

"I wish I knew, Madeline. I wish I knew."

CHAPTER 41

It was a bright Wednesday morning four days after Madeline, Louisa and I were terrorized by the stalker on our way back from the Warhol exhibit. I was sitting in the office, listening to the commotion in the trees on the other side of my windowpane. It matched the confusion in my brain. Outside, the crows were trying to force the magpies out of the evergreens. A territorial dispute in Birdland? Inside, I was scribbling on my notepad, seeking answers to a question that had become even more puzzling.

I had called Sarah at seven o'clock on Monday morning, hoping to catch her before Dave arrived. She sounded agitated when she picked up the receiver. "Dave will be here any minute," she whispered. "You have my home number, please use it." So much for not wrecking her weekend. I promised to call her at home from now on, then explained I needed her to review the company's fleet car records to determine the whereabouts of Marty's car. She hesitated. "What if someone asks me why I want it?"

Oh please, Sarah, don't waffle on me now. "Look, Sarah, I need to piece together what happened in the hours leading up to Michelle...and Marty's...deaths. Marty's movements that morning are a critical part of that." I cringed with the realization that I'd just told Sarah a small lie. I knew what Marty's movements were, he drove to Timmies to meet Michelle, then someone drove him and Michelle to the right-of-way where they died. What I didn't know was what happened to his car during this time.

Sarah had called me back first thing this morning with answers that weren't answers at all. I'd made notes of her call on a yellow pad covered with doodles, all feathery lines and stars. There was a quick knock at my open door, and AJ slipped into my office and shut the door quietly behind him. He grinned, bouncing lightly on the balls of his feet.

I looked up. "Just the man I was looking for—"

He winked and raised a finger to his lips to shush me. "Just give me a moment," he whispered, "I'm avoiding Madeline."

My eyebrows shot up. "Really, what did you do to incur her wrath?"

He pressed his lips together, suppressing a smile, then said, "She told me about your run-in with that guy on Saturday night; apparently she almost broke her ankle when you two dragged her into an intersection."

"A classic Madeline overstatement, but go on."

"She spent the entire weekend with an ice pack wrapped around her ankle and said it still looked fat. Then I said her ankles looked equally fat to me."

"AJ, you didn't!" I wanted to scold him for teasing her but found myself chuckling instead. We kicked around some off-the-wall ideas to placate Madeline before my mind returned to my earlier conversation with Sarah. "Well, I'm glad you're here. I found out what happened to Marty's car."

Instantly AJ's lighthearted mood evaporated. He pulled out the chair opposite me and sat down.

I didn't bother looking at my notes. The story wasn't complicated, just bewildering. "Sarah pulled up the fleet car log sheet and made a few calls. Marty's car is back in the plant fleet."

AJ leaned back and crossed his arms behind his head. "That's where it's supposed to be, isn't it?"

"Yes, but that's not the point. What's interesting is how it got there. Sarah says another plant employee returned Marty's car. He found it abandoned on the side of a service road about twenty kilometres from the Elliot Lake plant. This was on the day of the explosion. Everyone was crazy busy and he didn't want to bother his supervisor about it so he called a towing company and they towed it back to the plant. Then he forgot about it."

AJ raised his eyebrows. "Twenty kilometres. There's no way Marty and Michelle would walk from the side of the road out to the right-of-way in that kind of weather. So how did it get there?"

"That, my dear Watson, is the burning question. Someone, I'm guessing Parka Guy, left it there, but why?"

The room was quiet except for the sound of a sheet of paper being ripped off a notepad, crumpled into a ball and dropped into the trash can.

CHAPTER 42

Just when you think things can't get any worse, they do. I was cursing like a sailor and glaring out the French doors off the kitchen at the office buildings shimmering in the distance when the front door thumped open and Louisa and Quincy tromped into the foyer in a blast of cold air.

"How was your walk?" I asked as she unclipped Quincy's winter jacket. He flicked his back paw and one of his booties flew into the powder room.

"Stop that," she said to the dog. "Who were you swearing at?" she asked me. "I could hear you through the door." She untied Quincy's remaining booties and wrestled his block head out of his harness. He took off like a shot, caroming off my legs into the TV room where he flopped onto his back, wriggling and moaning in front of the fireplace.

I watched him for a couple of seconds. "I swear that dog's demented," I said and returned to the kitchen.

"Says the woman standing in the middle of the room, swearing at her phone." Louisa pulled a cookbook off the shelf and called over her shoulder. "Pasta primavera?"

I nodded. A headache was building behind my eyes. A chinook was coming in. "Ray called," I said. "He lost Jack's bloody pipe."

"Oh God, you're kidding!" She stopped rummaging in the fridge to stare at me. "Jack's going to kill you."

"That's what I told Ray." I slumped at the kitchen island and watched Louisa work. She's a very efficient cook, she always lines up all the ingredients in front of her before she begins, unlike me: I'm usually halfway through a recipe before I discover the onions have gone bad.

"What did Ray say?" she asked.

What *did* Ray say? "Well, the conversation didn't last long and was very disjointed… he said he had bad news and Jack's pipe was missing." Every time I said Jack's name his tight little face and furious eyes floated into my mind.

"How can it be missing?" Louisa asked. "The TSB must have massive storage facilities and foolproof tagging and identification protocols given the kinds of investigations they conduct. Did they lose it, or heaven forbid, break it?"

"Ray says they never got it in the first place." I was even angrier now than I had been when I hung up on Ray.

Louisa was standing at the sink, washing a large bell pepper. She patted it dry with a paper towel and set it on the chopping board. "I don't understand," she said. The knife sliced cleanly through the pepper's firm red skin, exposing the spongy white pith inside. "How could they not have received it? I thought you delivered it to Ray yourself."

"I did, and he delivered it to Dave Bryant. At that point, Louisa, I lost it. I flew into a rant about not trusting Dave as far as I could throw him and said all sorts of things that the Law Society would censure me for." I pressed my fingers over my right eye. My head was pounding.

She wiped her hands on her apron and said, "I don't understand. Why did Ray give the pipe to Dave?"

I felt sick to my stomach. "Because it's company pro-tocol. Had I given it any thought I would have known that. Dave's in charge of the regulatory group as well as the legal group now that he's taken over from Michelle. Any communication between Phoenix and the TSB runs through Dave." My cheeks burned. "Louisa, this is my fault."

Louisa reached across the kitchen island and gently patted my hand. I looked down and realized I was shak-ing. "Would you like a cuppa?" Our dad used to say that to Mom when she was angry. Mom said with his British accent it sounded like a risqué Hungarian word; it always made her smile.

I nodded, starting to feel a little calmer. "Ray's going to talk with Dave to see if they can track it down, but at this point, the pipe's vanished."

She pushed aside the cutting board and pulled some mugs out of the cupboard. Quincy materialized at her feet. *Cookies?*

I reached down and patted his head. "You know what's really upsetting? I think Ray might agree with Kirsten about the chevron markings." I remembered the look on Ray's face, puzzled and concerned, as we lifted the pipe out of my trunk and set it on the dolly in the parkade.

The tiny black bird on the spout of the kettle whistled. Louisa poured boiling water into my mug and handed me a small spoon, a souvenir of Niagara Falls, one of Mom's favourites, to stir the tea bag around. "So, what are you going to do now?"

"There's nothing I can do." I wrapped my fingers around my mug. "I persuaded Kirsten to let Ray deliver the pipe to the TSB, so he could convince them to reopen their investigation. Without that pipe, there's nothing new for the TSB to examine. The investigation is closed, its findings were inconclusive. End of story."

Quincy stopped snuffling along the bottom edge of the counter and collapsed at my feet. "All that's left now is for me to call Kirsten and tell her I lost Jack's pipe. She'll be disappointed, but that kid is going to be furious." I exhaled a long, slow breath. "Who said no good deed ever goes unpunished?"

CHAPTER 43

Kirsten ate at the Cozy Coyote Café every Tuesday evening while the boys were at hockey practice and Amy went to dance class. She still didn't know why she liked the restaurant so much. Under different circumstances everything about the place would offend her sensibilities. Kevin would have characterized the decor as 'hippy dippy western' but she'd developed a fondness for the rodeo posters on the walls, the horseshoe napkin holders and a ratty stuffed coyote staring balefully down at customers from its perch high in the rafters.

Gretchen, the proprietor, nodded at Kirsten when she came through the creaky red door. Gretchen was cajoling two middle-aged men in parkas and woolly hats to make up their minds: were they going with their usual or would they take a walk on the wild side and try the Tuesday night special, which was exactly the same as the Monday night special but with frozen carrots instead of frozen peas. After much hemming and hawing the men settled for their usual. Gretchen smiled a small self-satisfied smile; she'd placed their order even before they sat down at their regular table.

She approached Kirsten's table, "K, honey, what'll it be?" then raised an eyebrow when Kirsten asked for a slice of apple pie and coffee, instead of her usual club sandwich.

Kirsten pulled a paperback out of her backpack and settled in. Over the last two years she and Gretchen had become friends. They were an unlikely pair. Kirsten was from Toronto, a worldly professional woman and mother of three. Gretchen was a childless, middle-aged woman who'd barely finished high school and rarely left Alberta. "K, honey, this is God's country, why would I spend a day of my vacation anywhere else?"

Fate brought them together. Their shared status, they were both widows, pushed them to the fringes of society. No one knew how to relate to them anymore. Were they merry widows after other people's husbands, dour spinsters who kept to themselves, what? When they were together, they could relax. They didn't have to guard their tongues to avoid saying something that would engender pity or raise suspicion.

Gretchen hustled over to the two men who were now bickering about the merits of lowering the speed limit on the highway out of town. She set down their plates, refilled their coffees and called over to Kirsten saying her order would be right up.

Kirsten smiled and wrapped her scarf more snuggly around her neck. Despite its name, Cozy Corner Café, Kirsten was always cold here. In the winter the icy air seeped through the large glass windows creating a draft and in the summer the air conditioner blasted frigid air down the back of her neck. Gretchen said the problem was with Kirsten, not the café, and they left it at that.

"How are the twins? How's Amy?" Gretchen slid into the beige vinyl booth seat across from her. The café was quiet, she could sit a spell. Kirsten and the kids had become minor celebrities after the pipeline explosion; no one in Crisscross had been that close to what Jack had taken to calling 'ground zero.' The children relished their notoriety, the local media splashed their photos across the front page, but when the larger newspapers sent interview requests, Kirsten refused. She couldn't risk falling apart in public.

Gretchen continued. "Someone was asking about you guys the other day. I sent him to your place."

"Not another reporter?"

"He didn't say."

Kirsten peeled the tinfoil lid off the cream capsule and her fingers trembled ever so slightly. *Just like the last time.* The San Remo explosion and the pain of Kevin's suicide were inextricably linked in her mind. It had taken years of expensive therapy for Kirsten to crawl out of the dark pit she'd fallen into and now here she was again, teetering on the edge.

She shivered and zipped up the bottom third of her parka and glanced around the room. "How's business these days?"

"Pretty much back to normal. The mini boom from the explosion is over. It didn't take long once they cleared the right-of-way. Bad pipe out, good pipe in and poof, the trades and techies were gone." Gretchen's eyes sparkled. "But it was great while it lasted. I made enough for a second trip to Vegas." This was the only exception to Gretchen's Alberta-vacations-only rule. "Come with us." They'd had this conversation many times before. The last thing Kirsten wanted to do was to spend a weekend in a dark clammy casino with Gretchen and two of her high school friends. She laughed and shook her head.

They were on their second cups of coffee when Kirsten's phone rang. She recognized Evie's number and said, "Sorry, I have to take this." Gretchen nodded and hustled back to the kitchen.

Evie wanted to come to Crisscross tomorrow for a visit. "Is something wrong?" Kirsten asked. Evie replied there had been a development and she would explain everything in the morning.

Kirsten placed her phone carefully in the small pocket of her backpack and rubbed her hands vigorously over her thighs. Her legs felt weak and she tapped the toes of her boots together a couple of times, hoping this would restore her circulation. Then she opened her paperback, cracking its spine to force the pages to lie flat. She still had forty minutes to kill before she picked up the kids.

CHAPTER 44

I spotted Kirsten's house the minute I turned down the lane. *We're off the grid, you'll never find it,* she'd said. It's funny how hidden things become obvious once you know where to look.

The air was unusually light and crisp for February. I stepped out of the car and crunched across the gravel driveway. The scent of crushed pine needles rose sharp and sweet under my feet. Amy squealed near the back of the house. She was splashing in a stream of water pooling under a snow ledge, her boots pumping up and down as if she were Godzilla ravaging the residents of a faraway metropolis.

We both lifted our heads when we heard a strange growl. Kirsten leapt out from behind a fir tree, her hands curled like claws, huffing and snorting and waving her arms about. Amy saw me and shrieked, "Save me, Heart Lady! Save me!" She jumped into my arms, her wet boots banging against my thighs.

"Fear not, Dragon Girl, you're safe with me," I said in a deep, melodramatic voice. Then Kirsten dropped her hands and we all dissolved into giggles.

Kirsten greeted me and said, "I hope you don't mind if we walk." She took Amy out of my arms and deposited her on the driveway. "It's just too nice to stay inside." Her tone was light, but tense. She glanced at me out of the corner of her eye. "What's going on?"

I squinted up at the sun-bleached sky and said, "Lead the way." We turned left at the end of the driveway and headed toward the dense wood beyond the glade. The lane narrowed to a slippery path overhung with heavy evergreen boughs. It felt like we were pressing through a dark tunnel.

"The kids come here all the time," Kirsten said. "Jack and Tyler built a snow fort there." She pointed deep into a thicket. "It's probably gone by now."

"No, it's not." Amy shot through the underbrush, ducking under branches still heavy with snow and showering us with snow crystals. We followed at a slower pace but it was impossible to have a serious conversation as we trailed, single file, behind Amy down the narrow path.

A few minutes later we emerged in a snowy meadow. Nestled under the blue green branches of a massive pine was what appeared to be an unusually uniform snowdrift. As we got closer, it revealed itself to be a well-constructed snow fort, accessible through a narrow slot carved into its thick snow wall. Amy giggled and scrambled inside.

"Can you see me?" Her voice sounded small but clear. "I can see you." Even in her red snowsuit it would have been hard to spot her if we didn't know where to look. She piled little mittfuls of snow on top of the wall, complaining that the snow was getting soft and mushy.

Kirsten and I stood side by side, watching her. "Kirsten," I said, "I have news."

"So I gathered. It's not good, is it?"

"I'm afraid not."

She listened quietly while I explained that Jack's pipe had disappeared after I delivered it to Ray.

"I knew it." Her breath came in shallow white puffs. "I knew we couldn't trust him."

"No, listen Kirsten, I don't think this is Ray's fault."

"Well it sure as hell isn't the TSB's fault. It's a federal agency, pipe fragments that are evidence in a catastrophic explosion don't just disappear." She pulled a tissue out of her pocket and blew her nose. "That's it then, it's over." She stamped the snow off her boots and called out to Amy, it was time to go home.

"Kirsten," I was clutching her elbow. "Wait, this isn't the end. I've made some calls." I didn't say more, it was too early to tell her my focus had shifted to Michelle, Marty, and Parka Guy.

She shot me a look brimming with skepticism. "That company is corrupt. Their safety protocols are crap. A dozen people died at San Remo; two at Elliot Lake. It's going to happen again and there's nothing we can do about it."

She glanced at Amy who was still piling snow along the top of the fort's wall and called her again. The little girl threw the last handful of snow high up in the air. It sparkled in the sunlight as it drifted down into her hair. She crawled out through the narrow opening and hopped back to us, making bunny tracks in the snow.

We trudged silently down the lane toward the house. A flock of tiny brown birds burst up out of the cotoneaster bushes planted in a tidy row at the top of Kirsten's driveway. Kirsten's hand flew to her throat. "God! They startled me!"

"Me too."

"Amy, slow down," Kirsten shouted as her daughter flung open the door and charged into the house. We were right behind her when Amy screamed.

CHAPTER 45

A lean, wiry man wearing a black knit sweater and khaki pants was standing in the kitchen, his coat tossed carelessly across the island. He'd hoisted Amy up onto his hip. His forearm, pale and corded with muscle, held her close. Something glinted in his hand. A butcher knife from the knife block on the counter.

"Welcome home, Kirsten, Evie." His eyes were calm and a watery blue, his hair a washed-out rust colour. "Take a seat." He indicated the stools tucked under the kitchen island. "Not you, Evie." He tipped his head at the wine bottle sitting on the counter. "We're going to get better acquainted."

Neither Kirsten nor I moved.

"Don't make me say it twice." His voice was low, gravelly. Amy's lower lip began to tremble. Kirsten sat down heavily at the kitchen island. I moved behind him, reaching for the wine bottle. I found a corkscrew in a drawer and a juice glass in the cupboard. The cork squeaked as I pried it out of the bottle and twisted it off the curly metal screw.

"Put her down," Kirsten said. "I'm listening."

Amy's eyes were round with terror. He bounced her up higher on his hip to get a better grip on her small body. "Evie," he said, "pour me a drink, that's a good girl."

My wet boots slipped on the wooden floor and the juice glass came down hard and brittle on the counter.

He glanced at Amy, then back at Kirsten. "You like living out here in Podunk? Keeping to yourself, all nice and quiet? It'd be a good idea to stay that way, don't you think?" *What the hell was he talking about?*

"It's time you stopped bothering people," his eyes slid in my direction, "with stupid ideas. Stirring up trouble."

Amy made a small snuffling sound.

"Put her down, please," Kirsten said.

Tears were rolling down Amy's cheeks. "Mommy...?"

"It's okay, sweetie," Kirsten said with quiet determination. "I need you to be strong now, Amy. Like the dragon."

Amy cast a desperate glance at her mother, hesitated, then whipped back her head, arched her spine and shrieked. Her tiny hands flew into the man's face, clawing at his eyes, ripping at his ears. He snapped his head back to avoid her nails. Her legs thrashed and she wriggled out of his grasp. Just as her feet touched the floor, he caught her red hood. She screamed. Kirsten leapt up, her stool crashed to the floor.

I gripped the corkscrew and raked it down his forearm. The pale flesh opened in a long bloody gash. He released Amy's hood and whirled around to face me. The butcher knife came up. I grabbed the wine bottle and smashed it in his face. He staggered back, blood spurting from his nose, arcing through the air and spattering across the granite countertop and the whitewashed floor. The bottle clattered to the floor, wine mingling with blood, and I screamed. "Run!"

Kirsten and Amy were already out the door and halfway down the driveway. Kirsten shouted frantically over her shoulder. "The car!" My Mini was blocking her SUV.

"My car! Get in my car!" I fumbled in my pockets, found my keys, and pressed the fob. The car doors clicked open. Kirsten flung herself into the front passenger seat, hauling Amy onto her lap. I jumped behind the steering wheel, jammed the gears into reverse and roared up the driveway before she'd closed her door. Gravel flew from under the tires and we fishtailed as I yanked on the steering wheel and tore down the lane.

Kirsten glanced out the back window. "I don't see him."

"Call the police." My heart was pounding so hard I could barely talk.

"We don't have police, just RCMP, thirty kilometres away."

"Call them, call them now!" I struggled to steady my breathing. It was coming in short, jittery bursts.

"First the school. The boys, I have to get the boys!"

Oh God, what if there were more of them? "Where? Where's the school?"

"Stay in this lane." Her voice shook. "Stay in this lane."

"Mommy?" Amy lifted her face to her mother. Kirsten gently straightened Amy's hood which was twisted around her neck.

"Oh sweetie, you were so brave." Kirsten squeezed her daughter tightly. "So very, very brave."

Amy's grey eyes sparkled. "You said be a dragon." She raised her hands, her fingers were curled into tiny claws.

Kirsten cupped Amy's hands in her own and buried her face in Amy's baby fine hair. "I did, didn't I."

"Like Jezebel when she came out of the lake." Then Amy growled through clenched white teeth.

"Yes, like Jezebel, just like Jezebel." Kirsten looked at me over the top of Amy's head, her eyes moist with tears.

We'd barely come to a stop in front of the school before she thrust Amy at me and leapt out the door. I strapped Amy into the middle of the back seat and we waited until Kirsten reappeared with the boys. Jack grumbled as she settled them on either side of Amy, embarrassed that he'd been dragged out of class by his mom.

Amy stopped him in mid-sentence. "A bad man came to the house. He grabbed me but I was a dragon. I screamed and we ran away."

Tyler told her to shut up but Kirsten stopped him, saying it was true. Amy was a brave little girl who'd saved us from a bad man. Amy interrupted, insisting his name was Spike. *I'm the Heart Lady, he's Spike. Yes, that makes sense.* Amy chattered about the butcher knife, the corkscrew, the wine bottle, and us screaming down the driveway to get to the car before he caught us. The boys stared at her, mouths agape.

"Call the police," I reminded Kirsten. My voice was low and thick with adrenaline.

She dialed 9-1-1 and after a long wait was connected to the nearest RCMP detachment. The police would send someone to her house but it was highly unlikely the intruder would still be there. Kirsten was to stay away until they'd had a chance to examine the house and the yard. No one knew when she could return, it depended on the availability of officers and techs. Kirsten made non-committal noises and hung up. "Well, that was pointless."

"Kirsten," I said quietly, "you're all staying with me until it's safe for you to return home." I expected her to argue but she acquiesced immediately, agreeing that would be wise.

The highway hummed under the tires. We'd be home in a couple of hours. I glanced into the rear-view mirror.

The boys stared out the side windows, watching the snowy fields shift from white to red to grey as the sun slowly dropped below the horizon. Amy was tucked up next to Tyler, struggling to keep her eyes open. Absent-mindedly he patted her knee.

By the time we reached the city limits it was getting dark and the children were asleep. Streetlights refracted across the windshield and the traffic lights glittered red, green, and amber in the cold night air. As we stepped out of the car in front of the house, I was surprised to discover I was still shaking.

*   *   *   *

Louisa and Quincy were waiting for us when we arrived. I warned the kids not to bend too close to Quincy when they patted him; the dog had a habit of bouncing up and cracking people in the nose with his rock-hard skull. Jack declared a silly old dog didn't scare him, but hung back, allowing Amy and Tyler to cross the threshold ahead of him.

After the commotion at the front door died down, Louisa announced that pizza would be arriving in a few minutes. Kirsten shooed the kids into the powder room to wash up, then settled them in front of the TV.

I changed out of my sweater—splotched with wine and blood from when I cracked the bottle across Spike's face—and joined Louisa and Kirsten at the kitchen island. Louisa was offering to take Kirsten and the kids on an outing tomorrow, perhaps the Warhol pillow exhibit, when Jack materialized at his mother's elbow.

"When do I get my pipe back?" he demanded.

I'd forgotten about that damned pipe. I raised my

eyebrows at Kirsten, signalling that I should be the one to tell him. "Jack, something's happened to the pipe. It's disappeared." His face crinkled and for a minute I thought he might cry. I lay a hand on his shoulder. "I'm not saying it's gone forever; I'm just saying we don't know where it is right now."

Jack let out an anguished wail. Tyler raced into the kitchen and Amy began to cry. This set off Quincy who started barking and running around, ready to attack whatever was upsetting the strange little boy standing in the middle of our kitchen.

"Stop it, right now!" Kirsten said to Jack as she hoisted Amy up into her lap. "Amy, sweetheart, everything is fine." Jack flared again, she raised one finger and said, "That's enough!"

Just then the doorbell rang. Quincy went wild, barking and charging the door. The boys chased him, which only made things worse.

"Jeez Louise," I raised my voice over the din, "catch him before he attacks someone." Louisa dragged Quincy off into the powder room. Kirsten shuffled Amy onto the stool next to her and ordered the boys to take their seats or no one was getting dinner tonight.

I paid the delivery guy and returned with the pizza boxes. Within minutes the children were quietly munching through an extra-large cheese and pepperoni pizza and eyeing the lava cakes sitting on the counter for dessert.

Kirsten smiled at me over their heads. I smiled back, pretending life had returned to normal, but I couldn't shake the feeling I'd seen Spike somewhere before.

CHAPTER 46

Steff's coffee is strong enough to dissolve a spoon. After last night—sleep had come in fitful spurts, escaping from a knife-wielding lunatic will do that to you—I really needed it.

I glanced around the BLV lobby. The sound of raucous laughter floated down the hall. Bridget and Madeline were in the photocopy room, where Madeline was demonstrating her cockatiel's excellent command of the English language. She threw her head back, her thick red hair flying, and squawked his name, "*Ru-pert! Ru-pert!*"

Chuckling, I said, "Madeline, I had no idea you were this funny."

She whirled around and looked me in the eye. "I beg your pardon. Clowns are funny, I am merely amusing." It sounded like something the Queen would have said.

Keith strolled into the photocopy room clutching what appeared to be a hockey schedule. He leaned against the door jamb, looking as weathered as a ranch hand, and said, "Who's screeching like a banshee? And more importantly, why?"

"Madeline was telling us a Rupert story." I lowered my voice, attempting to mimic her, "Nope, I can't do it justice. Over to you, Madeline." Everyone, except Madeline, laughed.

Keith raised an eyebrow. "Who's Rupert?"

Bridget replied, "Rupert's Madeline's nasty bird, he's"—she poked a finger into the back of the paper tray—"hold on, who wrecked the photocopier?" The lights on the machine started flashing like angry bees as she wrestled with a sheet of paper stuck deep in its innards. Everyone swore they'd been nowhere near the photocopier in the last twenty-four hours.

The last twenty-four hours. My sense of unease returned. Despite the terror of yesterday Kirsten refused to talk about it. At first I thought she was shielding the kids, but when I broached the topic after she'd tucked them into bed, she just shook her head. *No. Not now.* It was as if she wanted to wall off the memory until it shrivelled and crumbled into dust.

Ignoring a traumatic experience might work for some people but it didn't work for me. Turning to Keith I said, "Got a minute?"

We were about to leave for my office when AJ appeared in the doorway. He scanned the four of us crowded around the photocopier in the windowless room and asked, "What's this, a staff meeting?"

"I've almost got it," Bridget said through gritted teeth. She tugged on the edge of a piece of paper. It ripped.

AJ pointed to the tiny shred of paper pincered between her fingertips. "Wait. Is that my memo?"

Bridget puffed a strand of blonde hair off her face and said, "If you guys are going to have a meeting, would you kindly take it somewhere else?" She dragged a weary hand across her brow leaving a sooty streak over her left eye. "Madeline, I need your help." She handed Madeline a roller thing. The look on Madeline's face when we abandoned her was pitiful.

Keith and AJ followed me into my office and made themselves comfortable in my visitors' chairs.

"What's up?" AJ casually hooked an ankle across his knee and raked his fingers through his hair; the cowlick at his crown stood straight up again.

"Something happened yesterday. I'm at a loss to explain it."

Keith folded the hockey schedule in half and slipped it into his shirt pocket. He sighed and said, "I'm almost afraid to ask." Keith had reason to be leery; in the last municipal election I'd become entangled with a corrupt politician and Keith made me promise to never, ever, go off half-cocked again. Unfortunately, this was easier said than done. At least for me.

I gave him a reassuring smile and started with Spike showing up at Kirsten's place. When I got to the part about stabbing him with the corkscrew, they both started talking and swearing at once.

"Wait," I held up my hands. "Let me get it all out first, then we can figure out what it means." Then I described how a few weeks earlier Madeline, Louisa, and I had been stalked after the Warhol pillow exhibit.

"Ah, yes," AJ said. "Madeline and her fat ankles."

Keith scratched his eyebrow, bewildered, then looked at me and said, "You know, when you said you needed to talk, I was afraid you were going to launch into a loopy conspiracy theory about the pipeline explosion—"

"Hey, that's not fair."

"Sorry, no, I didn't mean to sound disrespectful." He hesitated a moment before continuing. "All I meant was I know you're frustrated that the TSB report was inconclusive."

"Frustrated doesn't begin to describe it, but while we're

on the topic of inconclusive findings, let's not forget that Jack's pipe, the fragment that could have cleared things up, has disappeared."

AJ chimed in, "And Parka Guy."

"What Parka Guy?" Keith eyes flicked from AJ to me.

Great, now we're freaking him out. I described our road trip to Red Deer and Crystal's description of Parka Guy talking with Michelle and Marty, and how Marty's car disappeared out of the Timmies parking lot and reappeared on the side of a service road after Marty was dead.

AJ leaned forward in his chair, elbows on his knees, and said, "Admittedly, there may be a rational explanation for these events, but we haven't found one yet."

"Don't forget how all this started." I reminded Keith and AJ that the Vesper compressors had been unreliable from day one and Chris Henzel, a Phoenix Board member, was so worried he called Michelle and me to an off-the-record meeting to ensure we understood the gravity of his concern. "Then Elliot Lake blew up and Bannerman wanted me to write a legal opinion with Dave Bryant to mislead the Board."

Keith crossed his arms and considered this for a moment. Finally he said, "Granted, these are troubling facts, but isn't it possible they're a series of random events you're stringing together trying to find an explanation for why Michelle and Marty died? Maybe it was simply a matter of being in the wrong place at the wrong time."

"So why did Spike threaten Kirsten after she contacted me? And why's she worried sick about Phoenix's crappy safety record?" I stopped; it was all I could do not to grab him by the collar and give him a good shake.

"Evie," Keith broke into my thoughts. "Before you do anything rash—"

"I'm not going to do anything rash."

"You know what I mean."

"Yes, I know exactly what you mean."

And that's when I made up my mind. I had intended to show them Michelle's CYA file, but I knew now that Keith would insist I return it to Dave as a matter of professional courtesy or something. Dave was a snake; he didn't deserve any courtesy and I'd be damned if I was going to give up the file. I didn't know how I could use it yet, but it was all I had to stay one step ahead of Bannerman.

A strained silence crept over us. AJ shifted in his chair, then jumped to his feet and in a hearty voice announced he was going to check to see how Bridget was doing with the photocopier.

∗   ∗   ∗   ∗

After dinner, Louisa, Kirsten, and I watched the kids toss a rapidly deflating beach ball at Quincy. They'd gone to the Warhol pillow exhibit that afternoon and perfected the art of bouncing the silvery pillows back and forth. Now they were determined to teach the dog the same trick. Quincy might be a relatively smart dog, but he's stubborn. Once he got his teeth into that beach ball, he refused to let it go. After five minutes of shrieking and cajoling and trashing our once pristine front lawn, the kids trooped back inside with Quincy trotting happily behind them.

They jabbered to Louisa who was busy in the kitchen placing oversized marshmallows into three mugs of hot chocolate. Kirsten took me aside to say the RCMP had called, they hadn't found anything helpful and she was free to return home. "We'll head out tomorrow morning," she said, "after we talk to Ray."

CHAPTER 47

Kirsten and I stood quietly on Ray's doorstep waiting for him to answer the bell. It was early Saturday morning and the air was alive with the sound of chickadees prematurely celebrating the return of spring. Ray lived about twenty minutes from my place, but the drive over felt grim and interminably long.

The doorbell continued to chime, echoing around inside the two-storey glass box that was Ray's foyer. When he saw us through the reinforced glass sidelight, he hesitated, then flashed a tight smile. He was wearing sweatpants and his face was flushed as if he'd just returned from the gym.

Last night when I'd called, he refused to see us, too busy he said. Eventually he relented on the condition that we arrive after Linda left for her morning yoga class and clear out before she returned home.

He unlocked the heavy black door and stepped to one side as it swung open, it was one of those modern doors that pivot on a pole in the middle of the door frame. A plume of icy air floated in behind us. The house reminded me of Kirsten's place but on a massive scale, all light wood, pale marble floors and clean, brightly lit spaces. A floating staircase scissored across the back of the foyer from the basement up to the second floor. A couple of feet above our heads was the enormous blown glass sculpture Ray had purchased in Rome. It rotated slowly on the freezing air currents, casting red and blue tendrils of light in lazy circles across the pale grey walls. It was like being underwater.

Ray led us through to the kitchen and asked us to make ourselves comfortable while he fiddled with the cappuccino machine hissing on the marble countertop. We settled in the kitchen nook, another glass box, this one smaller than the foyer and jutting deep into the garden. It was a pretty winter garden with lots of evergreens of varying shapes and sizes, all covered with a soft blanket of snow.

"I knew your husband, Kevin," Ray said to Kirsten. "He was a good man."

"Yes, he was." Anger flashed behind her eyes. Whatever she'd come to say to him, she wasn't ready to say it yet.

"Counsellor, how have you been? I haven't seen you since, since..."

"Look Ray, let's get right to the point. We need your help."

He shot a wary glance at Kirsten, then back at me. "Sure, whatever I can do."

I took a sip of cappuccino. It was too hot and I pushed it away. Quickly I outlined what I'd learned from Michelle's CYA file: Marty was worried about the Vespers, he'd raised his concerns with Ray who'd ignored them, so he called Michelle. "She wanted to get to the bottom of it... and now they're both dead."

Ray tapped his finger on the side of his cappuccino cup, it wobbled, splattering a few drops of coffee onto the table. He mopped it up with the sleeve of his sweatshirt.

I continued. "AJ and I retraced Michelle's steps the day

she died; she met Marty at Timmies just south of town. It's a regular hangout—"

"Yeah, yeah, I know the place." Ray cut me off.

"Crystal, the owner, saw Michelle with Marty, they met some guy she didn't recognize."

Ray's head jerked up, but he didn't speak.

My eyes strayed to Kirsten who nodded, *go ahead.*

"Ray, a couple of days ago, a thug showed up at Kirsten's place and threatened us with a butcher knife. He knew who we were, Ray. He was there to give us a warning."

"What kind of warning?" Ray's eyelids fluttered but his focus never wavered.

"I don't know. Stay quiet, stop poking around in other people's business, something like that. He was talking about the Elliot Lake explosion, Ray, I'm sure of it."

Ray exhaled. "Fuck."

CHAPTER 48

"Look, whatever you two think you're doing, stop." Ray rose and stood in front of the glass wall, his back to the chilly garden. "Stop now."

"Are you kidding me?" A sudden inexplicable emotion bubbled up in my chest.

He glowered at us, elbows on hips, looking large and intimidating. The veneer of the welcoming host was gone. "Listen to me, both of you. There's a lot riding on the Vespers. You don't mess with these people."

"What people—" I demanded.

Kirsten slapped her hands on the table, the loud, hollow sound echoed in the glassy space. "For the love of God, Ray. Two people died in that explosion. You can't fudge this like you did San Remo."

Ray's eyes became hard, black slits. "What the hell does this have to do with San Remo?"

"Everything!" Kirsten was practically vibrating with rage. "You set Kevin up: a promotion, fast track, what a joke. Kevin was your patsy, your dupe. Anyone with real operational experience would have blown the whistle on you guys the minute they got down there. But Kevin didn't know any better. 'Don't worry Kevin, I've got operations covered,' you said. Then the bloody pipe blew up." She took a deep breath. "Kevin blamed himself, but it was your fault, cutting corners. It's always about the money with you guys, isn't it?"

"Shut up, shut the fuck up!" Ray shouted, looming over us. "Just drop it. Let it go."

It clicked. This wasn't just about the money. Ray was terrified.

"Ray?" He tore his eyes away from Kirsten when I called his name. "Something's happened. What is it?"

His eyes darted to the front door and I was afraid he'd throw us out. He turned to face the garden, so close to the window that his breath fogged the glass. "Someone approached Linda at the gym last week. Some random guy. 'How are you and your lovely daughter doing?' he says. Linda swears she's never seen him before. Then he pulls out his phone and shows her a photo of Olivia walking across the quad at Trinity. They followed her all the way to fucking Ireland!" Ray turned to face us, his head shook a little, like a tremor. "He tells Linda to say hi to her charming husband and that was it."

"Who was it? Are they okay, Linda and Olivia?" I asked.

"Yeah, everyone's fine." He gripped the back of a chair, pulled it out and slumped into it. He looked small as if he'd collapsed into himself. "I told her it was an old college buddy playing a stupid prank." He picked up his cappuccino. The cup trembled in his hand and he had to set it back down again.

I examined his face. There was more. He still hadn't told us everything. "The pipe. The regulator didn't get it because you never gave it to Dave, did you."

Ray exhaled slowly and said, "I destroyed it."

Then, without warning, *whump!* Ray's head jerked up. Kirsten and I froze. Something had smashed into the window and dropped with a plop into the snow. A broken magpie lay lifeless on the other side of the glass.

"Jesus," Ray leapt up. "Damn birds. Always trying to fly through the glass." He yanked at the white muslin curtain, the wooden rings clacked along the rod, shrouding the garden from view. A British nursery rhyme came randomly to mind, something about magpies, one for sorrow.

"You destroyed Jack's pipe?" Kirsten was incredulous. "You finally had a chance to fix this, and you destroyed the pipe. God damn it, Ray! A dozen people dead at San Remo, two dead at Elliot Lake. How many more are going to die before you finally do the right thing?"

He held up his hands. "Stop right there. This isn't like San Remo. The regulators didn't blame Phoenix for the explosion at Elliot Lake."

"They didn't have enough evidence!" Kirsten made a snort of disgust. "You want me to spell it out for you, Ray? Fine. The contractor used a downhand weld on Jack's pipe. This weakened the seam up to the hot-tap tee, but it held because you never ran that piece of pipe at full pressure. Then you installed the Vespers, you cranked up the pressure and the seam burst." She was on her feet, pacing behind me. "Are you with me now, Ray?"

"You always were a damn fine engineer, Kirsten. Understood the laws of physics better than most." Ray gave a rueful laugh. "The Vespers' AI pinpointed the flaw in the weld. We could have fixed it, instead we...we..."

Kirsten finished his sentence for him. "You, Ray, you bypassed the alarms, took the Vespers to full pressure and what, prayed the seams would hold?"

Ray stared over our heads out into the foyer where the glass blob turned slowly around and around. He shrugged. "Something like that."

"Did Bannerman order you to shut off the alarms?" I had to know.

Ray shied away, refusing to meet my gaze. "No... not in so many words."

Of course not, I thought, Bannerman didn't need to order his underlings to do anything. All he had to do was make it clear that their bonuses were gone if they failed to meet his deadline.

"But he knew about the bad welds?"

"He knew about the *possibility* of bad welds," Ray said quietly.

"Possibility, probability; now we're playing word games," I said with exasperation. "You have to tell the TSB what happened."

He flared. "No fucking way."

"Why the hell not?"

"Well, let's see. First, I've got a thug threatening my family, then there's the fact that that fucking contractor worked all across the system... for the last ten years..." Ray went back to the window where he started yanking on the thin white drapes. Was he trying to open them or close them more tightly?

"Surely not everything he touched is defective?" Kirsten said.

"We won't know until we inspect the entire pipeline." He snorted derisively. "You want to see something kill the share price overnight? Tell the market the net-zero Vespers we just installed turned the pipeline into a fucking time bomb."

Ray glanced at his watch. "Linda will be home soon. You have to leave."

He hustled us out into the foyer, pulled our coats out of the closet and all but threw them at us. "You have to go. Now." I was still trying to push my arm into my sleeve when he shoved us out the door. The lock snicked shut behind us and it was as if we'd never been there.

CHAPTER 49

The Mini was an ice box. The hinges groaned as the doors swung open and we slid inside. We struggled to click into our seatbelts, our breath coming in a cold white fog. I turned on the rear window defroster and waited for the glass to clear so I could back out of the driveway.

"Evie, let's go," Kirsten said impatiently. As we looped through the narrow streets, snow fell out of the trees in brittle clumps and shattered on the windshield.

"If Ray won't help us, we'll find another way," I said.

She stared out the front window. "I don't want to talk about it."

"You heard what he said. That pipeline is a ticking time bomb." We slowed at an intersection and I glanced over at her stony face. "Kirsten, this is serious—"

Her face contorted in horror, eyes wide, mouth open in a soundless O. My heart lurched when I glanced back out the windshield. A black SUV on the wrong side of the road was hurtling straight at us. I clutched the steering wheel trying to pull up onto the curb to get out of its way, but a woman with a tiny dog appeared and stepped into the crosswalk directly ahead of us. I blasted the horn and pumped the brakes. She jumped back onto the sidewalk, her dog barking frantically. The Mini bounced off the curb back into the path of the SUV.

I could see the driver—sunglasses, toque low over his face—he was so close. Then he veered sharply back into his own lane. The SUV clipped my headlight with a sickening thud, glass splintered, flying everywhere. The impact spun the Mini around on the ice, flinging me forward, the seatbelt cutting into my throat. We juddered to a stop in the middle of the intersection, pointing back in the direction we'd come. The woman and the little dog were just a few feet behind us, the SUV nowhere to be seen.

"Kirsten! Are you all right?" I popped my seat belt, reaching for her. Her seat belt was pinched across her chest, her head flopped sideways, wedged between the window and the headrest. "Kirsten, can you hear me?"

Someone thumped on my window. The dog lady. "Are you okay?" Her voice was muted on the other side of the glass. The dog barked and barked.

Kirsten bent forward and moaned. "I'm going to be sick." She fumbled with her seat belt, then pushed the door open and tumbled out onto her hands and knees. I staggered out the driver's side, slipped on the ice and caught myself just before I went down. The dog lady was hovering over Kirsten when I reached her. That stupid dog wouldn't stop yelping and whimpering.

"I'll call 9-1-1," the dog lady said.

Kirsten shook her head, no, then threw up. I pulled a Kleenex out of my pocket and told the dog lady we'd be fine. "You sure?" the dog lady said. "You don't look so good to me." I said we lived down the road and she said, "Then I'll take Maurice home, he's had a rough day."

A man and a woman all bundled up and equipped with walking poles materialized by my side. "I'm calling my son," the man said. "He's an EMT."

Kirsten lifted her head. "No, really I'm okay."

But it was too late. The man pointed at a young guy, parka open and flapping, sprinting down the sidewalk. When he arrived, he asked Kirsten a few questions. She insisted she was all right and eventually he let us get back into the Mini.

The fob key in the ignition fired up. "Are you really okay?" I asked. She said now that bloody Maurice wasn't barking his fool head off, she was fine. For some strange reason that made us laugh.

I was wondering what it would cost to repair the head-light when a horrible thought struck me. "We have to go back." I pressed the gas, too hard, and the wheels whined, fighting for traction before we lunged forward.

Kirsten braced herself against the dashboard and her window. "What is it?"

"We have to go back." I pointed in the direction of Ray's house and accelerated. "That SUV—"

"Evie, stop. You're going to get us killed." I continued to accelerate. "I mean it!" she said, "Slow down!"

I careened wide around a corner onto Ray's street. His magnificent modern house was in the middle of the block. The road on both sides was clear. No sign of the SUV.

Kirsten said, "You see? Nothing. Let's go home."

I rolled up into Ray's driveway. A high-pitched keening sound pierced the air. "Come on, come on!" I flung my door open. Kirsten's door opened with a reluctant pop.

As we ran up the front steps the keening grew louder, more wretched.

The massive front door swung open at my touch. "Oh Jesus!"

CHAPTER 50

Ray's wife Linda was crawling around on the floor, her face and hair smeared with blood. Her mouth was open, wailing and gulping for air.

Ray lay on his back, his head turned toward her, eyes still. The enormous glass blob was on top of him, hunched over his body like a glistening glass spider. Its tentacles were buried in his neck, his torso, his thighs. Shiny splinters sparkled on the marble tiles. Blood spatter arced up the grey walls and pooled under the baseboards. His limp body jerked violently; Linda was yanking on his arm, frantically trying to haul him out from under the sculpture.

"Oh God, Oh God, Oh God," Kirsten moaned behind me.

I yelled, "Get her out of here before she cuts herself!" and pulled my phone out of my pocket.

Kirsten half led, half dragged Linda into the kitchen, murmuring nonstop, it's okay, it's okay.

I felt lightheaded, my heart beating too fast as I waited for 9-1-1 to pick up. Look away, look outside, don't look. The glass blob was bathed in sunlight, bouncing red, yellow, and purple prisms off the pale walls, off the floors; off Ray's face. The wall was dirty, smudged with scuff marks. *Why was the door open?*

Linda tried to push past me when I entered the kitchen. I caught her and crushed her in my arms, her blood-soaked top stuck to my open jacket and my sweater. "The police and ambulance are on the way," I said. She allowed me to lead her back to the kitchen island.

Within minutes the foyer was overrun with police and EMT personnel. Men and women talked to each other, mobile radios crackled, rainbow-hued glass crunched underfoot. Everyone moved carefully, watching the shiny glass spikes out of the corners of their eyes as if they might come to life and slice everyone to ribbons.

An officer took Kirsten and me to one end of the kitchen while another questioned Linda. She was shaking so hard she could barely talk. Twenty minutes later we were hustled outside and the officers put Linda into a police cruiser. They'd call us if they needed anything further. "Linda doesn't have anyone here," I called after them as they got into their vehicle. "Her daughter lives in Ireland." Someone assured us they'd take care of her.

We climbed back into my car. The air inside was thick with the scent of blood. Kirsten rolled down her window. Neither of us said a word until we arrived home.

CHAPTER 51

Quincy scrabbled across the tiles at the sound of my key in the lock. Louisa glanced up but the kids didn't budge from their places at the kitchen island, too busy eating grilled cheese sandwiches with pickles. The dog lifted his snout when we entered, sensing the metallic smell of blood. Louisa's smile faded when she saw our grim faces. "Guys," she turned to the kids, "if you finish everything up, I'll make you some cocoa." They cheered and wiggled in anticipation.

As she approached us, she raised her hands and mouthed *what happened?* Keeping my voice low I asked her to go upstairs to get us some clean tops, then led Kirsten downstairs to the basement laundry room where we rinsed our blood-stained garments in the laundry tub and tossed them into the washer.

"Mommy!" Amy shouted from the top of the stairs. "Are you down there?"

"Be right up, sweetie," Kirsten said as she plunged her hands and arms under the faucet. The water ran red, pooling and swirling down the drain. Louisa came downstairs clutching two sweatshirts. Kirsten was pulling one over her head when Amy trundled down the stairs into the laundry room. She froze when she saw her mother's face, there was a smudge of blood at her temple.

"Mommy?" Amy's grey eyes clouded with fear.

I handed Kirsten a damp cloth and pointed to her face. She nodded and explained to Amy that everything was fine. The twins appeared at the top of the stairs, demanding to know what was taking us so long. Louisa ran back up the stairs, distracting them with questions about marshmallows, big or minis for their cocoa. Kirsten shouted up to them. "Finish your lunch, then get your stuff together. We're going home."

Jack groaned, he wanted to take Quincy to the park. Kirsten didn't respond. Louisa was doling out mini marshmallows by the time we got back upstairs. She caught my eye, *what's going on?* I shook my head, *later.*

After lunch when the children were upstairs safely out of earshot, I explained about the SUV running us off the road and returning to Ray's place where we found Ray dead under a six-foot blown glass sculpture. "Kirsten," I said, touching her hand. She pulled away. "You don't need to leave right away. Stay until tomorrow, just to give yourself some time to recover from the shock."

Louisa stared at Kirsten's drawn face and said, "You're not going anywhere until you eat something." With classic efficiency she assembled two more sandwiches and put the kettle on to boil.

Kirsten leaned forward on the counter and dropped her face into her hands. A tiny fleck of blood was stuck under her fingernail. She raised her head and said, "Evie, I'm done. I'm so done. We're going home."

At first, I didn't register what she was saying. "I don't get it," I said. "How could the glass blob fall out of the ceiling? Ray designed the hydraulic lift for a multi-level garage. That stupid sculpture would be child's play for someone with his skills."

Kirsten pushed her sandwich away; she hadn't touched it. She noticed the spot of blood under her fingernail and scratched it off as if it were a drop of paint.

In a faraway voice she said, "Linda thinks it's her fault. The blob"—we were all calling it that now—"was suspended by a mechanism, like a chandelier lift. Ray didn't want the housekeeper falling off the stepladder when she cleaned it so he installed a winch in the attic and put a locking switch in the foyer, it looks like a light switch. All the housekeeper had to do was turn the key to unlock the switch and flick it to lower the blob."

I thought about the foyer, long pale walls, prisms of lights bouncing this way and that. "I didn't see a key."

The sadness on Kirsten's face deepened. "That's because there wasn't one. Linda removed it when her parents came for Christmas. She didn't like the look of it sticking out of the wall. She never got around to putting it back."

Louisa said, "Without the key there was no failsafe. Am I right? The blob would drop down if someone accidentally flicked the switch."

"That explains the marks on the wall," I said. "When we got there the first time, Ray was alone, Linda was out, the place was spotless." Kirsten nodded, remembering. "But when we came back and found Ray"—suddenly my mouth was dry and the words were sticky—"there were scuff marks and smudges on the wall, like someone wearing boots or dirty clothes had brushed against it." As I said it, the pieces fell into place. "That's why the door was open. Someone came to the house, Ray let them in. They fought. In the scuffle someone hit the switch, the glass blob dropped down from the ceiling and crushed Ray."

Kirsten narrowed her eyes; her analytical brain considered the possibility. "Yes, that makes sense."

"We have to tell the police." I reached for my cell phone.

Her face hardened. "No, Evie, we don't." She slipped off her stool and glanced toward the stairs leading up to the bedrooms. "You can do whatever you want, but I'm going to check on the kids, make sure they've got everything, then we're heading home."

"Kirsten, you heard what Ray said about the faulty weld, the hot taps. Phoenix—"

She whirled around, her face close to mine, and hissed, "*Phoenix?* That fucking company destroyed my husband; I'll be damned if it's going to destroy me too."

Louisa shot me a warning glance and I caught myself. Kirsten squared her shoulders, then paused to look at Louisa who was by the sink plopping tea bags into mugs. "Louisa, Evie, thank you both for your hospitality, we'll take the bus back."

Louisa raised her head. "Absolutely not, I'll drive you."

Kirsten protested, the bus would be just fine. Louisa insisted; she enjoyed the kids and wanted to spend as much time with them as possible. Kirsten sighed and accepted Louisa's offer of a lift back to Crisscross.

After Kirsten went upstairs, Louisa became sombre. Slowly she poured boiling water into our mugs and turned to me. "Evie, will you stop pacing around like that? Slow down, for God's sake." She pushed my mug across the counter to me and pressed a spoon into my hand.

I said, "Promise me you'll check the house when you drop them off, make sure there's no one lurking about."

"Yes, yes, of course," she said, "but that's not what I'm

talking about." She sat down beside me, squashing her teabag with a spoon until the steaming water was amber.

It took me a moment to catch her meaning. "*Seriously? We're really going to have this conversation now?*"

"No, we're not having this conversation now. I'm simply sending up a flare. Like we agreed. When you dig in like this, you miss the signals and push too hard. Kirsten just spent the morning trying to keep a hysterical woman away from her husband's lacerated body. This is not the time nor place to lecture her about what she should do in the interests of public safety. You have to back off."

I hadn't thought about it for a long time, but Louisa was right. I had been brutalized in the past; any violent encounter can cloud my judgment. Louisa and I had a pact, she would 'send up a flare' when she thought I was losing perspective. I slumped down beside her at the island.

"Cookie?" She slid the cookie jar closer to me. "Or would you like the other half of my grilled cheese?" Chastised, I picked up her sandwich and took a bite. It was cold and a little greasy.

I harrumphed. "I hate it when you're right."

Louisa smiled and went into the foyer, pulling her parka and boots out of the hall closet. "Why don't you put your feet up and relax until I get back." She checked her phone. "Google says the drive to Crisscross is just over ninety minutes. I'll be back before dinner. Take Quincy for a W-A-L-K or something."

The dog cocked an ear at us, his tail wagged tentatively.

"I think he's learning to spell," I said. Louisa chuckled and equilibrium was restored.

Ten minutes later Kirsten and the kids trundled down the stairs. The boys were shouting and swinging their backpacks around, excited to be heading home. Amy kissed the top of Quincy's head and he had the decency not to bounce up and break her nose.

After they drove off, I sank into the teddy bear velvet sofa in the TV room, pulling a throw over me. It's an angora blend and sheds worse than the dog. Quincy sighed and flopped at my feet. I rubbed my temples, slowly, methodically. I'm the big sister, I'm supposed to set an example for my little sister. And yet Louisa's the steady one, the balanced one, sending up flares to get me back on track when I become too aggressive or too angry.

Drill down, identify the cause of your anger, my therapist had said. Three people were dead: two died trying to prevent a disaster, the third died trying to cover it up. The only person who could fix this mess was the man who created it: Bannerman.

Stalemate.

CHAPTER 52

News of Ray's death spread quickly. By Sunday afternoon it was featured, admittedly as a small story, in all the online media outlets. The reports were brief and singularly uninformative:

> Raymond Montgomery Cook, 46, has been found dead in suspicious circumstances around 11:35 a.m. on Saturday. Homicide detectives are investigating. Anyone who may have home security footage or dash cam footage of any unusual activity in the Mount Royal area should contact police.

Raymond Montgomery Cook. I hadn't known him long but he was a gentle albeit moody man who loved his family. I smiled, remembering his joy at discovering that horrible glass sculpture in Rome. 'Linda's going to love it,' he'd said. Not anymore; she'll cart it to the dump the first chance she gets.

My mind turned to Matteo. Ray described him as a dear friend, I had to let him know Ray was dead. But how? I had Matteo's business contacts through Vesper, but not his personal information. I sent a text to Faro and asked him to relay the news to his client. Faro didn't reply to my text, but it was well past midnight in Rome so that wasn't surprising.

*   *   *   *

Later that evening Louisa placed the cribbage board in the middle of the kitchen table and challenged me to a game. "Come on, it will distract you," she said. The 'tournament' is part of our Sunday evening ritual when Louisa isn't working nights. Dad loved the game and we'd inherited his cribbage board after he died. It's more than fifty years old. When I was small, he told us it was made from honey wood; it had such a luminous warm colour we believed him. Some of the paint was worn off but the red skunk marks were still visible and Louisa was stuck behind the double skunk line. This had never happened before and I was poring over my cards, plotting how to finish her off in one merciless hand, when my phone rang.

"It's Sarah, Michelle's admin, I have to take this."

"Aw what a shame," Louisa said as she plucked her pegs out of the board.

"Oh no you don't, you put those back, we're not done yet." She rolled her eyes and I wandered into the study to take Sarah's call.

Sarah's words were rushed. Dave had dragged her into the office this afternoon to do some urgent work. "I didn't put two and two together until I heard about Ray's death."

My heart quickened and I started pacing again, my reflection gliding smoothly across the glass panes in the French windows. "Start at the beginning."

She took a deep breath. "Dave parked me at my desk, went into his office to make a phone call, then came out and dictated a memo to be sent to all the vice presidents and their direct reports, ASAP."

I stood at the window, peering at my glassy image. "What was in the email?" This really was none of my business.

"He wants them to send him all their files, hard copy and digital, texts, voicemails, anything they have with respect to the Vesper transaction."

When a company gets sued the first thing the lawyers do is lock down anything that could be evidence, just in case an employee decides to destroy relevant information in a misguided attempt to protect the company...or themselves. "Is someone suing Phoenix?" I asked.

"No, the only thing that's changed since Friday is Ray is dead." She hesitated, then said, "Evie, he wants me to pull all the x-rays out of storage."

"For Elliot Lake?"

"For the entire system, starting with Elliot Lake."

All pipeline companies x-ray their welds, it's a regulatory requirement designed to show the welds are up to code. Newer pipelines take spot x-rays, capturing five to ten percent of their welds, but some older companies like Phoenix x-rayed their entire system. If Dave was pulling all the x-rays, he must be worried about the integrity of all the welds. Ray was right, the entire pipeline could be unstable.

Louisa was glaring at her cards when I returned to the kitchen. "I've got garbage," she said. "Go ahead, finish me off." I misread my hand, didn't get the cut, and she crowed as she limped across the double skunk line. That's what happens when you don't keep your head in the game.

CHAPTER 53

I hate it when the law, codified by centuries of learned minds making reasoned decisions, falls flat on its face.

"The law is an ass; did you know that?" I swept into Keith's office. His back was to me, he was rummaging through a messy stack of files on the bookshelf under his window.

He spun around, spluttering. "Jesus, don't sneak up on me like that." I muttered an apology and sank into a chair. He said, "The law is an ass? Are you quoting Dickens or simply expressing your present state of mind?"

Madeline's voice floated over my shoulder before I could reply. "Darlings," she stopped at Keith's door, her long fingers working the square buttons on her Prussian blue coat. "The law is, and forever shall be, an ass." Satisfied with her pronouncement, she floated into her office and shut the door.

"Why is the law an ass?" AJ came up behind me and tapped tentatively on the metal arm of the other visitor's chair. He'd just peeled off his coat and was bristling with static electricity. I leaned away from him to avoid getting zapped.

We usually start the week in Keith's office sharing light-hearted stories about our weekends. But not today. Today I told them about Ray: how he admitted he'd destroyed the pipe, and how he refused to ask the TSB to reopen its investigation, and how a few minutes later he was eviscerated by that monstrous glass squid of a sculpture. "He knew the pipeline was riddled with defective welds but he didn't say anything. And now it's too late."

Keith and AJ quizzed me on the details, how did the blob fall, why was Ray under it.

I raised my voice to focus their attention on the only thing that mattered now. "Did you hear what I said? The Vespers will turn the pipeline into a fucking time bomb. And there's nothing we can do to alert the authorities and shut it down."

"No, that can't be right." AJ turned to me, leaning an elbow on Keith's desk, this knocked a file off the top of a shaky pile. He picked it up off the floor and carefully repositioned it on the stack.

Keith said, "I get that we have an obligation of confidentiality, even to a former client like Phoenix, but this is a threat of imminent death or harm, it's an exception to the rule."

"Yes," AJ said, "the TSB has no discretion here, it must reopen the investigation when presented with material new facts." He held his phone in front of my face and recited a section of the legislation word for word.

"And your 'material new facts' are what, exactly?" I tried not to snap at him, but I'd already gone down this rabbit hole. "Jack's missing pipe fragment and the words of a dead man? Trust me on this. I spent most of the weekend combing through the legislation and rules of conduct." Here Keith's gaze flickered, registering caution. In the past we'd had some rip-roaring arguments about whether a lawyer's conduct, mine in particular, violated the Law Society rules.

Keith pivoted to his computer, clicking the keyboard, while AJ continued to scroll through legislation on his phone. I shook my head. "Without any material new facts to give to the TSB, we can't force them to reopen the investigation... and without Jack's pipe, we've got nothing." I sighed. "The law is an ass."

Keith pulled his eyes away from his computer. "What about Kirsten? She's an engineer, she saw the markings on Jack's pipe. Can't she talk to the TSB?"

"After yesterday, she wants absolutely nothing to do with Phoenix...I can't say I blame her."

I listened as Keith and AJ muttered softly, scanning the same rules, admonitions, and ridiculously naïve statements I'd pored over yesterday. Of course you can report the company's illegal activity to the company lawyer and of course he'll take it up the line to his CEO and the Board and of course they'll drop everything to fix it. *Of course they will.*

Finally AJ set his phone down on Keith's desk and said, "I got nothing." Keith looked up from his computer and shook his head. The stack of files in front of me shuddered and I put my hand on top of the pile to steady it.

"At this point I'm almost ready to buy a full-page ad in the local paper, exposing Phoenix and its benighted Vesper project as a danger to public health and safety."

"What?" Keith's head jerked up with alarm.

"I said *almost* ready. I'm not actually going to do it." Was that true? I didn't know anymore.

My cell pinged. A call from Faro. "Look, I've got to take this." I picked up the call on my way back to my office and Faro blurted out the one question I hadn't anticipated. "Ray didn't commit suicide, did he?"

"Oh my God, Faro, why would you say that?"

"So it's not suicide?" He repeated. "You're sure? Matteo is very worried." The image of Ray pinned under the glass blob; no, definitely not suicide.

"Faro, Ray did not kill himself. Why would Matteo think such a thing?"

Faro exhaled slowly. "Matteo is frantic. He promised Ray that Judy Jango's AI patch would sort out Vesper's reliability problems." There was a pause on the line before he continued. "Evie, you may not know this, but Ray called Matteo about a month ago. The Vespers were acting up again. Ray said he had a lot riding on the successful installation. And Matteo, he wondered whether the pressure was too much and Ray took his own life."

Oh, Faro. Nothing could be further from the truth. I held my tongue and listened while Faro reminisced about Ray, the cowboy with the larger-than-life personality. Then Faro said something that stopped my heart: Bannerman was hosting an Investor Day next week, he'd invited all the heavy hitters, the likes of Goldman Sachs and Morgan Stanley, all the big name analysts and investors, as well as the national and international press, to witness the launch of the world's first net-zero pipeline.

But instead of putting four or five Vespers online and giving them a month to settle, Bannerman was rushing all twenty-six compressors into operation, at the same time, on the same day, putting the entire pipeline under maximum pressure, faulty welds be damned.

Faro was still talking. "Bannerman's invited Matteo to be there as the face of Vesper." He chuckled, "Matteo says he feels like a movie star being trotted out to launch a new makeup line."

"Faro," it came out as a whisper. "We have to stop him."

CHAPTER 54

"Come on, we're going for a walk." Louisa flung a mitten at me, hitting me squarely in the face.

"Stop that!" I said. I was huddled under the throw on the sofa, wallowing in the dark mood triggered by my conversation with Faro.

Whap, another mitten, this one bounced off my chest and onto the floor. Quincy seized it in his jaws and skittered off in the direction of the kitchen. "Now see what you've done," I whined. "It's getting covered in dog slobber."

Louisa assumed a look of fake contrition. "Well, you'd better get it back then, hadn't you, because we're going for a walk."

There's no stopping Louisa when she gets like this. She takes after our mom who would frog march us around the block if she caught us moping or indulging in self pity. *The fresh air will clear your head.* I sighed and crawled off the couch to help Louisa corner Quincy under the kitchen table where I wrestled my soggy mitten out of his mouth.

"Don't forget the Cardinal," Louisa said. It was getting dark and Quincy's new toy, complete with running lights, was a better choice for a nighttime workout than his neon green tennis ball.

The Cardinal was a Christmas present from Faro

to Louisa, they'd been emailing and texting each other since our Drumheller trip. When it arrived, we had no idea what it was. Louisa grabbed the parcel out of my hands, tearing through the sturdy brown butcher paper and dumping plastic packing peanuts all over the floor. Inside the plain blue box, sheathed in bubble wrap, was a delicate red bird nestled in soft pink tissue paper. It looked like blown glass. "A Christmas ornament," I whispered. "It's beautiful."

"No." She picked it up. "It's too heavy." She rummaged through the wrapping paper and found Faro's note. Smiling, she read it aloud: "*When Canadian birds freeze and drop from the sky, this Cardinal will sing for your pleasure.*"

I squinted, trying to decipher the instructions printed on a small pamphlet tucked under the bird. "Huh, what do you know, it's a drone."

We pored over YouTube videos, learning how to operate our little drone before taking it to the playground for its inaugural flight. Louisa jiggled the joystick, jog wheels, and gimbal; within hours she was using it to exercise the dog. Quincy raced up and down the field barking and snapping as the bird swooped low over his head. God help him if he ever caught it and chewed it to bits.

We were heading back to the house, the dog panting from his Cardinal workout, when a black SUV crunched through the frozen snow and eased to a stop under a bright white streetlight. The tinted window whirred down. Bannerman was sitting in the back; in his soft camel coat and red cashmere scarf he looked every inch the pampered CEO. "Good evening, Evie," he said. "Can you spare a minute?"

I peered through the window. "Sure, let's walk." His smile faded at the prospect of leaving the warmth of the

SUV, but I'd be damned if I was going to get trapped in the car with him. Louisa slipped Quincy's toy into one oversized pocket and gripped his lead with both hands. The dog's body stiffened, his ears twitched, sensing my apprehension.

"Louisa," I said, "why don't you take the dog home." She started to say something. I held up a hand, *it's okay.*

"I'll give you five minutes." Her eyes never left Bannerman's face. "It's too cold to be standing around out here." She tugged on Quincy's leash, half dragging, half walking him back to the house. I turned smartly and marched up the sidewalk toward the small park at the end of the cul-de-sac. For a moment I thought Bannerman wouldn't follow, then I heard the car door creak open and thunk as it slammed shut. The SUV's engine revved once or twice, but the car did not move.

I stopped to give Bannerman a moment to catch up. He lost his footing, slipped and caught himself. His expensive brown leather shoes were totally unsuitable for this climate. It didn't help that my neighbours did a terrible job of shoveling their walks, there were icy skiffs of snow all over the place. "Careful," I said. "You don't want to fall and break a hip." He glowered at me.

The tip of his nose was red by the time he came abreast of me. I hadn't noticed it before but in my winter boots we were roughly the same height. I continued walking but at a slower pace so he could keep up. Tiny white puffs swirled about his head as he spoke. He talked about Ray's death, such an unfortunate accident, the company life insurance plan was excellent, his wife Linda and his daughter would be well cared for. He peered at me out of the corner of his eye. "I understand you and that other woman saw Ray the morning it happened..."

We stood on the pavement next to the little park sandwiched between the cul-de-sac and the river. The river runs behind my house then curls around a bend to flow past the park and down to the weir. In the summer it's packed with kids noisily launching canoes and rubber rafts but in the winter it's quiet, the ice is too unpredictable for skating.

"I'm sorry, what were you saying?" I asked.

Bannerman tried again, this time phrasing it as a question: Had my friend, Christine, Kirsten, whatever her name was, and I seen Ray the morning he died? Yes, I said, Kirsten and I had coffee with Ray that morning. A small line appeared between his eyes as he stared across the river at the snowy escarpment on the other side. The terrain was steep, just like the slope behind my house. The City leaves it in its natural state, the gradient being too sharp for fussy flower beds and lawn mowers.

"Interesting," he said, "any particular reason for the visit?"

It was the studied nonchalance of the question that gave him away. If I'd had any lingering doubts whether Bannerman knew about the danger posed by the faulty welds, they were gone now.

Litigation. The word popped into my head. I stopped in my tracks, surprised I hadn't figured it out sooner. Bannerman was two steps ahead of me before he realized I was no longer moving, he turned, waiting for me to catch up.

I had it now. Dave dragged Sarah into work the Sunday Ray died because he was worried about litigation. Not litigation arising from the Elliot Lake explosion—Phoenix paid off anyone who'd made a claim for compensation—but litigation that could arise in the future. Dave was scouring the electronic and hard copy files looking for two things: references to damning x-rays that would prove the welds were unsafe, and incriminating internal correspondence that showed Bannerman was aware of the danger and was determined to launch the Vespers anyway. This evidence, like the evidence in San Remo, had to disappear.

I rubbed my mittens together—the wind had picked up, gusting snow crystals around the streetlights—and fixed Bannerman with a cynical eye. "You're wondering if Ray told us about the cost-benefit analysis, aren't you?" Bannerman's gaze hardened, then he glanced down, tugging one soft leather glove over an exposed wrist. *Gotcha!*

Like the profit-driven CEOs who'd gone before him, Bannerman was ruthless. He'd run the numbers and calculated it would be cheaper to risk an explosion here and there and pay out millions in lawsuits than pull the entire pipeline out of service to repair the defective welds.

He assumed a bland expression. "I'm not following you."

"Oh, I think you are. It's the Ford Pinto case, the exploding gas tanks, all over again. Ford's CEO decided it was cheaper to pay the lawsuits than recall the cars and spend a few bucks to fix the faulty gas tank design."

I braced for an onslaught of denial and righteous indignation. Instead, Bannerman continued to stare at me. Thoughtfully. As if he were making yet another careful calculation.

He rubbed his smooth lambskin glove along his jaw. "You know," he said slowly, "sometimes we don't pay people what they're worth. An unforgiveable oversight on our part. You've done fine work for the company. This might be a good time to revisit your retainer. I'm sure we could come to a satisfactory arrangement."

That's when I lost it. "Are you fucking kidding me? You want to buy my silence?"

Immediately he realized his mistake. He'd interpreted my reference to paying off litigants as a signal that I'd stay quiet if he made it worth my while. In Bannerman's world everyone has a price.

His sharp black eyes flicked around my face, recalibrating the situation: if he couldn't buy me off, what did I know? Had Ray told us something significant?

I should have left it there, but the words tumbled out before I could stop them. "So what are you going to do now, send someone to kill me too?"

He froze, his face almost as grey as the dusky sky, and gazed at me with such intense malevolence that I stepped back. Then without another word he stalked off toward the heated cocoon of his car.

CHAPTER 55

It was Monday morning and Kirsten watched as the twins charged out of the SUV, grabbing their backpacks and flinging hasty goodbyes over their shoulders to Amy and their mother. She hadn't seen them this excited to go to school in a long time. She'd refused to let them out of the house all weekend, afraid they'd come to harm, and they were bristling with pent-up energy. Kirsten knew it was irrational, an overreaction to Ray's death, and resolved to do better. She turned to Amy who was humming to herself in the front seat.

"What do you think, sweetie, did you want to stop at the playground before we go home?"

The little girl bounced out of the SUV and was halfway to the swings before Kirsten finished unclipping her seat belt. They can't get away from me fast enough these days, she thought.

"Slow down!" Kirsten shouted as Amy flung herself into a swing, scrabbling her bulky boots across the frozen gravel to set it in motion.

"At least she's not on the flying fox," Kirsten muttered under her breath. The school debated for months about ripping out the pint-sized zipline. It was too flimsy to support the big kids who hung on until they were dragged through the gravel on their knees, and too complicated for the little ones who couldn't release the hand grip fast enough to avoid smacking face-first into the support pole on the opposite side. The damn thing sent kids to the ER on a regular basis.

If we can't protect our kids on the playground, how the hell are we going to protect them from exploding pipelines?

Kirsten was uneasy about her decision to walk away. Ray confirmed that nothing had changed at Phoenix since San Remo. The company cared more about profits than people. Evie wanted to keep fighting and Kirsten had left her in a lurch. No, she couldn't go through it all over again. She wouldn't allow Phoenix to smother her, to drag her down, deep into the shadows like the last time, after Kevin died.

"Push me, Mommy!" The swing's chain was twisted and Amy was spinning around in lazy circles, the tips of her boots carving arcs in the icy gravel.

Kirsten pulled her gloves out of her pockets and slipped them on. The playground was tucked into a grove of trees behind the school, sheltered from the cutting wind, but still the air was cold and harsh. How far was the pipeline from here? She hadn't seen any pipeline markers along the property line, so it wasn't directly beneath her feet⊠ assuming the markers had been properly situated in the first place.

Kirsten positioned herself behind Amy, watching a young woman enter the far corner of the playground. She was carrying a small child in a baby carrier strapped to her chest. They were heading this way.

"Push me high!" Amy squealed. Her quilted mittens gripped the chains, her clumsy boots kicked energetically back and forth.

Kirsten bent down to adjust Amy's jacket across her

back. "There, now you're not hanging out all over the place. Ready?"

The little girl giggled.

"Are you *sure* you're ready?"

Amy shrieked and Kirsten pulled the swing way back. "Hang on tight." The swing was suspended for a brief moment, like a memory floating in the air, then Kirsten pushed it out with a mighty shove. Amy swooped down in a magnificent arc. On the opposite side she leaned into the chains and flung her arms wide open. "I'm flying, I'm flying!"

The young woman with the baby stood shyly to one side, watching Amy sail back and forth. She said hello and sat down in the next swing, adjusting the baby carrier to settle the infant more comfortably. "Hi," she said, "I'm Samantha. And this is Liam." Liam was wearing a shiny hooded snowsuit. He looked like a miniature astronaut with teddy bear ears. "We don't like being cooped up in the house, do we Liam?"

Kirsten introduced herself and Amy shouted hello. The little boy's bright blue eyes followed Amy as she swooped up and down beside him. Samantha moved her swing gently back and forth.

"Amy?" Kirsten called out. "Ready to go higher? Hang on tight." Amy bobbed her head and her red hood slipped down to her shoulders. She chortled as she soared up into the dove-grey sky.

"Were we ever that carefree?" Samantha asked, tugging one small boot back onto Liam's foot. Samantha said she'd recently moved to town from the east coast. Her husband had landed a good job with an oil service company. "Don't ask me what he does, something to do with moving equipment around." They'd arrived just before the Elliot Lake explosion. "Please tell me that sort of thing isn't a regular occurrence around here. It scared the living daylights out of me"—she glanced down at the toddler in her lap— "and Liam. We thought it was an earthquake or something... then we saw the pictures on TV..."

Is it a regular occurrence? No, but it could be. "It's the first time it's happened since we've been here," Kirsten said. The memory of the ominous vibration under the lake hit her so hard, she gasped.

Samantha looked down at Liam and stroked his downy cheek. "I've become such a worrier since this little guy was born." Liam's eyelids fluttered. He was almost asleep. "My husband says I'm being silly."

Not really. Kirsten shook her head, trying to dispel images of fireballs, explosions, charred bodies. Pipelines covered the province like a spiderweb, snaking under roads, next to schools and hospitals, worming their way deep into quiet neighbourhoods.

Amy's swing was slowing down. "Again!" she demanded.

"No more," Kirsten said, "we have to be on our way."

Amy twisted around in the swing, her face crinkled in disappointment.

"Is that a bunny nose?" Kirsten asked with a pretend scowl.

Amy pressed her lips together, fighting off a smile. Kirsten crossed her arms and made a serious face. "Did you just give me a bunny nose?"

Amy laughed and Samantha laughed with her. Liam stirred but didn't awaken. Kirsten reached over to the baby, taking his small mittened hands in her own. "Goodbye little Liam, I hope I see you again soon." She gave Samantha her phone number and suggested they meet up for coffee at the Cozy Coyote Café, then hustled Amy into the SUV.

"We have a busy day ahead of us," Kirsten said as she pulled out her phone and dialed a number. After she finished her call, she checked Amy's seat belt and tweaked the little girl's rosy cheeks.

"Okay, let's go. We've got things to do, people to see." She started the ignition and backed out of the school parking lot.

"Which people?" Amy asked.

"The Heart Lady."

∗   ∗   ∗   ∗

Kirsten went home to pack: two days of clothes for everyone. She picked up the boys after school and dropped them off at Gretchen's place. Jack didn't like the idea at first, complaining it wasn't fair that Amy got to visit Quincy and they were being left behind. He stopped fussing when Gretchen promised to take them up into the restaurant's attic. In addition to the coyote she had a stuffed owl and some kind of weasel-y thing up there. She offered to babysit Amy as well but Kirsten wouldn't hear of it.

Traffic was slow for a Monday and Kirsten didn't reach Evie's place until after dinner. Evie flung open the door, pulling Kirsten and Amy into a tight embrace. Amy giggled at Quincy who pushed his fat head into her tummy, begging for a rub. After Amy finished a glass of water and a cookie, Kirsten carried her and her favourite stuffie, a bedraggled rabbit, upstairs to bed.

Evie set two wine glasses on the kitchen island while she waited for Kirsten to come back downstairs.

The high-rise towers sparkled across the river. Kirsten returned to the kitchen and picked up her wine glass, "Ah, this is exactly what I needed." Her deep brown eyes locked into Evie's. "Right, what's the plan?"

CHAPTER 56

I raised my glass to Kirsten. "You're the plan."

Her eyebrows shot up. "Okay, take me through it."

I thought back to when I told Faro everything: how we'd found Jack's pipe and how Ray admitted the entire pipeline could be riddled with faulty welds that would rupture, sooner or later, after the Vespers went online.

"Bannerman knows?" Faro was incredulous. "He knows and he's going ahead with the launch anyway?" He made a choking sound; the words were sticking in his throat. "I will inform Matteo and get back to you."

I had filled the slow, anxious days waiting for Faro's call developing a plan. If Bannerman wanted to put on a show for Investor Day, then by God, I'd give him one, but I needed Matteo's participation and Faro had made it clear that Matteo would not become involved until he talked to Kirsten. I was jotting down all the reasons why Kirsten should agree to talk with him when she called. "Evie, I'm in. I'll do whatever it takes to stop that bastard." And a couple of hours later she and Amy appeared on my doorstep.

I took a small bowl of hummus out of the fridge and set it on a cutting board next to a package of pita bread. Kirsten shook her head. "No, really, I'm not hungry."

"All the more for me then," I laughed. I always eat

when I'm stressed. What I was asking Kirsten to do would put her squarely in Bannerman's cross hairs.

I cut the pita into eight skinny slices. Scooping up a garlicky glob of hummus I joined her at the island. "You need to see something." Faro had sent me Bannerman's Investor Day agenda. "Bannerman is taking the Vespers, all of them, live on Thursday."

"What?" She grabbed the agenda out of my hand, reading the first line aloud: *9:00 to 10:00 Media event—Vespers Go Live (open to all).*

I could hear Bannerman's spiel now: sure, there had been a few hiccups. Elliot Lake came online last September only to experience a 'rupture' in November. But the TSB's report, issued in January, exonerated Phoenix, and now at the end of March all twenty-six Vespers were ready to go live. Behold: The launch of the world's first net-zero pipeline.

Kirsten crumpled the agenda into a tight ball. "This is insane. Bannerman knows the risks."

"He knows there is a risk," I said. "What he doesn't know is the timing or magnitude of the risk. Will every weld burst the minute the Vespers go online? Likely not. He's gambling he'll have a couple of weeks, maybe more, to take advantage of the bump in share price, then cash out and disappear."

"How do you know that?"

"I don't, I'm guessing based on what I've seen of the man." Michelle's CYA file described Bannerman as a reckless risk taker who was financially over-extended. He'd be prepared to play the odds in return for a big payoff.

Kirsten reached for a pita slice and smeared it with hummus, gnawing on it like a piece of cardboard. "Where do I fit in?"

I pulled the wine bottle closer and topped up our glasses. "Tomorrow we have a conference call with Faro and Matteo. Matteo wants to hear your story firsthand." She tipped her head like a small bird. "Kirsten, you need to start with San Remo. I know it will be rough, but you have to convince him that Bannerman is a reckless man, that he's more than prepared to plow ahead with the Vespers, regardless of the risks, because he has a history of putting profits over people."

She popped the pita in her mouth, then fixed her deep brown eyes on me for a long moment. Finally she said, "Yes, I can do that."

I brought my hands to my face and rubbed my eyes, pressing hard to keep the tears at bay.

"Evie?" Kirsten's voice was gentle. "What is it?"

"Just stress. Stress and relief." I flashed an optimistic smile. If Kirsten could get Matteo on board, I would do the rest.

Kirsten raised her glass and clinked it to mine. I picked up what was left of the hummus and pita and carried it into the TV room so we could sit by the fire. Quincy curled up like a fat sausage at Kirsten's feet. His ears pricked up when her phone pinged. She clicked on a text, smiled, and handed me her phone. It was a picture of Jack and a motheaten stuffed weasel. Both of them had their eyes crossed.

CHAPTER 57

Tuesday morning is garbage pick-up day at the office. A large beetle-shaped truck wheezed and clanked in the parking lot as it lifted the bin over its shoulders and banged out the contents. We don't have much real garbage anymore. Bridget knows exactly what goes into which bin and God help those who don't follow the rules. Even Madeline is resigned to trudging into the coffee room with anything that belongs in the compost bin. Kirsten, Amy, and I weaved around the garbage truck and past the wooded hill that rises at the edge of the parking lot into the building.

The call was booked for 8:00 a.m. and we had a half an hour to kill. We found Keith milling about in the coffee room. He introduced himself to Kirsten, stooped to shake hands with Amy, then watched, bemused, as I rifled through the stationery supplies in search of photocopy paper and coloured markers to keep Amy entertained for the next hour and a half.

Amy was sitting at my desk, humming to herself as she taped sheets of paper together, when Kirsten and I went down the hall to the conference room. The sound of a snowplough grinding down the street gave way to voices in the reception area. AJ, Bridget, and Madeline had arrived. Madeline gave a small shriek of dismay as she passed my office. She poked her head into the conference room and said, "Are you aware there's a child parked behind your desk?"

Bridget bustled past Madeline to the stationery supply cupboard and returned with multi-coloured streamers fluttering in her wake. "You can't expect a child to amuse herself with whiteboard markers," she scolded. Madeline looked at her, nonplussed, then disappeared into her office, no doubt hoping that Amy would be gone by the time she resurfaced.

AJ strode into the conference room. "Hi," he said, "I just met Amy. What a cute kid." AJ is one of the few men I've met who isn't intimidated by small children. Kirsten's smile widened. When he shook her hand, a small spark of static electricity crackled between them. I'm not sure what it is about AJ, but the man is a human lightning rod. "Let us know how it goes," he said as he strolled to his office.

Kirsten and I sat at the far end of the table, facing the large screen on the opposite wall. Behind us, cold air lay heavy on the windowpane and the wind picked up, sprinkling ice crystals against the glass.

This was going to be a tricky conversation.

I had to convince Matteo to back me in saying the Phoenix pipeline was so unsafe that launching the Vespers would make the Deepwater Horizon catastrophe look like a firecracker. And we had to do that without creating the impression that the source of the problem was the Vespers themselves.

I glanced at Kirsten as we waited for Matteo and Faro to come on the line. She sat ramrod straight. She'd brought nothing to the meeting other than her searing memories of San Remo and Elliot Lake. I pulled up my yellow pad and made a few notes, but soon the page was filled with stars and wavy lines; what do doodles reveal about the doodler, I wonder.

Faro and Matteo appeared on the big screen. *Here we go.* They were seated at a wooden table with sunlight streaming over their shoulders from tall windows behind them. It looked like the meeting room at the Vesper plant in Salerno. I introduced Kirsten.

Faro wore a light blue tailored suit while Matteo was casually dressed in a cream-coloured polo shirt that set off his swarthy complexion and curly black hair. If either of them smiled, it happened so quickly I missed it. This was the first time we'd met without Ray's boisterous presence and the room felt strangely empty. We talked a little about Ray and how much we missed him. Then after a hollow pause, it was time to begin.

"Matteo," I said, "Although I represented Phoenix in the Vesper transaction, I'm not here today in the capacity of Phoenix's lawyer. Kirsten and I are simply concerned citizens. We're extremely worried about the stability of the Phoenix pipeline once the Vesper compressors go online."

When I mentioned the Vespers, Matteo leaned forward, pushing a large black ashtray to one side. Its presence on the table was jarring; I wondered whether either of them smoked or it was simply an artifact left behind many years ago.

I continued. "Kirsten is a pipeline engineer. She worked for Phoenix many years ago, her husband was in charge of the San Remo operations when that pipeline failed. She's familiar with Phoenix's operations and has information that will shed light on the cause of the Elliot Lake catastrophe."

Matteo interrupted. "Faro briefed me," he said. "These are very serious allegations; Ray was an excellent engineer.

Now that he's gone, he can't defend himself against accusations of unprofessionalism...or worse."

We knew this would be difficult for Matteo. He and Ray worked together and partied together, bent on achieving a common goal; the bond of mutual trust and respect was strong.

He took a deep breath and continued. "That being said, Ray called me a month ago. The Vespers were acting up, he said, nothing serious, but trending in the wrong direction. My team combed through the Judy Jango test results. We are convinced the Vespers are solid, even more so now with the AI patch." He cleared his throat. "I told Ray the Vespers are not the source of his problem. Now Faro tells me you have a theory."

So far Matteo had held his emotions in check, but he winced at the suggestion that Ray had not been honest with him. He knew Ray much better than he knew me; which of us would he believe? He stared into the camera. I had to make him focus his anger not on me, not on Ray, but on the person who deserved it, Bannerman.

To do that, Matteo had to hear Kirsten's story, starting with the San Remo explosion and ending with the threat to Ray's family, which in Ray's mind gave him no choice. He'd launch the Vespers knowing full well they could transform hundreds of miles of towns and villages into a death zone.

I asked Matteo for his patience, then nodded at Kirsten. "I believe you're up."

Kirsten lifted her chin. In a voice devoid of emotion she explained how Phoenix's decision to cut corners created the horror of San Remo and drove her husband to suicide. Then she moved on to the day she took her children skating at Elliot Lake and the pipeline exploded under the ice. She described how her son Jack found a pipe fragment that, in her opinion and likely Ray's, proved the seam had been improperly welded and would burst once the pressure increased beyond a certain point.

Matteo shook his great curly head. "No," he said, "that can't be right. The pressure can't increase because Vesper's AI shuts down the compressors if it senses the pipe is unsafe."

"Matteo," I interjected. "Ray told me and Phoenix's Chief Legal Officer that he'd shut off the alarms. He told Kirsten and me on the day he died that he interfered with the AI. He overloaded the system, the weld didn't hold... and Elliot Lake exploded."

Matteo inhaled sharply. "This useless contractor? He worked all over the pipeline?"

"Yes, that's what Ray said."

"Bannerman knows?"

I nodded. "Ray said as much the day he died." Matteo clasped his hands under his chin and closed his eyes. Faro glanced at him but didn't speak.

"Matteo," I said gently. "Ray also said a thug threatened his wife and daughter. You know how much he loved his family. Sadly, he thought this was the only way to protect them." In my heart I now believed this to be true. Ray exploited the grey zone when it came to buying exotic cars, but he'd never endanger the public, not unless he thought he had no choice.

They sat very still for a moment and I wondered whether the screen had frozen. But then the screen flashed and brightened as a shadow passed in front of the sun.

Matteo spoke quietly. "How could he live with himself?" It was a rhetorical question.

I explained my plan for Investor Day. Sarah had

confirmed the kick-off media event was open to all employees; I would use the crowd to slip in. Matteo would already be there, having been invited by Bannerman. Then if everything went well, I could discredit Bannerman without trapping Matteo and his company in the backlash.

Matteo cocked his head when I finished. He spoke to Faro in rapid Italian for a few minutes. I willed myself to stay still, not to interrupt. There was nothing more I could do. Either Matteo would help us or he wouldn't.

Finally, Matteo turned back to the camera. His lips parted and he laughed.

CHAPTER 58

Two days later at 8:40 in the morning Kirsten, Amy, and I were battling our way through a pack of angry protestors blocking the entrance to the Phoenix building. It was clear from their placards they didn't believe Bannerman was truly committed to net-zero. Given the conduct of some of the major energy companies—lots of lip service, little meaningful action—their skepticism was understandable.

A police van was parked across the street but there wasn't a cop in sight. The media trolled the sidewalk searching for someone, anyone, to drop a pithy quote. The mood was chaotic and I wondered, not for the first time, whether it would have made more sense to leave Amy at home with Louisa. But after our encounter with Spike, Kirsten refused to let Amy out of her sight, so here we were jostling our way through the revolving glass doors to hear Bannerman announce the company's leap into a net-zero future.

Inside, the air crackled with anticipation as reporters, employees, and Investor Day attendees got their bearings and slowly funnelled into the auditorium. I need not have worried about Amy, she grinned as if she were entering a circus tent, and in all the excitement no one paid the least bit of attention to the little girl in the red snowsuit inching her way into the room.

The auditorium was designed like a small concert hall, complete with a state-of-the-art stage facing rows of seating which banked steeply up to the back wall. It could seat about two hundred from the looks of it. The first row was reserved for the press, who'd come from all over the world to report the biggest story of the year. The analysts, investment bankers, executives, and employees were free to sit wherever they liked. I scanned the crowd searching for Matteo and Faro, fearful that Matteo may have changed his mind, and finally spotted them taking their seats at the far end of the second row.

Wires secured with duct tape snaked under the seats to a standing microphone positioned in the middle of the apron separating the stage from the audience. Distracted by a flickering image at the back of the stage, a stylized phoenix glowing red in the darkness, Amy tripped on a thick electrical cord. We climbed higher up the stairs to the back row.

The auditorium lights dimmed when Bannerman crossed the stage and walked into the spotlight illuminating the podium. The phoenix on the back wall spread its wings, throwing bursts of sparks across the blue-black screen.

Amy complained that she couldn't see anything and Kirsten hoisted her up onto her lap. "That's not a dragon," Amy whispered, pointing at the logo.

"No, darling, it's a bird. Now hush, I want to hear this."

The podium mic made a muffled thump when Bannerman picked it up. He looked dapper and confident in his dark blue suit and brilliant white shirt. He patted his hair, his scalp gleaming in the yellow light, and welcomed the crowd with a wide smile. "Thank you all for joining me on this historic day: the day Phoenix spreads its wings and leads the world into a net-zero future."

Behind him the phoenix burst into flame; sparks floated across the screen before coming together in brilliant red streaks that slowly formed a shape. The audience held its breath. Was that the new company logo?

"That's not a dragon," Amy repeated.

She was right. The phoenix was still a phoenix but with razor-sharp claws and blazing outstretched wings.

Amy squirmed in her mother's lap. "I don't like him."

"Shhh!" Kirsten patted Amy's hair.

Bannerman stepped to one side of the podium and directed our attention to the big screen behind him. The phoenix faded and an image of a Vesper compressor appeared in its place. The Vesper gleamed, a gargantuan jet engine with sharp blue blades. "This is a Vesper compressor, one of twenty-six state-of-the-art compressors we've installed across our system. This will transform Phoenix into the world's first net-zero pipeline. Today we become the first and only pipeline company on the planet to meet climate change head-on."

Sounds of applause, awe, and excitement from the audience.

Bannerman moved on to a few simplified drawings, arrows tracking natural gas entering the compressor system, greenhouse gases being siphoned off, and clean natural gas exiting the plant, then he shifted his pitch. Technical jargon was too much for the media, analysts, and investors. Let's tell them something they'll all understand: this transformation will make Phoenix piles of money. After ten minutes of glowing financial predictions he stopped, inviting questions from the press.

If I've learned one thing from my colleagues at the criminal bar, it's this: The art of seeding doubt starts with a seemingly innocent question. As the mob of reporters scrambled for the microphone, I edged down the stairs and fell in behind them. As luck would have it my turn at the mic came right after *The Guardian* reporter who asked about the Transportation Safety Board's investigation of the Elliot Lake explosion. Bannerman deflected the question with ease, but his smile faded when the reporter stepped away, revealing me at the mic.

"Ms. Valentine. Unless you're a member of the press, you must step aside."

"No," I smiled at the reporters. "I'm not with the media, I'm an investor. This is Investor Day, isn't it?" Madeline, bless her heart, reminded me that our firm's savings plan included investments in mutual funds which in turn invested in Phoenix and other energy companies.

While Bannerman shifted his weight from one foot to the other, considering how to respond, I gripped the mic.

"Just one quick question, Mr. Bannerman. The Vesper compressors require extremely high pressure to deliver net-zero natural gas; what steps has Phoenix taken to ensure the pipeline can withstand this increased pressure?"

This was the hook.

He looked thoughtful, no doubt running through various canned answers the legal and PR departments had vetted for him. Before he could respond Matteo rose from his seat at the end of the second row, making eye contact with Bannerman who smiled broadly and said, "That's a good question. The pipeline's SCADA system is integrated into the Vesper's AI. Matteo Vianelli, Vesper's CEO, is here with us today. He can explain the Vesper's safety protocols much better than I can."

The line.

Matteo played it out, thanking Bannerman for the opportunity to address the question and turning to face the reporters. "Yes, that is correct, the Vespers require extremely high pressure. When we tested the prototype at Elliot Lake, the pipeline experienced a dangerous pressure surge. The Vesper's AI technology will trigger alarms and automatically cut off gas flow to reduce pressure before the pipeline can become unstable." Matteo grimaced. "To put it bluntly, our software stops the pipeline from exploding."

Bannerman's smile froze, but Matteo wasn't finished yet. He gestured up at Bannerman and said, "As long as no one interferes with the alarms or the Vesper's AI, the Vespers will operate in an entirely safe manner."

Faro sat next to Matteo. His head was bowed, he was nodding. He and I had worked on Matteo's answer for hours to keep it accurate and so simple that even the thickest reporter would understand what was coming next.

The sinker.

I stepped back up to the mic. "Mr. Bannerman, can you, as Phoenix's CEO, confirm that the company has not in the past and will not in the future do anything to interfere with Vesper's failsafes in any way that would make the pipeline unstable or cause it to explode?"

The seconds ticked by as the implications of my question sank in.

The reporters focused on cause and effect. If Bannerman launched the Vespers today and the pipeline exploded anywhere on the system, the first thing they'd ask was did Phoenix interfere with Vesper's failsafes?

The investors focused on a different issue: the security of their investments.

Bannerman was skewered. It's one thing to ask your pet lawyer to conceal evidence that would harm your position in a lawsuit. It's quite another to lie to Goldman Sachs and Morgan Stanley and Credit Suisse; double cross them and they'll destroy you.

Bannerman shot me a venomous look; his fingers drummed the edges of the podium. "Today is about the future, not the past—"

"Elliot Lake?" The reporter from *The Guardian* cut in. "Mr. Bannerman, a follow-up question please. Can you comment about the 'dangerous pressure surge' at Elliot Lake as described by the CEO of Vesper, specifically whether Phoenix interfered with Vesper's failsafe mechanisms?"

The media scrum bubbled with excitement. They'd come to cover a great story about the future of net-zero and now realized there could be even more to the tragedy at Elliot Lake.

Bannerman frowned, glanced at his watch, and said as much as he'd like to chat about hypotheticals, it was time to move on to the Investor Day part of the agenda, which was for invited guests only. He shifted his gaze to someone standing in the shadows at the edge of the stage. A lean wiry man emerged. A security guard to shoo us all out? He loped down the short flight of stairs from the stage to the apron, raised a hand, pointing to the auditorium doors.

That's when Amy let out a piercing cry.

CHAPTER 59

Amy was curled into a tight ball in her mother's lap, shrieking and rocking back and forth. The young woman beside Kirsten reached out and touched Amy's shoulder. The little girl screamed and twisted away, burying her face in Kirsten's neck.

Kirsten held Amy tightly, whispering in her ear, then lifted her head, anxiously scanning the room. Amy's anguished cries roiled the crowd who reacted with confusion and alarm. *What is it? What's happening?*

The wiry man summoned by Bannerman extended his arms wider like a bouncer corralling a bunch of unruly drunks, then stopped in front of the mic and looked right through me. Pale, watery eyes, dirty red hair. Bannerman's bodyguard. *Spike.*

A jolt of anger shot through me. I had to protect them. I turned, plowing through the media scrum back up the stairs. Kirsten was struggling to her feet with Amy clinging to her neck. Spike turned away, shoving the reporters toward the auditorium doors. They continued yelling questions, "Mr. Bannerman! Mr. Bannerman!" but Bannerman had disappeared into the shadows at the side of the stage. Spike banged the doors open, forcing the reporters out into the lobby.

Investment bankers and analysts gathered in confused

clumps, glancing up at the now vacant stage, leaning in to talk to each other. One demanded to know what the fuck was going on.

Finally I reached Kirsten who was trying to push past the people blocking her aisle. "We're leaving!" she yelled to me.

Just as Amy lifted her tear-stained face to look at her mother, a shrill noise pierced the air, ricocheting off the auditorium walls. Bright white lights started flashing high in the ceiling. Amy squeezed her eyes shut and pressed her hands over her ears. Kirsten wrapped her arms around her daughter and edged past me.

Confusion overwhelmed the room. "Fire drill? Is it a fire drill?"

A metallic voice came over the intercom: *There's been an incident. Proceed to muster stations. This is not a drill. Repeat. This is not a drill.*

Kirsten hoisted Amy higher on her hip. I stayed close as we pressed through the mob of people filing down the stairs and piling up in front of the stage. Some were panicking, blocking the exit. Others milled about, dazed and frightened. With grim determination we pressed forward, squeezing through the doors, only to be overwhelmed by the mayhem in the lobby.

"Kirsten, be careful," I yelled. "He could still be out here."

The alarms were so loud I didn't hear her reply.

CHAPTER 60

The lobby was jammed, the crowd heaving with fear and confusion. A group of placard-waving protesters had forced their way past the security guards, their chants adding to the din. Employees poured out of the stairwells, pooling in front of the elevators. A barefoot woman clutching her pumps was doubled over next to the security desk. Her friend took her arm, urging her to keep moving.

"Kirsten?" I turned but she was gone.

The security desk was mobbed. People demanded information; the hapless guard simply repeated what the robotic voice on the intercom was saying: Proceed to muster stations.

Outside, protestors thumped the glass curtain wall singing something no one could hear. Two firetrucks roared up in front of the building, lights strobing and sirens blaring. Firefighters scrambled down from their trucks only to be engulfed by the protesters who appeared to think they'd been sent to break up the rally.

Inside, the crowd became more agitated. *Muster stations? What muster stations?* A handful of employees decked out in red hard hats and reflective vests appeared, shouting and waving their arms, desperately trying to get everyone's attention.

There! I caught a glimpse of Amy's golden head bob-bing on Kirsten's shoulder as she plowed through the crowd. They made it to the revolving door on the far side of the lobby and disappeared outside.

Three sets of revolving doors faced the street. Peo-ple rushed across the lobby, piling up in front of each door, unable to pass through. The crowd behind them pressed forward, desperate to escape. A woman screamed. A revolving door was jammed. "Stop," someone yelled, "her hand, she's stuck!" One exit blocked; the mob stam-peded to the two remaining revolving doors. Shoving and screaming. It was hopeless. My heart beat loudly in my ears. I cast around for another way out and spotted the exit at the back just beyond the koi pond.

I was almost there when I saw them. Spike and Ban-nerman, standing just inside the storage room built into the wall, a tiny room lined with narrow shelves filled with chemicals and fish food for the koi pond.

Bannerman's voice floated over the wail of the sirens. It sounded strange; stress had sharpened his Boston accent. He was shouting, "...get the fucking press out of there, not burn the fucking place down!" Spike stepped back, his arms loose by his sides, fists bunching. Bannerman raised his chin, a smirk on his lips. "Oh, now you get it." Bannerman tapped a pointy finger on Spike's forehead. "At last, light dawns on Marblehead." That's when Spike exploded, driving his fist into Bannerman's face so hard that Bannerman stumbled backwards. One heel caught on the lip of the koi pond and he plunged in. Spike lunged after him, arms outstretched.

At first I thought he was trying to pull Bannerman out, but he clamped his hands around Bannerman's throat and shoved him deeper in the water. Blood poured from

Bannerman's nose, forming a thin red cloud that obscured his face. He flailed and splashed, the fish scattered in all directions, but still Spike wouldn't bring Bannerman up.

"Stop!" I screamed. "We're not animals!" I ran around the pond and wrapped my arms around Spike's neck and yanked backward, again and again. "Let him go, for the love of God, let him go!" Spike didn't look up, he simply whipped back one elbow and sent me flying. I slipped on the wet floor and went over the side of the pond, plunging headfirst into the cool blue water. Bannerman thrashed; Spike hauled him out of the water and rammed him back in again. The water surged, tugging me under Bannerman's body until I was pinned beneath him. *These assholes are going to drown me!*

Suddenly Bannerman was gone and two strong hands clutched my suit jacket and dragged me up out of the water.

"What the hell is wrong with you people?" A burly firefighter pinned Spike against the wall. A second firefighter flipped Bannerman onto his back on the smooth terrazzo floor and was about to administer first aid when Bannerman spluttered to life. I slumped on the floor, head resting on my knees, gasping for breath. A small knot of people gathered around us. The burly firefighter pointed to the exit. "Folks, this is an evacuation, get out!"

Bannerman struggled to his feet, sloughed off his soggy jacket and dropped it in a sodden heap on the floor. He glanced at Spike, then turned away. Spike blinked, water dripped from his ginger hair into his pale blue eyes. *What's with these two?* I inhaled, coughed again, then got to my knees. A firefighter gave me his hand and pulled me to my feet.

A third firefighter appeared, carrying a couple of silver

space blankets. She draped one gently across my shoulders then stopped next to the burly firefighter to say, "Looks like it started in some wastepaper baskets behind the stage in the auditorium. Lots of smoke and damage from the sprinklers, but no one's hurt as far as we can tell."

She tried to pass Bannerman a space blanket but he dismissed her with a flap of his hand. He leaned close to Spike, speaking quickly and softly. Spike's eyes were firmly fixed on the floor, but he was listening. A police officer materialized out of nowhere, talked to the firefighters, then turned to Spike and said a few words before cuffing him and steering him toward the revolving doors. Bannerman fell into step beside Spike, and I moved up next to the officer. The crowd, which was much thinner now, watched our sodden trek across the lobby with open mouths and bewildered eyes.

As we neared the exit, I stopped. I told the officer I wouldn't press charges. I was done with the lot of them. Bannerman lifted his hands, palms up and said he wasn't pressing charges either. The officer said Spike was going to the station whether we pressed charges or not. Bannerman protested, then fell silent. Just as Spike passed through the door Bannerman called out to him, "I'll take care of it, just you remember what I said."

Spike glanced back over his shoulder then strode across the street to the police van.

CHAPTER 61

To hear Matteo tell it, Investor Day was a fiasco. Bannerman's staff prowled the lobby gathering up the analysts and investment bankers and cajoling them back into the auditorium. Bannerman reappeared in a fresh suit and new shirt, determined to push the meeting back on agenda—Phoenix is a fantastic company heading into a bright new future, not to mention a great investment—but the investors weren't buying it. All they wanted to talk about was Elliot Lake and whether the Vesper compressors were too powerful for the pipeline.

Matteo repeated his message all day long, the Vespers were perfectly safe, as long as no one tampered with the failsafes. When Bannerman couldn't produce a senior engineering executive—what with Ray being dead and all—to describe Phoenix's safety protocols and assuage their fears, they drew their own conclusions. By the end of the day, the investors were firmly entrenched in their position that 'out of an abundance of caution' it would be prudent to delay bringing the Vespers online. Was there any harm, they asked, in waiting a couple of weeks, perhaps longer, to give them the assurance they needed before they would bless this transaction with a BUY recommendation?

Bannerman knew it would take more than 'a couple

of weeks' to appease the investors, but he had no choice: delay the launch or they'd trash the stock.

Then to add insult to injury photos of Spike throttling Bannerman in the koi pond appeared all over social media and in the regular news. Even the stodgy newspapers couldn't resist a flashy headline. FRACAS IN FISHPOND was my favourite.

All good, right? And yet I was twitchy and spent the night obsessing about the bobcat that prowled the woods along the river's edge. I was looking for him now, peering through the pink morning glow that illuminated my office when I heard AJ's tuneless whistle announce his arrival. He stopped in my doorway, an impish grin on his face, and said, "What are you doing here? Shouldn't you be off schmoozing with your adoring fanbase?"

"I have an adoring fanbase?" I swiveled away from the window and waved him into my office.

He plunked down in a chair and pulled his cell phone out of his coat pocket. "Yep, you're trending on Twitter."

"What?"

"Hashtag splish splash." He flicked through his screen. "Here, I bookmarked it."

I grabbed his phone out of his hand and stared in disbelief at a clip of me clinging to Spike's neck as he throttled Bannerman, then going headfirst into the koi pond before two firefighters fished me out—all to the tune of a long-forgotten pop song.

"Perfect." My face burned as I pushed his phone away. "That will do wonders for my reputation."

AJ eyed me carefully, his initial amusement shifted to concern. "When you said there had been an altercation at Investor Day, you didn't mention this." He tapped his phone which was lying faceup on the desk, the clip on constant replay. "Seriously, what happened?"

I took a deep breath. Where to begin. Louisa and Kirsten were frantic by the time I pulled up in front of the house and dragged myself up the front steps swaddled in my mylar space blanket. Kirsten had returned to the house two hours earlier and no one could reach me on my cell; not surprising as it was at the bottom of the fishpond. Louisa marched me into the bathroom. "Before you say another word, you're having a hot bath and something to eat." She ran my bath and stuffed me with tomato soup, a chocolate cookie, and a shot of apricot brandy. Mom would have been proud.

I told the story to AJ the same way I'd told it to Kirsten and Louisa, starting with the fire alarms and the confusion in the lobby and ending with Bannerman and me in the koi pond; only this time I left out the bit about the fish.

For some strange reason, all I could think of when I was on the verge of drowning was Hindenburg, the magnificent bronze koi fish. *Are the fish okay?* I'd asked the firefighter as I trembled under the silver blanket. He raised an eyebrow and said, *Ma'am I'm sure they're fine.* I stared into the pond and Hindenburg appeared, glittering bronze and gold against the soft blue tiles. And I started to cry. He hovered on the surface and blew a few bubbles at me as if to say: *See this water line, you stay there, I'll stay here, and we'll be just fine.* Then he flicked his tail and darted away. And I cried some more. Louisa said it was a delayed shock reaction. I said it was because I really liked that silly fish and was afraid that with Bannerman and me thrashing around in the pond, we'd killed it.

"Wow," AJ said, "that was quite an ordeal." The front doors banged open and voices filled the reception area.

Bridget and Madeline came straight through to my office. "You're famous!" Bridget said, holding up her cell phone. Her eyes sparkled with excitement.

"Yeah, for fifteen minutes," I replied. "What kind of idiot films someone falling into a fishpond when the bloody building might go up in flames?"

"To be fair," AJ said, "they were filming one guy trying to drown another guy with a crazy woman clinging to his back."

"You know, Evie," Madeline said slyly, "you missed a great marketing opportunity. You could have flashed your business card when they dragged you out. 'Braxton, Lawson, Valentine! Nothing keeps us down.'" I raised a disapproving eyebrow, she chuckled and said, "At least you'd have gotten a better theme song."

"I'm never going to hear the end of this, am I?"

She was humming the tune *I Will Survive* as they waltzed out of my office, leaving me alone to peer into the urban wilderness on the other side of the glass. Still no sign of the bobcat. He had to hunt, I get that, but couldn't he do it somewhere else?

Keith pressed the 'start' button and flashed a satisfied grin as the fan on his Kona whirred and the engine sparked to life. This morning we were in traditional business attire and I was somewhat surprised at how dapper he looked in his tailored suit and brand-new overcoat. I'd worn high-heeled dress boots which made the icy pavement treacherous as we darted across the street from the restaurant back to the parkade. Women's fashion is the bane of my existence.

"You know," I said, "had we given it some thought we'd have realized the lawyer suits weren't necessary." After all, the client asked us to meet her at Galaxie, a trendy breakfast place, not the Fairmont Hotel.

Keith disengaged the parking brake and pressed the accelerator. "Speaking of giving it some thought, did you see today's paper?"

"That was a bit of a leap. No, why?"

"Check in my briefcase." Keith tilted his head toward the backseat and reversed slowly out of the parking stall. "City section, top of the second page."

I poked around in his briefcase, it was as messy as his office, and found the paper wedged between a file and a large Tupperware container. "What's for lunch today?" I asked.

"A baguette and gruyere with some kind of special jam." He smiled a slightly exasperated smile.

"I'll eat it if you don't want it." Keith's wife is an artist, but she became a first rate cook too when she discovered Keith was grabbing lunch from the food trucks parked outside our building—junk food in her opinion. So now when AJ or I order from Keith's favourite Greek food vendor we have to pick up a little extra to share with him.

Keith laughed and rolled smoothly up the ramp, holding the car on the incline while the garage door clanged open and pedestrians hustled to clear the sidewalk.

The story was right where Keith said it would be, city section, top of the second page:

MAN ACCUSED OF ARSON FACING NEW CHARGES

A man who allegedly tried to set fire to a Calgary office building is facing additional charges in connection with the deaths of two individuals who perished last November during a natural gas pipeline explosion. Both individuals were employees of Phoenix Corporation which owns the natural gas pipeline that exploded on November 12. Their bodies were discovered on a right-of-way near the Elliot Lake compressor station, east of the town of Red Deer. Police say Sully Sullivan, also an employee of the company, is cooperating with the police. The cause of the explosion, which caused millions of dollars of damage, was investigated by the Transportation Safety Board, but its findings were inconclusive.

Sully Sullivan, so that was Spike's name. "Cooperating with the police? Keith, what do you think that means?"

Something tightened in my chest; I adjusted the pages of the newspaper and folded it in half and then in half again.

Keith kept his eyes on the road as he spoke. "Sounds like Sully isn't the only one the police are looking at in connection with Michelle and Marty's deaths."

Spike hunched over Bannerman. His face fierce with rage. Determined to hold Bannerman under the surface of the water until his body went limp and his life drifted away like the blood pooling in a pink cloud around his head. Then the mystifying part where Bannerman talked to Spike gently, as if he'd assaulted Spike, not the other way around.

"You all right?" Keith shot me a glance, then turned his focus back to the traffic which was building steadily as we cruised through the downtown core.

"Yeah, I'm fine." I slipped the newspaper into the side pocket in his briefcase.

He lifted his foot from the accelerator and we glided to a smooth stop at an intersection. He loved his Kona but its quietness unnerved him. His biggest fear was that he'd injure someone who stepped in front of the vehicle as it floated soundlessly through the streets.

I shoved his briefcase into the space between us, allowing it to flop onto the backseat. "Evie," he said, "Bannerman will not go down gently; you know that, don't you?"

"I know. Investor Day was a gong show. They took Matteo's comment about 'dangerous pressure surges' to heart. And so they should."

Keith took his eyes off the road and looked at me carefully. "Matteo isn't the only one who's cost Bannerman a bundle. You played a role as well."

I considered this for a moment before replying. "I hardly think being the conduit that connected Kirsten to Matteo counts as playing a major role in Bannerman's fall from grace. I'm not the one who got him financially over-extended or forced him to cover up structural problems on the pipeline for well over a decade."

He shook his head. "Yes, but don't forget. Bannerman is one of those guys who measures their place in society by how many zeros they have in their bank accounts. He's so rich he's never wrong."

Keith was right. We'd worked with many wealthy CEOs at Gates, Case and White and to a lesser degree in our own practice. They believed they're rich because they're smart, and if they're smart, they're never at fault.

Keith started weaving down a series of one-way streets as we got closer to the office.

"Fair enough." I watched the people standing at crosswalks waiting for the light to change or ducking into coffee shops to pick up breakfast on the way to work; hundreds of millions of people were doing this exact same thing all over the world.

We were driving beside the river now, approaching the pretty bridge that spanned it. The ice was melting, soon the ice shelves along the shore would collapse and float downstream in jagged chunks. Keith's eyes were cautious as he said, "This brings us back to where we started. Bannerman."

"What about him?"

"For Bannerman, wealth is the ultimate yardstick. How much do you think he expected to make by cashing out after Investor Day? Thirty million, fifty?"

"At least fifty." Sarah said he'd spent the last week ridiculing the 'gutless wonders' on his executive team who cashed out their options in September when the first Vesper was launched, rather than follow his lead and wait until Investor Day. Had everything gone to plan, glowing reviews from the likes of Goldman Sachs would have pushed Phoenix's share price into the stratosphere.

Keith flicked the indicator. It clicked so quietly it was barely audible above the sound of the tires hissing on the pavement. "Bannerman needs someone to blame for stopping him from taking what he thinks is rightfully his. He can't blame Goldman Sachs, they're richer than he is, but he can certainly blame you."

He cruised into a parking stall, frightening a magpie pecking at something shiny stuck in the dead grass at the edge of the lot. Indignant, it ruffled its black and white wings and stalked away.

I unclipped my seat belt and scooped up my briefcase which was lying in a small damp puddle at my feet. "Don't you worry about me, Keith. I can take care of myself."

Famous last words.

CHAPTER 62

Chris Henzel, Michelle's director friend, called two weeks later. He was in town for a Board meeting and wondered if we could touch base. Of course, I said, my curiosity rising. Other than a rushed conversation with Sarah who said Spike was out on bail and 'get this, Bannerman's gone AWOL,' I'd heard nothing from Phoenix.

So that afternoon I bundled into my winter coat, heavy boots, scarf, and mittens and trudged over to a coffee shop close to the office. It was mid March and we were in the grip of another cold snap, although as far as I'm concerned four straight days where the temperature doesn't rise higher than minus twenty-one Celsius is more than a 'snap,' it's a disaster.

I arrived first and carried my coffee over to a small table next to the windows. These trendy coffee shops with their bright shiny interiors try so hard to stand out from their competitors but once you get inside they all have the same upscale vibe. I preferred Campana's which is down the street from my house. Its décor is stuck in the 1970s and it makes the worst avocado toast in town, but it's comforting, like home.

The café door opened; Chris stomped the snow off his boots and brushed a few flakes out of his wiry hair. He gave me a cheery wave before proceeding to the counter to place his order. Despite his additional workload—Sarah said the Board had had three unscheduled meetings in the past two weeks—he looked calm and unhurried.

He stuck out his hand for a shake just as I went in for a hug, and we covered over the awkward moment with idle chatter about the weather. Quickly, Chris turned to the reason for his call. Phoenix was augmenting its legal team and the Board wanted to offer my firm a retainer.

I took a sip of camomile tea before replying. "Chris, thank you for considering BLV but, and I'm putting this as delicately as I can, as long as Bannerman is CEO and Dave Bryant is the Chief Legal Officer, my firm will not consider accepting a retainer from Phoenix." In other words, we wouldn't touch it with a barge pole.

There was a quiet moment where we listened to the logs popping and snapping behind us. The fireplace was a nice feature, especially on a bitterly cold day.

He eyed me carefully, then laughed. "Can't say as I blame you, but that won't be a problem."

"Why? Because Bannerman is missing?"

He coughed, his coffee had gone down the wrong way. "News gets around fast."

"Nothing beats the office grapevine." I smiled.

He set his cup down and leaned back in his chair. "Well, you heard right. Bannerman's been MIA since Investor Day...but we'll be hearing from him soon." In the quiet, close atmosphere of the café it felt like we were spies having a clandestine meeting. "Ah, what the hell, it'll be common knowledge soon. The Board is meeting with Bannerman tomorrow. We're offering him early retirement."

"Bannerman is getting fired?" I struggled to keep my voice down. "Really?"

He nodded. "The Chairman of the Board will step in on an interim basis until we find his replacement." The image of that sleepy old bear of a man came to mind. "Dave Bryant is also leaving the company."

I laughed. "Well, Chris, when you put it that way, how can I refuse?"

He flashed a quick grin, then turned somber. "Before you accept, there's one more thing you should know. When Bannerman sees his package, he's not going to like it."

A log slumped in the fireplace, producing a burst of sparks. The fire was dying down and the café was practically empty.

"Why not?" I asked. "Given the mess he's made of the Vesper deal, what did he expect, accolades?" Keith's comment about Bannerman refusing to take responsibility for his actions came back to me.

Chris scowled. "He's hired a flotilla of lawyers. They've advised the Board that their client expects to be fully compensated on all the 'at risk' components of his pay...and then some." Chris' voice was tinged with bitterness now. "Bonuses are paid out in February based on calculations made last December. Back then we thought Bannerman had exceeded all his targets except safety. Now we know better. We're clawing back pretty much everything except what he's entitled to under his base pay and pension plan. He failed to act in the best interests of the company and his payout will be reduced accordingly."

It made sense to me, but then again, I wasn't a self-absorbed, entitled senior executive. "What's the difference between what he's expecting and what you're offering?"

"Before everything blew up, pardon the expression,

Bannerman was in line for a payout of around sixty-five million; the Board is offering thirty, max."

I let out a low whistle. "That's still a tidy sum, considering."

Chris snorted. "I've known Alistair Bannerman a long time, he used to work for Meers, remember. Thirty million is nowhere near enough for that guy; hell, he's probably spent the full sixty-five mil already."

Outside, the snow was coming down hard and fast, blanketing the contours of cars parked at the curb and the edges of the shops across the street. I was about to say we should leave soon, before the roads became impassable, when Chris smiled and said, "Bannerman won't land another CEO job after this debacle. Word on the street is his judgment isn't what it used to be." He beckoned me closer. "Those Goldman guys, they're royally pissed. And scoring directorships with big name companies? Pfffft, up in smoke. His reputation is shot." Then he chuckled. "Matteo is doing all right, though. The Goldman guys liked his candor."

It was getting dark now. I slipped into my coat and pulled my mittens out of my pocket. I told Chris I'd discuss the retainer with my partners; I was quite sure we'd accept. He smiled broadly and said the Board was looking forward to working with me.

As I left the warmth of the café and marched out into the gathering wind, I wondered why I wasn't elated by news of Bannerman's downfall. It was certainly a long time coming. But Keith's words haunted me. *Bannerman needs someone to blame. He can't blame Goldman Sachs, but he can certainly blame you.*

CHAPTER 64

The following day, the day of the Board meeting, wound down slowly, seconds ticking by like minutes, minutes ticking by like hours. I'm not sure what I was expecting, it's not as if Chris promised to call if Bannerman flew into a rage over his 'meager' pay package and was holding the Board hostage in the men's room.

After I'd read a court document for the third time and still had no clue what the judge was saying I decided to pack it up and go home. I was so focused on the prospect of having a quiet hour to myself—Louisa wouldn't be home until 7:30 p.m. and I didn't have to pick up Quincy from doggy daycare until 6:00 p.m.—that I didn't notice the black SUV parked at the end of the street.

I hung my coat in the hall closet and was about to untie my boots when a voice floated out from the kitchen.

"You're home early. Banker's hours?" The hair on the back of my neck stood on end. I looked up to see Bannerman sitting at my kitchen table. The French doors off the kitchen were ajar, a slight breeze stirred the edge of the newspaper laying open on the table. The room was cold and he'd flipped up the collar of his camel coat. One gloved hand rested on his knee, the other was curled around the handgun lying on the table. He nodded at a kitchen chair opposite him. "Please, join me."

I walked stiffly across the room and sat down. He crossed his arms and said, "Evie, Evie, Evie. What am I going to do with you?"

"You could get out of my house for a start."

His eyes were as bright as shiny pennies. "You cost me a lot of money today. A lot of money." Then he glanced dismissively around the kitchen. "You and your tiny life; you could never pay me back." He heaved a theatrical sigh.

My tiny life? I shoved my hands under the table, clenching my fists to stop them from shaking.

He spoke quietly, his tone even, his eyes on the gun. "I lost it all. Thanks to you. My company, my reputation—"

"What reputation? You kill people. A dozen innocents in San Remo. Two at Elliot Lake. Ray." My mother's voice sounded a warning in my ear: *Evie, this isn't helping.*

He gave a derisive snort. "I didn't kill anybody. Some people have the bad luck to be in the wrong place at the wrong time."

"Michelle and Marty didn't accidentally end up on the right-of-way, they were tricked or dragged out there by your bodyguard, Sully Sullivan." It was strange to say his name, he was still Spike to me.

Bannerman lifted his eyes slowly from the gun to my face, registering mild surprise. "What tipped you to Sully?" He appeared to be genuinely interested.

"The cars. Michelle's car was found in the Timmies' parking lot and Marty's car was abandoned on the side of a service road; someone had to drive them out to the right-of-way." I remembered Crystal's description of Parka Guy. "A random guy was seen talking to Michelle and Marty outside of Timmies. It doesn't take a genius to figure out this guy drove them out there and left them to die." *I have to get him out of here before Louisa gets home or he'll kill her too.*

Bannerman grew more reflective. "Ah yes, Sully. Poor Sully. We grew up together in Dorchester, not that you'd know it to look at me now. We lived on the same squalid block in the same miserable apartment building." He smiled, almost indulgently. "Sully's a loyal guy, but not too bright."

He touched the gun, stroking it gently so it rocked back and forth. "We were quite the pair back in the day. Brains and brawn. Makes the world go round, always did, always will. But you have to be careful when you're dealing with brawn." He glanced up at me like a teacher confirming a student was paying attention. "Spell out your instructions or they'll fuck it up." He pulled the gun closer and sat back in his chair. "'Create a distraction,' I said, not 'burn the place down,' threaten them, not—"

"Sully was pretty damn threatening when he showed up at Kirsten's place."

His lips stretched in a thin smile.

"Your goon held a butcher knife on a four-year-old girl. Was that your idea?"

Irritation flashed across his face. "It's Sully's call, he does what he must in the moment."

"And 'in the moment' he decided to kill Marty and Michelle on the right-of-way?"

"Sully was delivering a message. Threaten them, scare them off, let them cool their heels at twenty below for a couple of hours. Then that fucking pipeline blew up and they were killed in the blast."

I leaned forward, resting my arms on the table. It was becoming clearer to me now. "You're saying he was going to go back for them?"

"Sure he was."

"I don't believe you," I said. "If they were alive when he left them, they would have started walking back to the plant, Michelle would be clinging to Marty's arm the whole way, trying to stay upright in her wretched boots. The searchers would have found them together, not twenty-five feet apart. Marty's body was burned, but Michelle was far away enough that she was untouched by the blast. She died of head and neck injuries...at the base of a rock outcropping. Why would she be heading away from Marty toward a pile of rocks instead of sticking with him? He was the only one who knew how to get them out of there."

Suddenly anger overwhelmed me, obliterating my fear. "I'll tell you why. She saw Sully kill Marty and was running for her life. He caught her and bludgeoned her to death. He was driving back to Red Deer when the pipeline exploded. And then he called you."

Bannerman's expression was unreadable.

"You told him to get Marty's car, to make it look like Marty drove them out there, just the two of them and they died in the blast. But by the time Sully got to the Tim Horton's parking lot, picked up Marty's car, and headed back to the site he couldn't get through the RCMP cordon. So he ditched the car on the side of the road, went back for his own car and left. How convenient for you that Elliot Lake exploded; poor Marty and Michelle, they just happened to be in the wrong place at the wrong time."

Bannerman's face hardened, he was bored with this conversation. "You may be clever, but you cost me, Evie Valentine, big time. Back in Dorchester if someone costs you, they gotta pay."

He picked up the gun and pushed back his chair.

CHAPTER 65

I leapt to my feet, hands raised in supplication. "No, wait! I have to call Louisa."

He stared at me, nonplussed. "I'm supposed to pick up the dog from doggy daycare. If I don't get over there"—I made a show of looking at my watch— "right now, they'll call Louisa at the hospital, and she'll know something is wrong."

His expression changed as he processed this new information. I figured he may be delusional but he didn't want to get caught, so I plowed on. "You don't understand these doggy daycare places. They go ballistic if you don't pick up your dog on time. They'll call Louisa, she'll tear back here, it'll be an awful mess." None of this made sense. But it was all I had.

"One more minute," I pleaded, "then you're outta here."

Risk-benefit analysis. It's what he did all day long. I prayed he'd decide a small delay, one tiny minute, was a small risk to take to increase the odds he'd get away clean.

"Make it quick," he said.

My legs were shaking, knees were jelly, as I walked toward the closet. "Just getting my phone from my briefcase." My back was to him; I could feel his eyes following my progress. I glanced at the kitchen island. Yes, it was still there, right where it was supposed to be. Quickly, I ran through what I would say to Louisa. *Please God, let her understand.*

I dialed her number. It rang and rang. The chair creaked as Bannerman shifted impatiently behind me. The call went to voicemail and I dialed again. It rang twice before she picked up. "Evie," she sounded agitated, no doubt rushing from one calamity to another. "You're not supposed to call me at work—"

I cut her off. "Yes, I know, Louisa, listen... *listen...* I can't pick up Quincy after all," I coughed. "And you know their cardinal rule... if we're late." I said it again more slowly. "The... cardinal... rule. You know it."

"What are you babbling about?" Now she was annoyed as well as harried.

Bannerman waved his gun at me. "Get off the phone."

I lowered my voice. "Louisa, darling, I love you." I blinked back a tear and turned to face Bannerman. Had she understood me? The *cardinal* rule.

I moved back to the table, desperate to draw Bannerman's eyes away from the kitchen island where, next to the fruit bowl, a small red bird tilted slowly to one side, then whirred and righted itself. The amazing thing about Faro's drone was it could be operated with a handheld controller or a cell phone. The Cardinal was powering up. Louisa could see us.

Bannerman cocked his head, hearing the metallic buzz behind him. He glanced over his shoulder. The drone was airborne and flying straight at his face. He pivoted, raising his gun. I bolted to the French doors, banged them wide open and flipped myself over the balcony railing, landing heavily in the prickle bushes that separate my garden from the wild slope angling steeply down to the river's edge. I started running the second my feet touched the ground.

The French doors crashed against the walls again. Bannerman grunted, heaved himself over the railing and landed heavily on the frozen ground below. I glanced behind me. He tried to stand but slipped and lurched drunkenly to one side. Torn ligament? Broken hip? Hunching, he raised the gun. A shaft of evening light winked off the barrel. The drone darted through the French doors, an angry red blur buzzing around his head. He lifted an arm to bat it away and lost his balance. The gun arced out of his hand, sailed through the air and landed with a plop in the snow beside the neighbour's peony cage. Bannerman half fell, half rolled, down the ragged slope, sliding faster and faster as he struggled to regain his footing, his Italian leather shoes useless.

The homeless guy who lives fifty metres away watched the whole thing from his rickety lean-to as if this was typical Thursday evening fare. "Call the cops!" I yelled. He shrugged. No cell phone.

Barely upright, Bannerman careened down the embankment, stumbled at the river's edge and fell face down on an ice shelf. He screamed in pain. One arm was outstretched, the other folded under his body. Head bobbing like a baby's, he looked around. Blood poured from a gash above his right eye.

Here the river flows fast and cold. It never freezes completely; the current is too strong. The ice slabs at the river's edge weaken in the Chinooks, breaking off and floating downstream like little icebergs. The ice creaked under Bannerman's weight. He flailed one arm; the other was still trapped beneath him. Panting, he raised his head higher, caught sight of me and screamed, "Get over here!"

"You've got to be kidding," I muttered as I scrambled through the snow to the peony cage and pocketed the gun. It was heavier than I expected, dragging down my filthy pant leg.

He became more agitated as I came closer, cursing and flinging that one arm about. The tips of his leather shoes tapped the ice.

I was about to tell him to stop flailing when the ice made a sound, *pop, pop, pop*, then silence. A long crack inched out from under Bannerman's coat, tracing a black line from one side of the slab to the other. If the ice cracked through, he'd go in and be swept downstream. Down to the weir where he'd be caught in the towback and drown.

I stopped, assessing the man spreadeagled on the ice. Would that be so bad? He was an evil man, responsible for so many deaths...

Louisa's drone flashed across my line of sight; she toggled her wings and hovered a couple of feet closer to Bannerman's prone body.

"All right, all right." I knelt on the riverbank and slid my hands slowly across the ice. It was so cold it burned. I grabbed his ankle and hauled back, hard. He screamed and without thinking I let him go. Pop. The thin black crack gaped wider. Black water bubbled out of the fissure, soaking Bannerman's coat and cashmere scarf. He whipped his head about, trying to keep his face out of the water. The fissure grew wider.

"For the love of God, stop moving!" I yelled, clamping both hands onto one ankle and hauling him back a few inches. He roared in agony.

Behind me, the sound of trampling boots: people scrambling down the embankment. A woman in a bulky EMS vest touched my shoulder. "We've got this," she said, edging me out of the way to make room for her partner. They maneuvered Bannerman off the ice slab and examined him. The lights of the ambulance and a police car flashed up on the road overlooking the embankment. A policewoman shooed away the neighbours who'd materialized out of nowhere. Another cop scrambled down the slope. Long and lean, I recognized him.

"You okay?" he shouted.

I nodded. I'd met Sergeant Pritchard over a year ago. He was thinner than I remembered, the lines around his eyes had deepened. I'd forgotten he had heterochromia, one brown eye and one blue eye. We watched in silence as the EMTs strapped Bannerman's sodden body onto a stretcher and maneuvered him slowly back up the slope. He screamed in rage and pain when they lifted the stretcher over a thorn bush and it snagged his pant leg. "Sir," the EMT said, "you may have a broken hip, try to stay quiet."

Pritchard turned to me. "So what happened?"

I described finding Bannerman in my house and how Louisa helped me escape. A look of awe spread across his face as he stared up at Louisa's cardinal which was hovering in the air over the EMTs loading Bannerman into the back of the ambulance.

"You got lucky," Pritchard said. "Can't say the same for Sully Sullivan."

"Did Bannerman go after him?"

"Yeah, this morning. Did a real number on the guy, but he'll survive. And let me tell you, he's pissed."

Pritchard is one of the most circumspect people I know, maybe because he's a cop, but I sensed he was about to share a crumb of information. We started picking our way back up the slope. The breeze rustled through the poplar trees, I wasn't wearing a jacket and the cold cut like razor blades.

Pritchard handed me his overcoat. "You saw the media reports, right? Sullivan helping us with our inquiries? Initially he didn't say much, he wouldn't stray beyond the attack at the fishpond. But at one point he slipped and made an oblique reference to the 'accidental deaths.' There was something about the way he said it, coupled with the fact that three Phoenix employees died in the space of eight months, too many to be a coincidence, that focused our attention."

Gravel shifted under my feet, my legs were rubbery and I stopped for a minute. "And you think the news story about Sullivan helping the police spooked Bannerman?"

"Who knows, that was days ago, but something pushed Bannerman over the edge."

Could be the loss of thirty million dollars.

We'd reached the steepest part of the escarpment, both of us struggling to stay upright. No wonder Bannerman went down headfirst. The exertion of the climb made me lightheaded. My pace slowed as I gulped in lungfuls of air. "What I still don't understand is why Sullivan tried to drown Bannerman in the fishpond in front of hundreds of witnesses?"

"He says Bannerman insulted him and he lost his temper." The image of Bannerman up in Sully's face, sneering and tapping his forehead, and Sully exploding, came back to me. I shuddered, wondering if Michelle or Marty had said something to enrage Sully and had paid for their mistake with their lives.

A branch snagged my foot and I stumbled. Pritchard caught my elbow, hauling me back to my feet. "After the beating Bannerman gave Sullivan this morning, he'll tell us everything he's got."

The policewoman stood next to the cruiser on the driver's side. The street was empty, the gawkers had gone home. Pritchard gave her a nod and walked with me to my front door. It was only after he asked me to come down to the station to make a formal statement that I remembered Bannerman's gun. With a small shake of his head, Pritchard took it from me and wished me a good evening.

Inside, the kitchen was cold. I closed the French doors; we'd have to find a window guy to repair the glass. Bannerman had smashed a pane to break in. I slumped at the kitchen table. My thoughts were scrambled and I couldn't stop shaking.

Then I heard a tap, tap, tap on the glass. Louisa's drone was on the other side of the French doors. It waggled its wings and dropped to the ground. I opened the door and cradled it in my hands. Looking right into its little glass eyes I whispered, "Thank you, Louisa." My phone pinged with a text. She was on her way home.

Later that evening we were sitting on the velvet sofa, warming ourselves in front of the fire, a bowl of popcorn on the coffee table. I was wrapped in the Angora throw, she was curled up at the other end of the couch, her feet tucked up under her. "Evie," she said, "you weren't really going to leave him there to freeze to death, were you?"

"Hell no," I said. "I was going to jump up and down on the slab until it broke off and he fell in." She leaned forward and smacked my knee. She didn't believe me when I said I was kidding.

"Well, the next time you call because you're being held at gun point, might I suggest you be a bit more clear?" I smiled and reached out from under my fuzzy throw to scoop up a handful of popcorn, accidentally scattering some kernels on the carpet. Quincy hoovered them up in a flash. Louisa gestured for popcorn. "You sounded like a lunatic."

I passed her the bowl. "The message was perfectly clear: cardinal rule, cardinal drone, Bannerman, scary man, interrupting our walk with Quincy, call the cops."

She raised a skeptical eyebrow and I said, "Okay, I'll admit it was a bit of a stretch. But I must say, your flying skills are amazing."

She pulled the other throw off the back of the sofa and smiled. "I was pretty impressive, wasn't I."

CHAPTER 66

The May long weekend arrived after a bitterly cold winter and a soggy spring. The air was fresh with the promise of pine-scented hikes and smoky campfires. Quincy was delighted when I suggested a visit with Kirsten and the kids in Crisscross. He sprang into the front seat of the Mini and allowed me to strap him into his dog seat belt with barely a whimper of indignation, then spent ninety glorious minutes barking at the horses and cows and snorting and drooling all over his window.

I'd been to Kirsten's place many times in the winter, but now the narrow country roads in the fast-greening countryside were strangely unfamiliar. Skinny black spruce and lodgepole pine poked up from billowing thickets of willow, hazelnut, wild gooseberry, and honeysuckle. I pulled over to the side of the road and clicked on Siri. She made a valiant effort, counting down the kilometres until I turned right at a T-intersection where she declared we'd reached our destination. "Seriously?" I said to her; there were no houses on either side of the road. We continued driving until Kirsten's mailbox appeared a couple of minutes later.

I was unstrapping Quincy when the kids barrelled out of the house, shrieking and jumping about. The boys threw themselves at the dog, Amy smiled shyly and lifted her arms. I was hitching her up onto my hip when Kirsten appeared, carrying a small backpack. "As you can tell," she said, "everyone is very happy to see you."

I hugged her, squashing a giggling Amy between us, and said, "I believe the welcome committee is for Quincy, not me."

"Perhaps," she said before announcing we were going on a hike. Amy wriggled out of my arms and we strolled to the end of the driveway and turned down the lane toward the forest on the edge of the glade.

The boys convinced me to let Quincy off his lead and they bounded ahead of us. "Don't let him get too far in front," I warned, "he's never been here before." Amy dawdled behind them, happily pulling leaves off twigs and slipping small pebbles into her pockets.

The sun-dappled path was cool and the birds, hundreds of them, were raucous. Kirsten touched my arm. "Have you heard the latest?"

"The conviction, you mean?" The city was buzzing with the news that Sully Sullivan—he'd always be Spike to me—had pled guilty to a number of charges in connection with what the press had dubbed the 'Phoenix Deaths': Michelle, Marty, and Ray.

Kirsten nodded and fiddled with the straps of the small backpack, pulling them more snugly across her shoulders. We talked quietly so the children would not overhear.

It turned out Spike was smarter than Bannerman gave him credit for. In exchange for a reduced sentence he told the police everything they needed to know about the Phoenix deaths, implicating Bannerman every step of the way.

I peered ahead; Amy was fifteen feet down the path. I could hear the boys shouting and the dog barking somewhere around the bend where the path curved deeper into the forest.

Kirsten and I walked slowly as I recounted what I'd learned from Sergeant Pritchard; he'd interviewed me three more times after I'd given him Michelle's CYA file.

Bannerman clung to his story: Spike was too stupid to understand his instructions. He'd been clear that Spike was to threaten Michelle and Marty, not kill them. Spike vehemently disagreed. He'd been told to 'shut them the fuck up, I don't care how.' And that's what he did.

My throat tightened, making it harder to speak. "Spike took Marty and Michelle to the right-of-way, beat Marty senseless, then attacked Michelle when she tried to escape. According to Spike, they were still alive when he called Bannerman to confirm he wanted them dead. Bannerman told him to finish them off, throw their bodies in Marty's truck and push it into a ravine." I shuddered, that was the part I'd gotten wrong with Bannerman in my kitchen.

Kirsten bit her lip. "So Spike killed them with Bannerman's blessing, then went back for Marty's truck to make it look like an accident?"

"Yep," I nodded grimly. "Spike picked up the truck and was halfway back to where he'd left them when Elliot Lake exploded, giving Bannerman a smokescreen for murder."

Something jabbed my ankle. I bent down and pulled out a twig that had gotten stuck inside my shoe. Kirsten rubbed my back. "Are you all right?"

I hadn't realized I was breathing so hard. I swallowed a few times and said, "Bannerman says he has no idea what happened to Ray."

"Naturally." Disgust flashed across Kirsten's face.

"Spike says Bannerman was convinced Ray wanted to slow down the launch of the Vespers. He sent Spike to

Ray's place with instructions to tell Ray to come to his senses or his widow would be living high on the hog on Ray's life insurance."

"How did Ray end up under the glass blob sculpture?"

"It was just as we thought. They fought, one of them accidentally hit the button. When the blob came down it caught Ray in the face, and that was it." It was such a sterile way to describe Ray's horrific death.

Amy was just ahead of us, galloping down the path, pretending to be a pony. Kirsten watched her thoughtfully for a few seconds, then said, "Bannerman must have been apoplectic when he discovered you and I talked to Ray just before he died."

"Yeah, Spike says Bannerman was dreaming up all sorts of crazy schemes by then, but with three Phoenix employees dead, he couldn't very well kill me or make you and your family disappear."

Kirsten was about to speak when a flock of crows burst up over the treetops, flapping and squawking high in the bright blue sky. A young boy screamed, "Quincy, no!"

CHAPTER 67

When we reached the clearing all we could see were Quincy and the boys. Quincy was rigid, every sinew taut. The boys were draped across his back, Jack clutching his collar, Tyler's arms wrapped around his neck.

Amy reached them first. She glanced into the heap of vegetation, made a snick sound, and positioned herself between the dog and whatever it was he was fixating on. Quincy craned his body from side to side trying to see past her.

"No," she said firmly, hands on hips. "No."

I raced to the dog and clipped his leash to his harness. Wrapping the leash around my arm I shouted for him to come. Jack and I hauled back on his leash for good measure and finally Quincy broke his stance and circled around behind me to sit quietly by my side.

Kirsten rushed up and crouched next to her daughter. Amy pointed. "Look." Their faces softened as they gazed into a cubby hole of space created by fallen evergreen boughs and piles of broken twigs. There, partially hidden in the long grass, were three bobcat kittens. Fat furry bodies, wobbly legs and marble black eyes. They flicked their tiny, tufted ears and eyed us with curiosity.

One opened its mouth, making a warbling, fluting sound, and the other two joined in.

"Quincy found them," Tyler said, "they started wailing."

Jack nodded. "Scared the crap out of us."

"Don't touch them," Kirsten said. "Their mom will be around here somewhere. It's best to leave them alone."

"Where's their dad?" Jack stood tall, keen eyes searching the thicket.

"Oh, he's long gone." Kirsten pulled her phone out of her backpack and passed it to Jack. "You can take a photo if you're quick about it." After a few careful snaps, Jack handed the phone back to her, then asked for the leash and led Quincy out of the clearing and back to the path.

The children ran ahead on the curved path. We lost sight of them but could hear them laughing and chattering to each other. Someone roared and Quincy started barking again. I smiled at Kirsten. "I'm beginning to think bringing the dog along wasn't a brilliant idea."

By the time we returned to the house, the afternoon sun was high in a crystal blue sky and the wooden deck off Kirsten's kitchen glowed with reflected heat. I settled in a Muskoka chair while Kirsten disappeared into the kitchen. Amy dragged a small wooden box closer to me and sat down. When she grinned at me, she looked like a little cherub.

Jack and Tyler announced they were going to the garage to work on their go-kart and Quincy was coming along to supervise.

"Don't let him chew up a two-by-four," I yelled as they slammed the garage door shut behind them.

I hadn't seen the boys for months; they were taller and lankier now. Tyler was more self confident and Jack seemed a little more relaxed around me, maybe because I wasn't hounding him to give up something precious.

Kirsten reappeared through the patio door carrying a wooden tray bearing a large pitcher of lemonade, three tall glasses and a platter of cookies. "Amy baked these especially for you," she said with a suppressed smile.

Amy watched me carefully as I inspected the pale little men with uneven legs. I picked the one with the chocolate chip cyclops eye and wiggled my eyebrows to convey pleasure. She beamed and said, "Do you want to see my portfolio?"

"Of course," I said.

She slid off her box and skipped through the kitchen to her bedroom.

Kirsten picked up a cookie, turning it this way and that as if looking for the right place to start, then said, "So what happened between those two? Why did Spike turn on Bannerman?"

"I think it was the other way around. Bannerman betrayed Spike."

Kirsten hoisted the pitcher; it was beaded with droplets and heavy in her hands, and she poured out two tall glasses of lemonade. "How do you mean?" she asked.

I lifted my glass in a silent toast, the lemonade sparkled like molten sunshine. "The boys from Dorchester had been together all their lives. The brainy one clawed his way out of the slums, bringing the brawny one along with him. The higher Bannerman went, the less brutal Spike's life became...until the Vesper deal."

The sharp sound of wood clattering off concrete followed by excited yipping startled us both. We glanced at the garage door. Someone started to laugh and we relaxed again.

"All Bannerman had to do was hold everything together until Investor Day so he could cash out. Sure, Michelle and Marty were fussing about the Vespers, but it looked like Ray could keep them in check. When that was no longer the case, Bannerman deployed Spike to get rid of them. Just like in Dorchester. When the pipeline blew up, they thought they'd gotten away with it."

"Then we showed up," Kirsten said.

"We took Jack's pipe to Ray and Ray finally understood the magnitude of the problem, the entire system was riddled with faulty welds. He started to have second thoughts."

Kirsten frowned. "Second thoughts? I don't think so, Evie. He destroyed Jack's pipe, remember."

I didn't want to argue with her. It didn't matter now, but I'd seen something in Ray's face the morning he died. A flicker of conscience that may have been enough for him to push back on Bannerman. Then Spike appeared on his doorstep and it was too late.

I stretched in the Muskoka chair, trying to ease the muscles that had tightened in my chest. "Remember Investor Day?"

Kirsten shuddered. "How could I forget? I didn't think we'd make it out of there alive."

"That was the day Bannerman went too far. Spike did everything Bannerman had asked. Intimidation, even murder. He became the thug he used to be in Dorchester. And what did he get in return? Bannerman's contempt.

"Bannerman confronted Spike by the koi pond. He was practically spitting in Spike's face. Spike just stood there and took it until Bannerman said something about the 'light dawning on Marblehead'—that's Boston slang for when a stupid person finally figures something out—and

Spike lost it. He drilled Bannerman and tried to drown him in the fishpond."

She nodded slowly. "And Bannerman didn't press charges because he was afraid Spike would expose his role in the murders?"

"Exactly." I squinted in the sunlight. Just thinking about this was giving me a headache. "Investor Day was a disaster. The share price fell, the Board was livid. Bannerman knew he was in trouble. That's why he hired a raft of lawyers, he wanted to put the Board on notice that he wasn't leaving without a fight. The Board didn't care. Two weeks later they slashed his payout and 'retired' him. That's when he went nuts. He attacked Spike and he came after me."

Kirsten topped up my lemonade glass and passed me the cookie plate. I selected another strangely shaped little man. This one fell to bits in my lap.

Something Pritchard had said came back to me. "Spike wasn't surprised when Bannerman showed up on his doorstep. He said you can't erase your past; you are who you are. In Bannerman's case it was like flipping a switch; goodbye Hamptons, hello Dorchester."

Faro had said the same thing about Calisto, his pompous, windbag partner who refused to retire because he liked the prestige of being a lawyer. As if what you do defines who you are.

I heard a shuffling noise behind me. Amy was dragging a red cardboard folio case across the kitchen floor. Colourful bits of paper were sticking out around the edges.

"Here," she said, awkwardly trying to hand me the folio's black mesh handle without dropping the pencil crayons clutched in her fist. Once I had it, she hauled her little wooden box closer and I opened the folio case on my knees.

It wasn't long before I came upon the drawings from the day it happened, when the glass lake exploded. Ugly dragons with blood-stained teeth marauded across the landscape scattering terrified animals before them. As I flipped through the drawings the ferocious dragons became smaller and softer until finally a fat, sparkly Jezebel appeared.

"That's what took me so long." Amy pointed proudly at the drawing stuck into a sleeve in the folio case. Jezebel the dragon was glorious, three shades of brilliant green. Beside her was a kitten with pink tufts for ears and long blue whiskers.

"It's beautiful, Amy."

Amy beamed. "They're best friends." One of her pencil crayons slipped from her grasp. I caught it before it fell between the cracks of the wood decking. *Lemon Glacier.*

Amy took the pencil crayon from me and used it to press yellow dots on the bobcat's iridescent green-blue fur, *Cornflower* and *Fiery Rose.*

I ruffled Amy's hair, she smiled without looking up, and a thought came to me: you can't erase your past, but you can use it to become something better.

ACKNOWLEDGMENTS

Writing is a solitary activity but the effort of getting a book out into the world takes many hands. I would like to acknowledge a few such "hands" here.

I'm grateful to writing community, particularly Crime Writers of Canada and Sisters in Crime—Canada West who provide endless encouragement and support.

Thanks as well to my brilliant editor Pip Wallace whose insightful comments and sense of humour actually make the editing process fun.

A nod of appreciation to my colleagues in the legal profession who fight for justice each and every day and those working in the energy sector to make net-zero real.

A special thanks to my friend Kirsten Jaron, a brilliant engineer who knows firsthand what it's like to grapple with an "unplanned event."

I'd also like to acknowledge my mother, Mary Szasz, the most important women in my life; I think of her every day, and my sisters Rose Marie MacKenzie-Kirkwood, Linda Maki and Joanna Vander Vlugt, we've been through a lot and supported each other every step of the way.

A huge thank you to my husband Roy, my daughters Kelly and Eden, and their various dogs and cats who continue to pop up on the pages of this book or under my feet when I least expect them.

And finally, thank you to my readers, undoubtedly the best readers in the world. I'm grateful for your support and look forward to meeting you some day

ABOUT THE AUTHOR

© Photo by Barbara Blakey

SUSAN JANE WRIGHT studied anthropology and architecture before settling on law. She worked as a litigator then joined the in-house law department of a multi-national firm. Her career has taken her from the boardrooms of Calgary to the streets of Beijing.

The Glass Lake is the second in the Evie Valentine legal thriller series. Her debut novel, *Box of Secrets,* was a Crime Writers of Canada finalist for best unpublished manuscript.

When she's not writing she's travelling with her husband and two daughters. Her favourite vacation was a trip from Prague to London on the Orient Express. One day, she'd like to take the train from Venice to Istanbul.